THE CHANCE YOU WON'T RETURN

THE CHANCE
YOU WON'T RETURN

Annie Cardi

CANDLEWICK PRESS

Copyright © 2014 by Annie Cardi

First edition 2014

Library of Congress Catalog Card Number 2013946619
ISBN 978-0-7636-6292-9

14 15 16 17 18 19 BVG 10 9 8 7 6 5 4 3 2 1

Printed in Berryville, VA, U.S.A.

This book was typeset in Filosofia.

Candlewick Press
99 Dover Street
Somerville, Massachusetts 02144

visit us at www.candlewick.com

Courage is the price that Life exacts for granting peace.
The soul that knows it not, knows no release
From little things;
Knows not the livid loneliness of fear
Nor mountain heights, where bitter joy can hear
The sound of wings.

—*Amelia Earhart*

CHAPTER ONE

Trouble in the air is very rare. It is hitting the ground that causes it.

—Amelia Earhart

I was sneaking a twenty-dollar bill from Mom's purse when I saw the empty space where the picture should have been. It was of my parents on their wedding day, and they were laughing under a dogwood tree. Mom's hair was pulled back in a neat bun, a style she couldn't wear now, with her hair so short. Dad was clean-shaven in the picture, which always looked weird to me. His rented tux was a size too small; it showed in the arms and shoulders. They were twenty-two years old. I used to try to guess what they were laughing about. Whenever I asked, Mom said she couldn't remember.

Mom's ChapStick, an overdue library book, a dusty box of Kleenex—everything else was there. I pocketed the twenty and inched toward the nightstand, scanning the floor to see if the picture had fallen off when Mom hit her alarm clock that morning. But the picture was gone.

Downstairs in the kitchen, Teddy and Katy were peeling oranges for breakfast. Teddy kept jabbing his thumb into the flesh of the orange, making juice drip down his arm and onto the floor. Jackson, our terrier, licked the tiles.

Katy pushed Teddy toward the paper-towel rack. "Mom," she said. "Mom, he's getting it everywhere."

Teddy shoved her back. "She's pushing me."

"Mom, he's not going to clean it up."

Standing at the sink, Mom held its sides as if she was at a podium. Her mouth was caught between a smile and nothing. She looked over the backyard, where the Kmart swing set was rusting and a few scraggly trees almost blocked our neighbor's property. Usually she looked tired, even if the morning had barely begun. But for a moment, her face was clear and her eyes were focused.

Jackson barked. Teddy reached out to push Katy again, but her longer arms stopped him.

Mom blinked and wiped her hands on her jeans. "Both of you," she said, tossing a sponge at Teddy. "No horsing around." Teddy neighed, and Mom laughed a little.

I tried not to eye Mom as I made toast. Jackson nudged my leg, so I tore him a corner of bread. "Where'd your wedding picture go?" I asked.

"Okay, that's enough," Mom told Teddy, who had cleaned up the orange drips and was now scrubbing the rest of the counter. She pried the sponge from his hand and attacked the dishes from last night's lasagna. A tiny *V* appeared in the middle of her forehead. Over the sink, her hands worked furiously. I wondered if she would crack a plate. "Alex, did you say something?"

"The picture on your nightstand. When you and Dad got married."

Katy giggled into her cereal. "The puffy dress."

"Isn't it there? Dammit." Mom snatched her hand away from the hot water and turned the cold-faucet handle. "George must have moved it."

Katy looked up from her breakfast and caught my eye briefly, while Teddy continued to suck on orange slices. "Who's George?" Katy asked.

"David. Dad," Mom corrected herself, but she spoke carefully, as if she was afraid of making the same mistake again. She turned to me. "And exactly why were you in my room, Alexandra?"

"I was looking for my striped shirt," I said, not blinking. "I thought it got mixed up in your laundry." Katy was suddenly fascinated by her breakfast. She knew my shirt was on our bedroom floor, after I had tried it on and flung it off in disgust, but she also knew better than to say so. Now that Katy was in middle school, we had an understanding: she kept my secrets so I would do the same when she got some worth keeping.

Mom stared at me for a moment before shutting off the water. I'd expected more of a fight. Sneaking cash from her purse wasn't a regular thing for me, but I knew she had noticed some missing before and suspected me. Katy hoarded her money, so I couldn't ask her, and Teddy couldn't keep his mouth shut.

"Driver's ed today?" When I told her yes, she asked, "Have you practiced at all? Dad hasn't taken you in a week."

Whenever my dad asked if I wanted to go for a drive, I said I was busy or tired or made some sarcastic comment that would keep him from wanting to spend time with me in an enclosed space. But the real problem was that controlling a huge, whirring hunk of metal terrified me. My heart raced and I couldn't breathe and I forgot everything I was supposed to do. Cars hadn't always scared me. It wasn't like I cringed whenever anyone drove above the speed limit. I'd never been in an accident—not a real one, anyway. But something happened when I was forced to get behind the wheel. There were too many parts, all hidden under the hood; any piece could come off or spark. The brakes, the gas, the wheel, the mirrors—how could I be expected to pay attention to so many things at once? It went too fast. Anything could happen. So I avoided being behind the wheel as much as possible.

"Who cares if I don't practice? I'm going to be, like, the worst one anyway."

"That's *because* you don't practice," Mom said. "It takes time. And it would be a big help for me if you could drive your sister to gymnastics—"

"Oh, yes, please let me cart around my little sister. That's exactly how I want to spend my afternoons." At the table, Katy insisted that she didn't want to ride with me, either.

It wasn't the first time Mom had tried to convince me to drive. She and Dad had even offered to pay for a cell phone if I got my license—in case I broke down while I was on the road. By now I was the only person I knew who didn't have a cell, so that had almost gotten me, but then I'd remembered the feeling of being behind the wheel and claimed I didn't want one.

I devoured my toast at the counter and brushed crumbs into the sink. "See you later," I said, grabbing my backpack.

"Hey, where are you going?" Mom said.

"School," I said. "They make you go every day."

"You've got ten minutes before the bus. And you haven't made your lunch yet."

I lingered by the door. "I'll buy it. And I was going to walk."

Mom's eyebrows knit together. "You'll never make it in time if you walk."

"Sure I will," I said.

"Only if you cut through the woods," Katy muttered, probably deciding that if she had to ride the bus, then so did I.

"Oh, no," my mother said as she arranged slices of bread for sandwiches. "You want to walk, that's fine, but you have to stay on the street, where people can see you."

I gave her a look like I didn't know how she functioned in the world. "What's going to happen? I'll get attacked by a squirrel?"

Teddy snorted a laugh. "Maybe Alex'll get rabies and she'll

get all crazy and foamy." Sticking out his lower lip, he made slurping noises.

Mom ignored Teddy, even as Katy threw her napkin at him and told him to stop. "Remember that man a few years ago?" Mom said. "The one who tried to grab that boy?"

"Yeah, I'm desperate to get raped and murdered," I said, slinging my backpack over my shoulder. "Can I go now? I'm going to be late."

Mom cut three sandwiches so aggressively that I thought she'd cut off her own finger. "I am so sick of this attitude of yours. Ever since you became friends with that Theresa Harbin, you do things like threaten people in chemistry class."

I laughed. "That was one time! And we didn't threaten people; we threatened stupid John Lacey's letterman jacket. He deserved it."

Mom shoved sandwiches into paper bags. "You think you're entitled to everything."

"Oh, my Lord, you are so melodramatic," I said. "Just because I want to walk somewhere, you make a huge deal out of it. Shouldn't I be getting fresh air?"

"It's the way you say it, as if we're all dirt to you."

"Yeah, right, I'm such a horrible brat. Tell me about all the things I can't do right, please."

"You *could* do anything if you tried at all. But you don't care about anyone but yourself."

"No, you just can't understand how anyone could not want to do everything your way!"

We were almost shouting now. At the table, Teddy and Katy exchanged looks.

"And I don't appreciate you going through my things when I'm not around," Mom said. "How would you like it if I did that to you?"

"I wasn't going through your stuff. I already told you." The twenty-dollar bill burned inside my pocket. "Why would I even want to go through your stuff? There's, like, nothing there."

The way Mom looked at me, her head tilted and lips pressed together, she must have been trying to remember a time when I didn't act like I hated her. When she thought I was trust-worthy. For that, she'd have to go back a while. I was about to tell her that we'd had this argument a million times, but suddenly her eyes were clouded with something else. The planes of her face relaxed, and she gazed beyond me, to the kitchen table and beyond even that, into nothingness.

"Never mind," I said, and strode out the front door before she could ask me to walk my brother home from school.

I was still annoyed as I made my way across the lawn and down the street, toward the woods. Storms had prematurely yanked all the leaves off trees, and now the ground was slick with color. Car horns blared—senior boys greeting one another. I wished they'd knock heads together. Maybe that way someone's skull would crack open and we would get to see if any of them actually had a brain. For a moment, I considered skipping school altogether to hide out in the woods. I hadn't done my math homework—big shock—and probably wouldn't have time to finish during homeroom. Stoners and couples escaped to the graffitied boulder out here during free periods, but it seemed like their activities involved at least two people. On my own, I'd probably just end up hungry and feral.

Then I heard something else—hissing, like someone using a can of hair spray. I held my breath. Someone was probably behind the boulder. But I was still too pissed to realize it was too early for stoners or couples.

A branch snapped under my clunky boot as I strode around the rock. "Hey," someone said.

I hadn't expected anyone to notice me, and my mind was still clouded by my mom and obnoxious senior guys. "What?" I snapped.

A crown of a close-cropped head popped up on the other side of the boulder. Jim Wiley stepped into view. I still wasn't used to seeing him with his hair cut so short. Last year he wore it long, kind of shaggy. But the shortness worked; it made his cheekbones seem more carved and his lips softer. I'd spent the last few weeks admiring his cheekbones and lips during gym, the one class we shared. He'd already been one of the best-looking guys in school, and now he looked like some kind of Greek statue. He was tall like me and had startlingly light-blue eyes. Staring into them was like getting an electric shock, and I felt the hairs on my arm stand up.

In his hand was a can of spray paint. He stared at me for a second. "Sorry."

"No, it's okay," I said, a little too eagerly. "I didn't expect anyone to be here." I wasn't sure if he knew who I was. Most likely he recognized my general shape as someone he probably went to school with, or even more generally as someone who wasn't going to bother him. But of course I knew who he was. Everyone at Oak Ridge did. Last year he became a school legend when he drove his parents' car into the side of their house. After that, he disappeared for the rest of school year. Then in September he showed up, a junior again and kind of an icon.

He tried to hide the spray can behind his back, although I wasn't sure why. It wasn't like this was the principal's car or anything. The boulder was already covered with decades of couples' initials and swears.

"What time is it?" he asked.

"I don't know." Another problem with not having a cell phone. "The bell's probably going to ring soon."

"Thanks, ah—"

I wasn't sure if he was searching his memory for a name, but I put it out there anyway. "Alex."

"Alex?" he said. "You're a junior, right?"

"Yeah. We have gym together."

He nodded and leaned against the boulder, shoulder jabbing the middle of someone's spray-painted heart. The handwriting was sloppy, so it might have been LK LOVES SP. Some declaration of love. As far as I knew, Jim wasn't dating anybody. Before he drove into his house, he always had a girlfriend.

Now either girls didn't know what to make of him or he wasn't interested.

It was too quiet. "What's with the spray paint?" I asked. "Did you write your initials?"

"Oh." He glanced at the can like he was surprised to find it in his hand. "I was just messing around."

I looked behind him to see if any of the graffiti matched the color on his can. One part did. I'd expected something quick and catchy like FUCK YOU or OAK RIDGE SUCKS, but it wasn't even a word. It didn't really look like anything—a bunch of sharp edges, curves, all in phosphorescent orange—but it felt deliberate.

"What does it say?"

He clicked the cap back on the aerosol can. "My initials. It was supposed to be this tag thing. But I can't really do anything good yet."

In the woods, with so many of the leaves fallen already and the ground bright with reds and yellows, his graffiti fit. The other names and colors faded into the rock. "It's like a phoenix," I said. Once the words were in the air, I wished I could grab them and stick them back under my tongue. Who said stuff like that, especially to Jim Wiley?

"A phoenix?"

"It's this mythical creature—"

"Yeah, I know what it is," he said.

I felt myself blushing. "The orange. It reminded me of fire."

Jim nodded. "That's actually what I was thinking about. The shape, I mean, not just the color, you know?"

"Yeah," I said. "It's got this movement to it. There are edges, but they still have a kind of flow."

"Right. Like watching a flame."

"But with more control."

"Yeah, that's totally it."

I'd barely heard Jim talk before, and now we were having this conversation about color and movement. Did he talk this way with everyone? I could have been the only person Jim Wiley talked to about this. My heart was beating fast. "You did a good job." In the distance, I heard a shrill buzzing. "First bell."

"Right. Thanks." He picked up his backpack from the side of the boulder and slid the can of spray paint inside. "I probably would have missed homeroom if you hadn't told me."

"Oh, tragedy," I said, and he smiled.

I thought he would walk ahead of me, but he kept pace, even though his strides were longer than mine. We didn't talk until we passed through the front doors of the school. Then Jim said, "Later, Alex," and headed down another hallway.

I tried not to notice kids looking at us. Tried to pretend this was a totally normal thing, Jim and I coming to school together. He was a legend, and I was barely anyone. I rushed to my locker, wondering if people were already inventing some kind of scandal about us.

CHAPTER TWO

Women must pay for everything. They do get more glory than men for comparable feats. But, also, women get more notoriety when they crash.

—Amelia Earhart

When I told my mother I was the worst student in driver's ed, I wasn't lying. I'd driven over more cones than anyone else in our class, or anyone in any class before ours, as our instructor, Mr. Kane, liked to remind me. Two weeks earlier, I'd blown out a tire while driving over a curb. Instead of letting us have a free period, Mr. Kane had made us spend the last half hour of class learning how to change a flat. I hadn't been allowed behind the wheel since.

"It's your turn today," Theresa told me as we climbed into the backseat of the '97 Volvo station wagon that served as our student-driver mobile. Someone's parents had donated it a decade ago, probably after their children refused to be seen in it. The dents I'd put into the fender weren't the first. Even though Mr. Kane vacuumed the vinyl interior, there were still crumbs between the seats. After an hour, we'd smell like old skin and damp, stale bread.

"He's not going to let me drive," I said. It wasn't fair, anyway. Most high schools cut driver's ed ages ago, but our principal insisted that proper instruction could make for safer teen drivers. It obviously wasn't doing anything for me. I slid into the middle seat, Theresa on my left and Caroline Lavale, in her First Presbyterian Ministry T-shirt, on my right. In the driver's seat, Edward Baker was texting wildly.

"Mr. Kane has to let you," Theresa said. "It would be like not giving you a test in math. You'd think, *Hey, great*, but then he wouldn't pass you and you'd fail out of school and be stuck at home for the rest of your life. Do you really want that?"

"You want to see me drive through the fence."

Theresa ignored me. "So you broke a tire. So what? You helped us learn a valuable lesson about car safety." She leaned across me. "Isn't that right, Caroline? Did you know how to change a tire before Mr. Kane showed us?"

"Not exactly," she said.

"There you go."

Mr. Kane eased himself into the passenger seat and slammed the door shut. He was six foot four, so his head scraped the ceiling of the car. He scribbled on a clipboard, probably giving Edward points for not having destroyed any part of the car yet. "All right," Mr. Kane said. "Start 'er up. Seat belts, everybody."

Theresa ignored him. She grasped the driver's headrest and hoisted herself forward, her chin practically on Edward's shoulder. "Hey, Mr. Kane. Alex gets to drive today, right?"

Mr. Kane was telling Edward to put away the phone already and pay attention. Today was three-point-turn day. "Now you're at a dead end. Visualize the street," he said once Edward's path was blocked by a line of orange cones. "What are you going to do?" Edward didn't hesitate, possibly inspired by Mr. Kane's voice. When he wasn't teaching driver's ed, Mr. Kane was also the theater teacher, coaching drama queens through the chorus of "Sunrise, Sunset" with his powerful tenor. Apparently he'd played various understudies on Broadway a decade ago but had to give it up because of his mother's heart disease. She was still dying, and he was directing *Oliver!* this spring.

"Very good, Edward," he said as Edward checked his rear-view mirror and eased the car into reverse. Smiling into his clipboard, Mr. Kane was probably complimenting himself on using theater techniques in driver's ed.

"Yeah, you're a regular car god," Theresa muttered at the back of Edward's head. "When is Alex going to drive?"

Mr. Kane sighed. "After Edward's done, it's Alex's turn."

"I don't have to. Edward needs more practice," I said.

"Edward's a champion," Theresa said. "You can be one, too."

"I can drive if Alex doesn't want to," Caroline said, her quiet smile directed at me. A small part of me wanted to throw my arms around her and claim her as my new best friend. But

14

mostly I wanted to tie her up and repeatedly run her over with the Volvo. As if I needed her pity.

"It's okay—I'll do it."

Edward parked the car neatly by the curb so we could switch places. (Of course it was easy for him to drive; he had two older siblings.) In the front seat, I felt like Alice in Wonderland, shrinking to nothingness. Could I even press the pedals from here? Even after adjusting the seat and mirrors, I didn't feel like I fit. Which pedal was which again? I remembered smashing into the curb, the sudden bang and hiss of the front right tire exploding. In classrooms, students had leaned toward rows of windows. Dozens of eyes watched as we got out of the car to assess the damage. How could that have happened? I thought driving would be easy, natural. Even the idiot senior boys could drive.

When I tried to focus on the dashboard, my vision blurred and I couldn't remember how to count. The veins in my throat throbbed. Maybe if I had an anxiety attack, I would be excused.

"We'll start out with something simple," Mr. Kane promised. "You don't even have to visualize anything. This is only a parking lot. All you have to do is pull away from the curb and make a left turn up there."

I could feel everyone's fingernails dig into the vinyl.

My hands groped for the key, already in the ignition, and I yanked it the wrong way a few times before starting the car.

"What are you doing?" Edward laughed, hyena-like. In the rearview mirror, I could see three fillings in his unnaturally large mouth. His cell phone was pinned to his ear as he told his freshman girlfriend what a spaz I was.

"Shut the fuck up, Baker," Theresa snapped.

Mr. Kane whirled around in his seat, straining against the seat belt. "Hey, settle down back there. And shut the phone off, Edward." I hoped he would add "or else everyone's out of the car," but he didn't. Instead he looked at me, his forehead suddenly huge and gleaming. "Ease your foot onto the gas and gently turn away from the curb."

I'd only seen one of Oak Ridge High School's plays, last year's *Annie Get Your Gun*. It was painful to watch—screeching sopranos and boys with no rhythm doing the box step. Buffalo Bill Cody kept forgetting his lines. Meanwhile, Mr. Kane smiled as he directed the orchestra, hand waving gracefully over the violins. Maybe he was a better actor than director. Right now his teeth were welded together.

"Come on, Alex. Just like riding a bike," Theresa said.

Yeah, I thought. *I've done that before.* I placed my foot on the gas, applied the smallest amount of pressure, and in a second, we were gliding over the asphalt. My hands rested at four and eight. Orange cones passed like troubled thoughts in a clear mind.

Beside me, Mr. Kane's breathing steadied. "Very good, Alex," he said. "Can you picture a road? This is how easy it'll be."

Easy. We were moving and not dying. It was just like riding a bike.

Except with more numbers and dials. Suddenly I was

imagining people on bikes getting hit by people in cars. Accidents like that happened all the time—screeching tires, mangled arms, heads cracking against pavement. Cars didn't even have to be going very fast to kill someone; we learned that in the written classes.

"Be careful," Edward grumbled. "I think we hit five miles an hour."

My arms felt heavy and rubbery, like they were filling with water. The windows were all up, all manual. I wanted to ask everyone to roll theirs down, but the words shriveled in my throat. Somehow it had gotten overcast since I started driving. Clouds pressed against the windshield.

Mr. Kane was making swift checkmarks on his clipboard. "Now you're going to turn the corner there. Watch out for the corner. The left."

"Alex, the left," Theresa said.

I yanked the wheel toward the left. My arms were so heavy, I couldn't correct myself. Then my knees were locked and I couldn't take my foot off the gas.

"Wrong side of the road," Mr. Kane said. He reached for the steering wheel, but it was too late. We careened through the cones, over the curb, and, barely missing the goalpost, onto the trimmed lawn of the football field. Everyone in back clasped one another and braced their feet against the front seats. The word "left" was stuck in my brain, so I tried turning again, but by the screams, I could tell that wasn't the right answer. Mr. Kane kept shouting for me to stop. Finally the word registered and my foot smashed the brake. For a moment, everything was quiet. We were still alive.

In the rearview mirror, I could see Edward shake his head and chuckle to himself. "Jesus, Alex, you fucking suck."

"Out of the car." Mr. Kane's voice was choked, as if he'd swallowed a beetle.

I grasped the door, swung myself out of the Volvo, and walked stiffly on the grass. Let Mr. Kane yell at me; I was just happy to be standing on my own two feet again. Everyone else followed, standing as far away from me as possible, except for Theresa. Mr. Kane turned from us, hands at his hips, clipboard wagging at his side. His breathing was deep but sharp. When he faced us again, his cheeks were flushed and his nostrils flared.

"Alexandra," he said through his teeth, stressing the last syllable and turning my name into a kind of wince, "were you visualizing a street?"

I glanced at Theresa for help, but she was studying her shoes. "Yes," I lied.

He had to choose his words carefully. "Visualize that street again for me, won't you, Alexandra? You have run over everyone on that street, Alexandra. They are all dead."

Edward snickered in his fist, while Caroline looked vaguely ill. I imagined it was them I'd run over. Suddenly being the neighborhood assassin didn't seem so bad.

Mr. Kane took another deep breath, and when he spoke again, his voice was clearer, hitting the deeper register of his tenor. "I'm not sure you should be in this class," he told me.

"I think we should call your parents and set up a conference. Maybe we can find an alternative."

Because of my dad's schedule at the post office, it was hard for him to make conferences. Most likely, it would only be my mom. I could see it, the two of them discussing how unfathomable it was that I couldn't drive. Shamefaced, Mom would assure him that she could parallel park anywhere. My lack of skill must have been from my father's side of the family. They'd laugh. She would thank Mr. Kane for bringing this to her attention and refuse to let me on the road at all, in order to save the lives of pedestrians across town. Afterward she would drive me home, asking why I couldn't do this one simple thing. It would be heinous if my mother came to school. I hoped that if she were at home right now, staring out the window, she would be too distracted to hear the phone ring.

Of course, by the next morning, everyone had heard that I'd plowed onto the football field. It was a small school— ninety-three juniors, ninety-four now with Jim Wiley—so I wasn't surprised they all knew. The lawn was choppy near one of the end zones, two straight patches torn from where I had hit the brakes so sharply. Football practice had been limited to one half of the field, so the players' cleats wouldn't do any additional damage. The football coach and two groundskeepers were out there, hands on their hips and shaking their heads at the bare dirt.

"Oh, please," Theresa said. "It's just grass."

The rest of the student body didn't seem to think so. Somehow our football team had managed an undefeated season so far—a first for the Oak Ridge Mountaineers. People other than the players' parents were attending games. Even my school spirit extended so far as to wear a maroon T-shirt on pep rally days (though it was really only so I wouldn't stand out). People were talking about going to the state finals. According to the rumors, state was out of reach now that I had destroyed the field. Which was totally ridiculous—the field was barely damaged—but they claimed it was a mental thing. Without a perfect end zone, they wouldn't be able to score. Because obviously that had been their problem all the years the team sucked.

"Hey, Alex," a sophomore boy called to me while I was getting books from my locker, "can I get a ride after school?" Before I could think of a clever response, he turned back to his friends, all hooting with amusement.

"Yeah, laugh your brains out," I said. I shoved a calc book into my locker so hard, the metal clanged.

From across the hall, Theresa heard the noise. "I hate math, too," she said, "but at the end of the year, they make you pay for the books you mess up." When only half my mouth rose into a smile, she shook her head at the sophomores. "Screw them, seriously. They'll be smoking pot in their parents' basements when they're forty."

"Forty needs to hurry along," I said.

A group of boys in letterman jackets strolled down the hall, and my stomach knotted. From kindergarten through junior year, I had tried so hard to be inconspicuous, to fly under the radar, and so far it had worked: I certainly wasn't going to be prom queen, but I had my friends and managed to avoid crippling social trauma. Now everyone seemed to know both my name and that I couldn't manage a simple task everyone else had mastered.

One of the senior football players, Nick Gillan, his neck as thick as his skull, smirked at me. "Better start gardening."

"Christ, it'll grow back," Theresa said.

"It won't by Friday." Nick leaned toward me, so close that I saw the scars from where he'd scratched his acne. "Better get to work, Alex. It's not going to grow back on its own."

I could smell the smoke on his breath under spearmint gum, stale and sugary. Behind him, the other football players chuckled. I swung my locker door shut. "Yeah, like your bald spot? That hair's never coming back."

Nick briefly touched the back of his head, where hair was already starting to thin. His mouth bent into a frown. "Fuck you, Winchester."

My eyes narrowed. "Asshole."

Mr. Hunter, the vice principal, appeared nearby. "Problem here?"

"Not with me," Nick said. Stuffing his hands into the pockets of his jacket, he sauntered away, the other football players behind him.

Mr. Hunter frowned at me. "Watch your language, Miss

Winchester." Then he walked down the hall, limbs swinging in a poor imitation of the strut in old cowboy movies.

"You've got to be kidding me," I said.

Theresa shrugged. "He probably has money on the game."

I hadn't known how bad things would be if the football team's winning streak was threatened. For years, they'd suffered humiliating defeats, ranked as the worst team in their league. And suddenly, after winning a few games, I was the one responsible for jeopardizing their chances of going to state. All day everyone kept harping on it, either as a joke or taking it seriously. People claimed I had hurt the team's focus, or that the cheerleaders had better watch out when I was behind the wheel, or that I was a plant from our rival schools, out to kill the quarterback. When I was calm, I could say their behavior was immature and irrational, and they'd be lucky if they passed geometry or managed not to knock up their girlfriends. But by the time I followed Theresa into the cafeteria and heard my name at various tables, the calm had burned out of me.

Even when kids didn't call out or approach me, I could feel eyes turn whenever I entered a room. At one table, girls from the soccer team pretended they'd been looking elsewhere when I turned to them. Last year when I was on JV, we'd all been friends. I quit when I finally got sick of my mom lecturing me after games about what I could have done better. Now I wished I'd stayed on the team just so they might stick up for me. I would have made varsity this year. In sophomore English, we read *The Scarlet Letter*, and although I hadn't liked it at the time, now I felt like Hester Prynne was my kind of girl.

Theresa and I sat in the corner, joining our friends Maddie and Josh. I'd been friends with Maddie since elementary school, when we were both into horses, and Josh since middle school, when we both were into hating math class. They'd been talking about some band coming to Richmond, but stopped once Theresa and I sat down. I was sure they'd say something about my driving, but instead Josh asked, "You know Jim Wiley?"

All three of them looked at me. "Yeah," I said. "Everybody knows Jim. He drove into his house, remember?"

"No, I mean," Josh said, "like, are you friends?"

I balanced an apple in my palm before taking a bite. "Not really. I mean, I saw him on the way to school yesterday."

"What'd you do?" Theresa asked, grinning. "Hook up in the woods?"

"Yeah, it was really romantic," I said. "Bugs and wet leaves. I'm super outdoorsy." My mind flashed to Jim's perfect mouth and how I bet he would be an amazing kisser. "If Jim Wiley wanted to hook up in the woods, that's what I'd be doing right now."

"Like Tarzan and Jane," Maddie said. She took out a pen and started drawing purple flowers on her hands. "Except fewer gorillas, more squirrels."

I looked at Josh. "Did Jim say we were friends?"

Josh explained that he had been in Spanish class when people started talking about me, the car, and the football field. And then Jim said, "Like you guys are any better." I thought that was surprising enough, but Josh went on to describe Nick Gillan arguing with Jim about me, Nick saying I was some dumb bitch and they were going to lose the game because of me. "So Jim goes, 'Whatever. You sucked to begin with.' Nick's face got all red and he tried to jump out of his desk, which didn't really work because he's too big. Jim was, like, staring him down. I totally thought Nick was going to flip desks over or something, but then Señor Oria came in, so everyone had to shut up and sit down."

Maddie nodded. "Jim Wiley totally stood up for you."

I chewed a bite of apple and tried not to smile. "Yeah, well, he demolished part of his house. He probably thinks messing up the football field is so minor compared to that."

A few tables away, Jim Wiley was sitting with his senior friends but didn't seem to be saying much. He hadn't been in school long enough after driving into his parents' house to deal with any of the rumors. Some people had claimed he drank a whole bottle of Jack Daniel's. Others said he hated his family, and another group insisted that he snorted coke with the lacrosse team in the boys' bathroom. Whatever he'd done, it was cooler than freaking out behind the wheel.

I swallowed a bite of sandwich, but it was hard in my throat. I barely knew Jim; the first time he'd said more than "hey" to me had been that morning in the woods. Except now he was sticking up for me when most of the student body thought I was an idiot. I hoped the rumors about him weren't true. I hoped he was mostly an okay person. That suddenly seemed important.

Just after last bell, Mr. Kane caught me in the hall. I thought he was going to tell me about more imaginary people I'd killed, but he'd calmed down a little since driver's ed. "Alex," he said, exhaling heavily. It was as if he'd been practicing how to say my name without swearing.

"Mr. Kane," I said.

"I just spoke with your mother about your situation. Your parents and I are going to have a conference and discuss our options. I really don't want to fail you, so be prepared—it's probably going to have to be a lot of extra work."

I could already imagine the lecture—how I wasn't applying myself, how I was totally capable, and how I had to get over it already. "What did my mom say?" I asked.

"She's concerned, obviously," he said. He paused, frowning at his clipboard, and then met my gaze. His voice was softer. "She said she'd been feeling a little out of sorts, so please let her know that I can work around her schedule if she's under the weather."

"Right," I said, remembering how my mother had glazed over at breakfast. It was nothing, I told myself. Not like when she'd been sick—or that's what we called it—years earlier. "She's fine. You can meet whenever."

"Excellent. Until then, you can observe."

I tried to smile. Observing driver's ed—such a thrill. Public humiliation aside, I wondered if it would be better to fail the class.

"We'll make a driver out of you yet," Mr. Kane said.

"Can't wait," I said.

CHAPTER THREE

Preparation, I have often said, is rightly two-thirds of any venture.

—Amelia Earhart

That night, I expected Mom to corner me about driver's ed, but it didn't happen. At dinner, we talked about Teddy's science-fair project—a baking-soda volcano, like every other kid in second grade—and how Katy felt like she was kind of over gymnastics. Mom asked me how school was that day but didn't bring up Mr. Kane, and Dad didn't seem to know anything, either. I kept quiet.

Walking up the driveway the next afternoon, I could hear Patsy Cline on the stereo, a sign my father was already home from work. Usually he didn't get home until six, after my mother if she was working at the dentist's office that day. He probably pulled a muscle on one of his routes and left early. Teddy, whom I'd grudgingly picked up after school, started dancing.

"Oh, my God," I muttered. "Not this shit."

"I like it," Teddy said. Then he smirked. "You said shit."

"No I didn't. You heard me wrong."

"I'm gonna tell Dad." He raced toward the house with unwarranted glee, sticklike limbs flailing.

Inside, our father was sunk into the reclining chair, still in his postal uniform, a bag of ice slung over his shoulder, Jackson at his feet. Teddy was by his side, jabbering at him about me and a math test he'd had at school and eight other things. Dad's eyes were half closed, but he nodded at Teddy. "Great multiplying, Ted. See how all those flashcards paid off?" he said, patting Teddy's shoulder. He saw me hanging back in the hall. "I'll talk to Alex about that, okay?"

"Alex!" Teddy shouted, even though I was right there. He smiled so all his mismatched adult and baby teeth showed. "Dad wants to talk to you."

"Oh, gee, I wonder why." I tried to mess up his hair, but he dodged my hand and rushed out of the room. When he wasn't trying to annoy me, he could be an all right brother; he even liked playing soccer with me in the backyard. (I used to let him win all the time, but now I liked showing him tricks.) At first, when my mom was pregnant with Teddy, I'd thought I wasn't going to like him at all. For six months, I complained when my mother couldn't make lunch or take us shopping because her back hurt or she had to lie down. When Mom came home with him for the first time, Katy fawned over his tiny hands and feet. I hung back, not automatically impressed. Teddy wasn't a cute baby; he looked long and thin, as if he'd been stretched. But when Mom had asked what I thought about my brother, I'd said he had her eyes. She'd smiled as if I'd called him beautiful.

Arms folded over my chest, I perched on the couch, facing my father.

Dad groaned as he readjusted the makeshift icepack. "Pulled a muscle in my shoulder," he explained without my asking. "This one box got me. And all those catalogs. Of course people are going to throw them away. I swear, tomorrow I'm going to sort through what I think people won't need and toss it. Do us both a favor." As he chuckled, his shoulders shook and jostled off the ice. He tried to snatch it but moved too quickly, wincing at the pain.

"Wouldn't that be a federal offense?"

He waved his hand as though brushing away a cobweb. "I'd call it efficiency. They'd love it."

My father was definitely not the typical disgruntled postal worker. "Walking in the fresh air, bringing people news, what could be better?" he often said when people asked about the job. "Better than being stuck in a cubicle all day." We lived in such a small town that he knew most people on his route. At Christmastime, he came home with cards, plates of cook-ies, and the occasional bottle of wine. And because he carried dog biscuits in case of unfriendly pets, Jackson followed him around the house, ignoring any other member of the family.

Nodding toward the door, my father frowned. "And speak-ing of getting in trouble, don't swear in front of Teddy, huh?"

"It's not like I'm saying anything he hasn't already heard."

"All the same, you don't have to say it in front of him. He's seven."

I heaved a sigh. "Fine, fine." Before I could get to my feet, Dad held a palm up for me to stay.

"There was a message on the machine when I got home," he said, "from a Mr. Kane. He wanted to know what time would be good for the conference."

My heart sank. I'd hoped that Mom had forgotten about the conference and Dad would never have to know.

Dad's face softened behind his beard. "I offer to take you out, practice, and you refuse. And in class, apparently you're one step away from taking out an entire building with a car. What's the problem?"

"There's no problem," I said, jumping to my feet. "I suck at driving—that's all. Who even says I have to learn?"

I made my way toward the kitchen, but Dad called out, "Hey, I'm pretty sure I'm not done discussing this." His tone was firm enough that I stopped at the doorway. He had to turn in the chair to see me. "Mr. Kane's willing to talk about options. You might not even have to repeat the class next semester."

"Woo-hoo."

"I know it's scary, but we can go out somewhere, just us, and you won't have to worry about hitting anything. You can go three miles an hour—who cares? It's something you gotta learn, Alex."

"I can get by without it," I said, sitting down again.

"Sure, but it's helpful. Besides, what are you going to do? Stay at home your whole life?"

Considering how popular I suddenly wasn't at school, that didn't seem like such a bad alternative. But I realized it would also probably lead to the grisly murder of one family member or another. Rather than admitting that my dad had a point, I rolled my eyes. Jackson nudged his head against my palm, allowing me to pet him.

Dad grinned. "Now, should I bring a helmet to practice driving with you?" He rubbed his beard, mentioning that Mr. Kane's message said he'd talked to Mom about this yesterday. "You guys didn't already fight about it, did you?"

"You'd know if we did. Teddy's brain would probably explode with joy to tell you all about it."

I thought this would make Dad at least chuckle, but his frown deepened. "Would you give her a call for me?" He fingered the ice pack. "Ask when she thinks she'll be home."

Scowling enough to seem put out, I dialed the number for the dentist's office where Mom worked as a receptionist most days. I expected her voice on the other end, but someone else greeted me with, "Good afternoon. Forrester Family Dental." The voice was clean and crisp. I imagined two rows of sparkling teeth. This must have been Georgia, the new receptionist — bubbly was how my mother had described her.

"Hi. Is my mom there? Janet Winchester?"

"Is this Katy?" I told her it was Alex. "Alex, right. Your mom isn't home yet?"

I assumed Georgia was still learning the schedule. "No, she works until five on Wednesdays."

I heard papers shuffling; it sounded like static. Then Georgia told me Mom hadn't been feeling well, so she'd left a little while ago. "Headache or something. Light-headed, you know? Kind of confused." Georgia thought Mom must have stopped at the drugstore for aspirin. "I know she was at the doctor's a few weeks ago, so I hope it's nothing serious. Tell her I say, 'Feel better,' all right?"

When I hung up the phone, Dad asked what Georgia had said. It was a simple answer—Mom was a little sick and went home early. This wasn't anything unusual. She got headaches sometimes. Lots of people had them. It was just like Dad and his shoulder. And going to the doctor's could have been nothing, a checkup. Mom wasn't sick again. Not like before.

Almost four years earlier, Mom had been expecting another baby. I thought three of us were enough, but since Teddy was old enough for preschool, my parents had decided to have one more. "I always wanted a big family," Mom said.

It was going to be a girl. Mom and Dad brought home the ultrasound pictures to show us. They'd picked out names already—Meagan Rose or Jenna Elizabeth. I told Katy she'd have to share a room with the new baby. Teddy scribbled all over sheets of construction paper and told us they were drawings of his little sister. Mom taped them to the crib so Teddy could welcome the baby when she came home.

Then one day, when Mom was at the end of her second

trimester, I found her in the bathroom, crouched on the bath mat. She kept insisting she was all right, but we had to mop up the blood with paper towels. I rode with her in the ambulance because no one else was home, and I tried to say things like, "It's okay," but she was pale and stared at the roof of the car. She tried to hold my hand, but her grip was weak, so I had to hold on enough for both of us.

Doctors swept Mom away. I was left in the hospital waiting room, mindlessly watching episodes of court TV shows and shivering under the harsh blast of the air conditioner. Dad appeared briefly, only to join Mom while she underwent tests. Mom's friend and our neighbor Mrs. Ellis picked me up, already having gotten Teddy and Katy from their after-school activities. Mrs. Ellis tried to smile as she drove out of the hospital parking lot. "Sometimes babies come early," she said. As if I didn't know that already.

At home, Katy, Teddy, and I watched Pixar movies and ate Milano cookies. Every so often, Teddy would ask when Mom was going to be done having the baby, and I would tell him that sometimes it took a while.

"Was I like this?" he asked.

"No," I said. "You were crazy fast."

He smiled. "I'm the fastest one in my class." He poked Katy. "I'm faster than you." Katy vehemently denied this, so they were distracted for a little while.

A few hours later, Mrs. Ellis was still around. She was the one who answered the phone when Dad called. "Yes, yes, of course. Anything I can do," she said into the phone, and hung up. I didn't ask why she hadn't let me talk to my father. I didn't need to. "There were some complications," Mrs. Ellis said.

The baby couldn't breathe. Infant respiratory distress syndrome — that was what the doctors called it. When my dad came home briefly to change and see us, he said the baby's lungs were too stiff to breathe on their own. Something about how they hadn't had time to develop. My parents spent weeks at the hospital looking through a huge window at shriveled babies in little plastic boxes.

I only saw her once. Dad asked me to come to the hospital. Katy and Teddy were too young, he said, but I could see my sister if I wanted. I was nervous but said yes. We drove to the hospital without talking, without even the radio on. Inside, we walked directly to the neonatal intensive care unit. Dad pointed her out to me — Meagan Rose. Although I knew it was a girl, I could only tell that from the little pink tag around her ankle. Her limbs were emaciated, and her face was strained as if it hurt to lie there. Her chest kept caving in when she inhaled and exhaled, each breath aided by a plastic tube winding in her tiny nose. The sight of her made me queasy. I didn't ask to go back after that. A week later, when my parents came home alone, my stomach churned with relief and guilt. I wouldn't have to see that fragile, withered body again. But maybe somehow, my revulsion at the sight of my sister had caused her delicate heart to stop beating.

After that, the doctors recommended that my parents not

have any more children. We were it. Mom went to bed for a week. I tried to be helpful—bring her glasses of water, change her pillowcases, get her books from the library—as if I could make up for what had happened. But she didn't say much to me, or anyone. Silence sent cracks through her room. Then she got out of bed and made coffee and acted like nothing had happened. It was over and I thought we'd survived.

Dad was waiting for me to tell him if Mom was still at the office. "She's on her way," I finally said.

As I spoke, a car eased itself into the driveway. I rushed to the door. But it was Katy, being dropped off from gymnastics by a friend's mother. Now in middle school, Katy was trading her old friends for new ones, and their families were unfamiliar. Along with Katy, the girl and her mother stepped out of their minivan and walked to our front door.

The mother was shorter than I was and had a mushroom-ish haircut. She smiled like we'd already met. "Hi. I'm Amy's mom. You must be Alexandra."

Katy shrugged at me as if to say that she didn't usually talk about me but this was a mother who asked questions.

"I wanted to introduce myself to your mom," Amy's mom went on to explain. "Is she around?"

I was about to say that my mother wasn't home from work yet when I saw her walking up the street. At first I wasn't sure if it was even her or not—something about her was different. Her limbs seemed longer and more languid with each step. She wore the same clothing I'd seen her in that morning—pressed khakis, a light navy-blue sweater—but now she had a new linen scarf wrapped carelessly around her neck as well. As she approached the house, she waved, a wide and slow gesture, as if she had to travel a great distance to reach us.

Katy's friend's mom smiled. "Perfect timing, I guess."

Where was Mom's car? She'd driven to work that morning. Her expression was friendly and somehow younger. There was no stress under her eyes or around her mouth.

"Were you waiting for me?" she asked.

"Only for a second. I'm Karen White, Amy's mom. We spoke on the phone last week." Mrs. White extended her hand, which Mom shook heartily. Mrs. White didn't seem to notice anything off, but I thought my mother's handshake was too enthusiastic, and her grip looked too firm. I felt like I was watching her underwater; everything was there and recognizable but distorted. I glanced at Katy, who was undoing her tight braid and hadn't appeared to notice anything wrong.

Mom let go of Mrs. White's hand. "A pleasure." She turned to the petite brunette girl at Mrs. White's side. "And this must be Amy."

Mrs. White's smile didn't leave her face, but it faltered slightly. "Yes, of course, you remember Amy. You gave the girls a ride after gymnastics last week."

The gentle hint didn't curb Mom's enthusiasm. "Wonderful," she said. "I've always thought it was necessary for girls to get exercise and fresh air. My sister and I used to out-climb the boys in our neighborhood."

That caught Katy's attention. She frowned, mouthing, "Sister?" so only I could see. Our mother was an only child. I studied Mom's face, but her expression was genuine—calm and vigorous at the same time.

"I remember those days," Mrs. White said. "Well, I hate to run, but I'm so glad I finally had the chance to meet you."

"Lovely chat," Mom said.

"And you'll get the girls next week?"

Only then did Mom hesitate. "What . . . ? Ah, yes, right. The girls."

Mrs. White, having started to her car, stopped. She tried to keep smiling, glancing between Amy and my mother. "From gymnastics. Was there a change in plans? If you're too busy—"

"No, no," my mother insisted. "It'll be splendid. See you next week." Mrs. White opened her mouth to press the issue but closed it again. She clasped Amy's hand as she walked toward their car. We watched them back out of the driveway, my mother waving until they disappeared.

"What sister?" I asked.

Mom snorted a laugh, holding the screen door open. "What sister? Pidge, of course. Now, what'll it be, in or out?"

We followed her inside. My father had turned off Patsy Cline and was now trying to read the newspaper with one hand. When he heard the door slam, he set the paper aside and hoisted himself out of his chair. My mother didn't look up as he stepped into the kitchen. Whistling to herself, she filled a glass with water.

"What's Pidge?" Katy asked.

Mom gulped half the glass, then set it on the counter, sighing with satisfaction. She blinked hard, like she had something in her eye, and looked at Katy again. "I'm sorry, what?" Finally she saw my father, who was holding the ice pack in place with one hand. "Did you hurt yourself?"

"Yeah, lifting this one package," he said. "Must've had about eight barbells in it."

"I didn't know you were buying any barbells."

My father glanced at Katy and me to see if we were in on some practical joke. When all we could do was shrug, he said, "No, I was just lifting it. Someone else ordered them."

"Well, that's good to hear. I don't really like weight lifting. A good hike, a nice game of golf, that's the kind of exercise you should be getting." She seemed so emphatic that I had to wonder if she'd ever played golf before. Maybe she had when she was in high school. My mother grew up in Florida, so I could easily imagine her wearing a pastel polo shirt and strolling in the sunshine with a set of clubs on her shoulder. And it was something I'd never asked her about, even though I was kind of sporty, too.

"Are you feeling all right?" Dad asked.

She bristled. "Never better." She stretched her arms high over her head, fingers interlaced. "That woman—she

38

mentioned the girls next week. It has to be Ninety-Nine business. Do you think they'll know how to handle the machinery?"

"Machinery?" I said.

Mom snatched her glass off the counter, but once she had it, she didn't seem to know what to do with it. "It's complicated," she murmured.

"Mom," Katy said firmly. It was one thing to mention a nonexistent sister; it was another to potentially embarrass Katy in front of a friend. "You need to drive me and Amy to gymnastics next week."

Mom stared at Katy for a second before something connected. She placed the glass on the counter again.

"I know that," she told Katy, her tone defensive. She put a hand to her forehead. "I'm not feeling well. I'm going to lie down."

Dad took a step toward her. "Do you want some aspirin?"

She held up a hand to him. "No, I'm fine."

Dad tried to smile, but his lips didn't quite obey, simply pressed together instead. Katy mumbled that she had to shower. As long as Mom had started to behave normally again, she wouldn't have to worry. I wasn't so sure. If Mom was so confused at home, what had she been like at the office? And now, even as she seemed to recognize her surroundings, it felt like there were still pieces missing. It reminded me of being in class and not exactly knowing the answer to a teacher's question. As long as I could compile enough information to get by, I was safe. I didn't know if Mom could do that.

She walked slowly, like an old woman unsure if her bones would support her. As she climbed the stairs, she tugged at the linen scarf around her neck but didn't take it off.

I turned to my father. "She wasn't driving."

He readjusted his ice pack, blinking at me. "What?"

"She didn't drive home," I said. "She must have left her car at the office—or somewhere else."

"Maybe she didn't drive because she wasn't feeling great. She didn't want to hurt anything," Katy said.

Dad groaned softly as he removed the bag of ice and set it on the table. Jackson had wandered into the kitchen and was leaning against Dad's leg. Dad bent to pet him, not looking at Katy or me. When we lost Meagan Rose, Dad was efficient—he called relatives, bought groceries, got rid of baby clothes, but he didn't talk much about what was happening. Whenever I asked him if Mom was all right, he would say, "Of course," and end the discussion.

"You know your mom," he said. "She tries to do everything. She hasn't been sleeping well. Once she gets a few good nights' sleep, she'll be fine." He ambled toward the reclining chair.

"But she was acting so weird," I said. "And that new receptionist said she was at the doctor's recently. Don't you think—?"

"Alex." His voice was sharper than I'd ever heard it. "I'll take care of it."

I looked at Katy for support, but she refused to meet my eye and I felt like I was being melodramatic. And what did I expect him to do, anyway? If Dad had asked me what he could do about Mom, I wouldn't have known what to say. But I was sure there was something he and Katy were refusing to see.

"Fine," I said, grabbing Jackson's leash off the counter. As I was hooking it to his collar, I added, "Maybe we can call Aunt Pidge and ask her to talk to Mom."

CHAPTER FOUR

Courage is the price that Life exacts for granting peace.
—Amelia Earhart

Mom never slept well. She would get up at two in the morning—
a few hours before Dad had to be at the post office—and
pad downstairs in her slippers to pay bills or fold laundry.
Sometimes, if I couldn't sleep, either, I'd find her sitting at
the kitchen table with piles of clothes scattered around her,
bathed in the glow of the single fluorescent light above the
sink. I'd slump into a chair beside her. She'd ask if I wanted
herbal tea or something to eat. (Her late-night snack was
peanuts.) Then we'd talk. There was something about being
awake when everyone else was asleep that made it okay to tell
her about things. How did I do on that math test? How was the
movie I saw with Maddie? Did I still talk to my friends from

middle school? At any other time of day, I found these questions annoying, but sitting together at the kitchen table late at night made me feel like I could open up. Her hands moved efficiently as she folded towels, but she would look at me with a kind of softness. It was like we'd stepped into an alternate universe, where she didn't nag me and I didn't get so irritated by everything she said. When I started to yawn and said I was going to bed, Mom would say, "See you later," and wave a little, as if I were traveling a distance farther than upstairs.

The night before my parents' meeting with Mr. Kane, I woke to the sound of her bare feet on the staircase. Earlier that evening, after Mom had had a nap, she was herself again and remembered the call from Mr. Kane. Of course an argument followed. Mom was furious that I'd been in an accident and didn't tell them. "I had to find out from some teacher. What if it happened on the road somewhere? You could have been killed." I argued that I wasn't on the road somewhere, and even if I had been, I wouldn't have told her anyway because she just freaked out about every little problem. We ended up yelling at each other so late that it kept Teddy awake. So hearing her in the middle of the night made me think it might be a good way to smooth things over.

At first I thought she kept hitting the creaky boards as she moved downstairs, but then I realized she was saying something. I hoped she was humming to herself, but there was no tune or rhythm. Then she moved into the kitchen and I couldn't hear anymore.

43

Katy turned over in bed to face the door. I hoped she heard it, too. "Katy," I whispered.

"What?" Her voice wasn't drowsy enough to make me think she'd been asleep.

"Mom's downstairs."

Katy shifted again, grasping her pillow. Most of the time I complained about having to share a room with my little sister, but now I was grateful to have her lying a few feet away.

I threw back my blanket and was halfway to the door when Katy asked, "What are you doing?"

"She was all weird earlier. She could burn the house down or something."

"It was just had a headache," Katy said. "She was confused and then she was all right, so she's probably making tea or whatever. Just go back to bed."

"I'll be right back."

"Alex." I heard her feet hit the floor. She stumbled after me, following close as we went downstairs.

In the kitchen, the overhead light was on, not just the one above the sink. On the floor, Jackson licked at his paw. Papers covered the table and the counters. At first I thought, relieved, that she was paying bills, but the pages were too colorful. My eyes traveled over the blue and green, small lines stretched across. Maps, I realized, printed out from the Internet and taped together. Dozens of them.

Where was she going?

Mom was leaning over the table with a contemplative frown. "Hmm," she said as she ticked off marks. "Too far for that." When she noticed us in the doorway, she started folding up the pages. "Did I wake you? Sorry, I didn't realize how much noise I was making."

I stepped closer, Katy trailing after me. Crinkled printouts of the United States, Europe, and the Pacific overlapped one another, so it looked like someone could go from Guam to Alaska to France in two easy jumps. Writing sprawled across nations, mostly numbers but a few notes, too—*high altitude, mountain range,* and *stop for supplies,* and *English?*

Mom tried to cover up the maps with her hands. "These are nothing. You don't have to worry about them."

"Are we going on vacation? Like to Florida again?" Katy's voice was hopeful.

Mom chuckled. "Why not farther than Florida? People can fly all over the world these days."

"Where are you going?" I demanded. "When?"

She stiffened at the harshness in my voice. When she put her hand on my shoulder, her fingers were too rigid. I shook them off and she sighed. "Well, not *now*," she said. "I've still got a lot of work to do, plans to make, people to contact." Her voice dropped to a murmur. "Must ask Bernt Balchen—but that's top secret; he's a decoy. We haven't even started fixing up the Lockheed." She snatched a pen off the table and scribbled a few notes on the edge of a map.

Katy bent down and swung Jackson into her arms. "The what?"

"The engine's completely shot."

"What engine? Do you mean the car?" I asked. What if she tried to fiddle with her car? I imagined a spark and an explosion. "I don't think there's anything wrong with it."

Mom pressed a hand to her forehead. "Of course not the car. Who mentioned the car? Sometimes everything looks fine, but there could be a leak or a crack and then you're fifteen thousand feet in the air and you'll feel it."

"In the air? Like a plane?" Katy asked.

"Obviously," Mom snapped, then drew a deep breath. "I'm sorry. I didn't mean . . ." She gathered up a few more maps. "Yes, it's like a plane."

Her expression softened so that for a second it seemed like the most natural thing in the world for her to say. But she had to be joking. I tried to imagine my mother in the cockpit of a giant plane, soaring briskly through the clouds. If I was worried about driving, imagine the problems that could happen in the air.

"Are you going flying?" Katy nudged me.

Mom laughed again. "I would hope so, yes." She untucked the corner of one set of maps. "It's late. Why don't you girls get to bed and I'll show you the plans later?"

Katy nodded. "Sounds great."

I wasn't as enthusiastic. Even if Mom was learning how to fly, why hadn't she just told us in the first place? She wasn't a huge sharer, but usually she didn't guard information like that.

Not that I knew of, anyway. For all I knew, there could have been a dozen different plans and ideas spinning in her mind. I studied her face closely, as though her cheekbones and eyelids were hiding something.

But nothing seemed different. And I didn't know what else to do except steal her maps. "All right," I said. "Show us tomorrow."

"You girls sleep well." She turned back to her work, sighing thoughtfully to herself as she made another note above Scotland.

Jackson still tight in her arms, Katy elbowed me out of the kitchen and upstairs. But when we passed the door to our parents' room, I stopped. "I'm going to tell Dad," I said.

"He's asleep," Katy said. "He has to get up in a couple hours. He'll be mad."

"No, he won't. He'll want to know Mom's planning an around-the-world tour at two in the morning. That's not super normal."

"She always wakes up and does stuff like that. It's just, I don't know, a fun idea or something. Come on, please, just tell Dad tomorrow."

I glanced at my parents' door, imagining Dad snoring lightly, one foot peeking out from under the covers. I wanted to go in and tell him that Mom was planning to run away, fix the car engine, or steal a hot-air balloon, but all of that sounded ridiculous. She wasn't slurring her words or talking about conspiracy theories or having seizures. She wasn't stuck in bed.

When I tried to put my anxieties into words, I couldn't. And if I couldn't even talk about how Mom's expressions and gestures were suddenly different and why that seemed so wrong, what would I tell my father when I woke him a few hours before his route started?

But I knew he'd was concerned, too. After he'd picked up Mom's car from the dentist's office, where she'd left it that afternoon, he was quieter, and he didn't joke around during dinner or anything, even though he'd said he'd take care of everything. And he would. I didn't need to wake him up right now for that to happen.

"All right," I grumbled, letting myself be led down the hall.

"He'll probably say it's nothing. Stress or something," Katy said. Jackson curled up on the floor between us.

I couldn't see her face in the dark. She wanted so badly for there to be nothing wrong. I wondered if she was thinking about Florida, of when our family had gone there for April vacation when Teddy was still a baby. Katy was probably hoping Mom's imaginary trip would be something like that. Mom made sand castles with Teddy while Dad taught Katy and me how to bodysurf. We threw ourselves into waves, riding them until we scraped ourselves on the shore. At night I would lie in bed and still feel the rocking sensation of the ocean. That was before Mom lost the baby.

But I didn't want to remember that part. I feel asleep, making myself think about wave after wave after wave.

I slept through my alarm the next morning, so by the time I got up, Dad had already left for work. I wouldn't be able to talk to him until after school, and the meeting with Mr. Kane. That would be fine; Dad would talk to Mr. Kane and then he'd figure out what was wrong with Mom.

For breakfast, Mom made a pile of toast slathered with butter and jam, not asking if that was what we wanted. Usually we made our own breakfasts. At least the maps were gone. For a moment, I hoped the previous twenty-four hours had been a fluke, just an off day for my mom. But when I reminded her about the meeting with Mr. Kane, she tilted her head at me. "Today?"

"Yes." Geez, how could she have forgotten? "You know, you don't have to—"

"No, no." She seemed out of breath as she grabbed a notepad and pen. "These things are important. Here, I'll write it down. What did you say? Kane?"

I repeated the information to her twice to make sure she'd gotten it down. As much as I wished this meeting didn't exist, it would be worse if Mom didn't show up at all and had to reschedule. She promised she wouldn't forget. "I've done so many of these things I can practically sleep through them."

"No, you haven't. I haven't failed a class before. I'm not a total idiot." I wanted to believe this was the kind of exchange we had every day.

She looked at me, bewildered. "I didn't say that you were."

I picked up my backpack and slung it over my shoulder.

49

"You know, you don't have to see Mr. Kane today," I said, hoping to make the meeting sound insignificant. "If you're too tired or something."

Mom shook her head vehemently. "No, I'm fine. Don't I look fine?" She reached for the notepad again and moved too quickly, knocking a glass of juice onto the floor. It shattered and juice pooled on the tiles. "Dammit," Mom said. For a second, she looked as if she were going to cry.

Mom pulled out the dustpan while I reached for larger shards of glass. From the living room, Katy shouted, "Alex, the bus!"

"Go ahead," Mom said. "I'll be fine."

I frowned but there wasn't enough time to argue. If Dad had talked to Mom earlier, he must have thought she was feeling all right; and as long as he would be there, too, the meeting couldn't get too bad.

Mom followed us to the door and waved as we ran across the yard. On the bus, I looked to our front door, hoping to catch a glimpse of her expression. But I was too far away, and all I could see was the vague outline of her face.

During homeroom, Theresa complained about her parents' recent announcement that they were going to spend Hanukkah at her uncle's house in Colorado this year. Sitting in the back row, she ranted to me as she scratched stars into the cover of her French notebook.

"It's like, do we even know these people? They could be totally obnoxious. My mom barely talks to them, and anyway, it's *her* brother, not mine. Why do I have to spend so much time with them? And my own *parents*, for God's sake. Usually we only get together to light the damn candles."

At the front of the classroom, Mr. Pianci was reading the announcements — football game on Saturday, pep rally on Friday, lunch today was pizza. "Colorado's supposed to be pretty," I said.

"Yeah, maybe I can make myself an igloo and hide out in it."

"Colorado's a little south for that."

Theresa shivered. "It's close enough. All of Hanukkah," she said. "That is such a long time. Do you know how long Hanukkah is?"

"Eight nights," I said. "I live in the world."

Theresa half smiled, then rubbed her pen deeper into the cardboard so that a star filled with dark ink. "That's practically all of winter break. It's like a bad movie. They think we're going to end up overcoming wacky obstacles and act like one of *those* families."

I didn't know Theresa's family very well. Whenever we went to her house, her parents were at work or a conference or a vineyard. At first I expected to see signs of a neglected child in her — confessions that she wished she saw more of her parents, acting out to get their attention — but she seemed fine with the setup.

"So now I'm kind of trapped," she said. "Can you just kidnap me or something?"

She was joking, but I thought about Theresa coming over to my house now. How would I explain my mother poring over maps in the kitchen, planning a trip to nowhere? "Sure," I said, trying to smile. "In fact, how about we just run away together?"

Mr. Kane had agreed to meet with Mom and Dad during the third lunch period, when my parents could get away from work. While Theresa and everyone disappeared into the cafeteria, I waited at the front door for my parents' cars to pull into the parking lot. Part of me hoped that Mr. Kane and my parents would come to the conclusion that I didn't have to learn how to drive. Logically, I knew there was no reason to be afraid, that in such a small town it wasn't likely I'd hit a lot of traffic, much less get into a major accident. But just the thought of sitting behind the wheel made me sick. I knew I couldn't control something so big. I imagined the car veering off the road of its own accord; the air bag would detonate; the alarm would blare. The car would start to flip, and all I would see would be the ground, the sky, the ground, as the car turned over and over, until the windows cracked and the metal frame crumpled as easily as a tin can.

I had to turn away from the parking lot.

The halls were empty by the time Mom rushed in. She held the folded note from this morning as if she would have forgotten without the details in front of her. She wore a button-down shirt and a pair of baggy khaki pants held up by a leather belt.

My mother was a tall woman, but the pants seemed odd some-how. After a second, I realized they were cut wrong—they were men's trousers. The linen scarf from yesterday was tossed over her shoulder, and she readjusted it when she saw me.

"All set?" she said cheerfully.

I was glad the halls were empty. "What are you wearing?"

She glanced down at her outfit. "What's the matter with it?"

"Those aren't your pants," I hissed, in case anyone was within earshot. "And where is Dad?"

She held out a note for me. "Your father . . . David . . . called earlier. He can't get out of work."

I took the piece of paper from her and saw her choppy handwriting, first the time and location of the meeting I'd dic-tated that morning, and then an addition below: *David at work, not able to get away, talk to Alex later.* I read the note three times before crumpling it in my palm. Mom watched me, smiling benignly. I wanted to shove her away. I couldn't believe Dad. He had talked to me about driving, sounded sympathetic, been willing to work out a plan, and now he disappeared at the last minute. Was the town suddenly mad for stamps? Did a package need to be delivered immediately or someone wouldn't get a heart transplant? How could he have left me like this? Looking at my mother in my father's pants, I wanted to push her out the front door and lie to Mr. Kane about why neither of my parents was present.

"Alex? Mrs. Winchester?" Mr. Kane was striding toward us.

Shit. "Hey, Mr. Kane."

He stuck out his hand at my mother. "Thank you so much for meeting with me today," he said.

"My pleasure," Mom said.

"Are we still waiting for Mr. Winchester?"

"He's not coming," I said. "Mom, are you feeling okay?" It was one chance to avoid all of this, at least until Dad could be there, too. I hoped it would be enough of a hint for her.

But she chuckled. "Never better."

Mr. Kane glanced at me, straining to smile. "I hope we can get all this worked out. My office is just down this way."

Mr. Kane shared an office with the Latin teacher and one of the English teachers. Three desks were crammed into a room not much bigger than a supply closet, with one frosted window at the far end. A few posters encouraging kids to read were tacked up on the wall. The office smelled like Wite-Out and generic soap. Mr. Kane's desk was the most cluttered of the three, covered with papers not yet graded and books of audition monologues. On the edge of his desk was a half-eaten sandwich on crusty Italian bread — brought from home, obviously. He even had a plant, although it looked like the soil was dry and the plant was resigning itself to a short life.

"Please, sit down," he said, dragging over the other teachers' chairs. Mom sat with her elbow propped on one arm of her chair. In a stiff wooden chair, I felt trapped. My heart thudded as I watched Mr. Kane shuffle a few papers around before he found the clipboard from driver's ed.

"So, Mrs. Winchester," he said, "as you know, Alex has a bit of a problem when it comes to driving."

His voice was so solemn and sympathetic that I knew he must have rehearsed this. There was none of the edge that he had when I drove onto the football field.

"That's unfortunate," Mom said. "But certainly there are lessons."

Mr. Kane eyed me as if I'd lied to my mother. "Ah, that's the thing. She's not doing well in driver's ed."

My mother sat a little straighter in her chair and folded her hands on her lap. "I hope that doesn't mean you're thinking of failing her. I think the idea that a female cannot learn how to drive is ridiculous. How will she ever learn how to pilot a plane if she isn't taught proper automobile skills?"

Mr. Kane snorted. "Pilot a plane?"

"Do you think that's so unreasonable?"

I thought of my mother's maps. Was she planning on taking me with her?

"Well, it's just that Alex isn't exactly talented at driving, so I think piloting a plane might be out of the question for now." He coughed into his fist, glancing between my mother and me as though he could see where I got my issues. "Now, as for driver's ed, there's no way Alex can pass the semester as it is."

"It's barely October," I said.

Mr. Kane sighed heavily. "Yes, but you've already gotten into two accidents. I'm not even supposed to pass people

who've had one." He looked at my mother. "Now, what I pro-
pose is that Alex take private driving lessons outside the school
during her free time. Also, you and Mr. Winchester will have to
take her out as often as possible — go to the Kroger parking lot
early in the morning, or a quiet neighborhood. If she's making
enough progress there, she can keep driving in school. Plus,
she'll have to take an extra written exam to demonstrate she
has some command of the road."

"You don't have to be so condescending," Mom said. For
a second, I was relieved; she wouldn't let Mr. Kane be such a
dick. Then she kept going. "Do any of the males in your class
have to get outside instruction?"

"No, but —"

Mom stood. "Mr. Kane, was it? I know just how important
technical skills can be when it comes to operating any kind of
vehicle. But it's insulting to suggest that this young woman is
incapable of learning. I don't know what kind of interview you
think this is, but I'm afraid it's over."

"Mrs. Winchester —"

Halfway to the door, Mom stopped. She whirled around,
face crumpling in frustration. "Why do you keep saying that?"
Her voice rose and cracked as if he were attacking her.

"I thought . . . It's your name, isn't it?" Mr. Kane looked at
his clipboard for a clue. "If I've made a mistake —"

"Mom," I snapped, "stop it already." Mr. Kane looked at
both of us like we were crazy. I was afraid of how he would talk
about this later in the teachers' lounge, telling everyone about

how Alex Winchester's mom freaked out at him when he tried to present her with a fair solution to her daughter's driving problem. And outside this office, classrooms full of students weren't too far away. I didn't know how I would restrain her if she became hysterical.

"Stop calling me Mrs. Winchester," she insisted, almost shouting.

Mr. Kane, on his feet to stop my mother before she left his office, froze. He opened his mouth to apologize but closed it again, then repeated the process, like a dying fish.

"I have to go," Mom said, rushing into the hall. Without a glance back to Mr. Kane, I followed my mother. Her strides were long but not fluid, like they had been yesterday. She might have been walking on stilts under those baggy pants. I called for her to wait for me, but she hurried toward the front door. A sharp ring echoed—the period was over. In a second, the halls would be flooded with students.

"Mom," I said, "slow down."

Doors opened and students rushed in. Mom tried to dodge them, occasionally bumping into a cluster and apologizing as she moved forward. She burst through the front doors, escaping into the sunlight. When I followed, a teacher tried to detain me but I ran into the parking lot. I heard the teacher call my name. Other people must have heard, too, and stopped to listen as they shoved books into their lockers. Maybe a few even came closer to watch.

Mom rushed to the car, which was parked in the middle

of two spaces. She fumbled for her keys and slid into the front seat. On the passenger side, I let myself in.

"Where are you going?" I said. Tears clogged my throat. "What the hell are you doing?"

She shoved her keys into the ignition. Her face was puffy, and she was breathing heavily. Her hands hovered over the steering wheel, then the gearshift, and then the dashboard. Eyes wild, she muttered to herself about wind speeds and dials. Finally she smacked the steering wheel, inadvertently hitting the horn. We both jumped.

"Dammit," she gasped. "It's all different."

For a second, I thought she might have the same problem I had. Cars were too complicated. If she could accept this, it would be fine. But as she clutched the steering wheel, I saw this was something different. She wanted to drive off, go somewhere, but for some reason, she couldn't remember how.

I felt a sudden pity for Mr. Kane as I slid the keys from the ignition. Although I expected a fight, she didn't seem to notice me.

Some people did notice, though. Seniors allowed off campus for lunch walked by, trying to peek into Mom's car. They must have seen her running through the hall, and me chasing after her. If I had been able to maintain control of the car, I would have run them over. My face burned.

But maybe I could drive. We had to get home fast, and Mom obviously couldn't do it. I looked at the keys in my palm, trying to visualize the drive home. But my heart was pounding and my hands were shaking and all I could hear was Mom crying. I hated myself for not being able to help us.

"Let's just go," I said, throwing open the door. "Just come on."

She followed with an odd obedience. I circled the car and grabbed her forearm in case she decided to run off again. Who knew what she was now? She said she wasn't Mrs. Winchester. Did that mean she didn't recognize me? That she thought I was some nice girl trying to help her? The idea made me want to leave her there to fend for herself. If she could forget me, I could forget her. But the seniors were watching and sneering from their own cars. I decided it was better to skip the rest of my classes and take her home myself. Not that I had any idea what to do with her once we were there.

CHAPTER FIVE

In soloing—as in other activities—it is far easier to start something than it is to finish it.

—Amelia Earhart

It was only a couple of miles from school to our house, but it felt longer with my mother in tow. She was quiet as she walked, her arms hugging her chest as if she was afraid she'd fall apart. I kept my distance by a few feet.

She started mumbling. I could only catch little pieces of what she said. "... respond to the telegram ... expecting ..."

"Stop it," I said.

"Pardon?" she said, forcing her lips to smile.

"Don't talk to yourself." I kicked a rock so that it skipped along the gutter. In front of a neat white house, an elderly woman was gardening, pressing large bulbs into the earth. When she saw us passing, she waved politely. My mother waved back with enthusiasm. I hurried Mom along in case she tried to start a conversation. She wasn't upset or frantic, or even pensive. Her face was serene again. Maybe she was all right.

She drew a deep breath and exhaled slowly, walking with her hands clasped behind her back. "Beautiful sky today, isn't it?"

Still stuck on this airplane idea. How far would she take it? What if she decided to open a window and jump? "It's supposed to rain later," I lied.

"Is it?" she said. "Well, bad weather can materialize in an instant. You need to be careful." She adjusted her scarf so the ends fluttered in the breeze. "Funny interview, wasn't it?"

"Funny?"

"Why even talk to me if he was going to be so judgmental and narrow-minded?"

I almost opened my mouth to argue. I wanted to tell her that the interview—which wasn't an interview at all—was about me, not her, and it was true that I couldn't drive a car, much less pilot a plane, not that that was ever up for debate. I was furious that she had embarrassed me like that, and terrified that this was something deep-rooted, not easily shaken by more rest. Fear kept my mouth shut.

Her mouth twitched, and she tried to inhale deeply but couldn't seem to get enough air in. "I didn't mean to get upset," she said. "I shouldn't have done that. I just can't seem to . . ." She sighed.

"Are you sick or something?" I asked, not really wanting her to respond.

She shook her head vehemently. "No, just tired. It's a demanding job. You know that. You'll show him someday, won't you?" she asked. Her smile was so genuine that I imagined myself behind the wheel of a car, as careless as I was supposed to be at sixteen. What she said should have been the encouragement of a mother, but her unusual outfit and behavior made the sentiment altogether different and unappealing.

I called the post office and demanded they contact my father, find him, hunt him down, anything. "It's an emergency," I told them. Postal workers probably imagined a sick child, broken bones, or a car accident. They didn't think of my mother, talking about people she didn't know and places she'd never been.

Mom dozed fitfully on the couch. While I waited for my father, I sat nearby, pretending to do my history homework but glancing at her every few seconds. Her face seemed strained even in her sleep. I thought about how happy she'd looked the night before, when Katy and I found her with those maps.

When Dad arrived, still in his postal uniform, he rushed into the house like he expected to find it on fire. I met him in the hall. "What happened?"

Suddenly the sight of him reminded me of how he'd missed the meeting. If he had been there, he might have been able to keep Mom under control. At least I wouldn't have had to do it. "She's just all weird again," I said, voice rising with each syllable. "She flipped out in front of Mr. Kane, and I had to take her home. You should have been there."

Dad rested his hands on my shoulders. "All right, all right," he said.

I tried to steady myself; it was embarrassing that he had to calm me down when Mom was the problem. I told him about how she'd stolen his pants, how she insisted she wasn't Janet Winchester, her fixation on flying, her maps, how she didn't walk or talk like herself.

In the living room, Mom groaned as she woke. Dad knelt beside her and spoke evenly. "Are you okay?" he asked.

"I'm so embarrassed. I shouldn't be napping now. There's so much to do. I've barely started at all." She sat up and tried to stand too quickly, then fell backward on the couch.

"I think we need to talk," Dad said.

She brushed her hands on her pants as if she had gotten them dirty while asleep. "Only for a minute." When Dad tried to adjust the pillows behind her, Mom wrinkled her nose at him. "For heaven's sake, I'm not an invalid."

Mom sat in the middle of the couch, one leg crossed over the other, arm draped over a cushion. She looked almost posed. Remembering her frenzy at school, I steeled myself for hysteria, dishes thrown against the wall. Instead, Mom smiled pleasantly at Dad, whose face was stolid as he asked simple questions.

"How're you feeling?"

"Fine, fine. A little tired, but that's the norm."

"Why?"

She looked vaguely incredulous. "The meetings, the lectures, the interviews, the plans. I hope you'd know my schedule, Gip."

"Gip?" My head felt heavy, filled with fog and sawdust. "What's Gip?"

My mother stiffened, waving a hand in my father's direction. "Not 'what.' *Who*. George."

"David." Dad's voice shook a little. "I'm David."

Mom frowned at him. "I don't know why you say these things."

I wanted to catch Dad's eye, but he wouldn't look at me. Instead, he took a breath and leaned forward in his seat. "Jan, you're not really thinking straight. Maybe we should take a ride over to the hospital and—"

"No. Absolutely not." Mom shot to her feet and started pacing. "I can't go to a hospital now. People need me. They expect things from Amelia Earhart. I can't disappoint them."

She said the name so naturally, I thought I hadn't heard her right. But it replayed over in my mind until the name took shape. I remembered vague details about Amelia Earhart from elementary school—female aviatrix, a mysterious disappearance in the Pacific. Her fatal flight was in the 1930s; Mom wasn't alive then. Earhart set world records and flew across the Atlantic; the only time my mother had been on a plane was when she was on her honeymoon. But Mom said her name with such reverence that it almost echoed throughout the house.

"Keys," my dad said, patting his pockets. "Where did I put them?"

I followed him as he searched. I didn't want to be in the same room as my mother, who was still pacing and arguing that Amelia Earhart had responsibilities. "Where are you going?" I asked. Since I didn't know how to drive, I couldn't follow him if he left without me.

"Hospital," he said, turning on his heel to survey the kitchen. "Where the hell did I put them?"

I snatched his keys from the counter and pressed them into his palm. "What's wrong with her?"

He didn't look at me as he spoke. "I don't know," he said. "Maybe some blockage in the brain. Or it could be Lyme disease. That happens sometimes; it messes with your head, makes you confused. If that's it, she'll be back to normal in no time." I didn't ask him what if it wasn't Lyme disease.

From the front door, I watched him guide Mom to the car. She argued with him as she went, continuing to call him Gip, or G.P. "Just call me Amelia, please," I heard her say. I wondered what she saw when she looked at him. Was it his face at all, or someone else's? If she was Amelia Earhart, who did that make me?

The house was too quiet afterward. Even when my brother and sister got home, I jumped at every small noise. I told them Mom wasn't feeling well, ignoring the details. Teddy wanted to know if she had the flu, while Katy retreated to our room without saying a word. At the sound of every car coming down the street, I rushed to the front door, thinking it would be them. Then I remembered my mother's car.

"Katy," I called. "Watch Teddy. I'll be back in a little while."

"What?" she said, incensed. "Where are you going?" I left before I could think of a lie to tell her.

Mom's sedan was still in the school parking lot, now deserted except for a handful of other cars. It was just after dusk, and everyone had left various sports practices. From a distance, I could hear the plunking of a piano and a chorus singing, "Consider Yourself" from *Oliver!* Halfway through the second verse, they stopped and started over again. Overhead, the sky was clear but there was too much light pollution to make out more than a few stars.

I circled the car once before giving the front left tire a solid kick. *I shouldn't even be here,* I thought. I should have been at home, or at Theresa's, or, hell, finding some guy to make out with, not kicking my crazy mother's stupid car.

The door was unlocked. I swung myself into the driver's seat and slammed the door behind me.

I pulled the key out of my pocket and shoved it into the ignition.

The engine growled and shuddered into life. Heart thudding, I couldn't control my breathing but tried to remember what Mr. Kane had taught us. Something about the gearshift. I yanked at it, trying to force it into place, matching the arrow on the dashboard up with something. *Please,* I thought. If I could only get this to work. Just let this one stupid thing work. Tears blurred my vision. The roof was sinking toward me. I would be crushed. I thought of Amelia Earhart, rotten corpse maybe under the weight of an entire ocean.

Screaming, I beat the steering wheel. The horn blared.

Then I saw Jim Wiley standing by the window. He tapped it with his knuckle.

"Hey," he said. "That's not exactly a fair fight."

I wiped my eyes with the back of my thumb. "Yeah, sorry, I'll stop." Fantastic. Jim Wiley saw me freaking out alone in the school parking lot.

He took a step back, and I assumed he was leaving, but then he strolled around to the passenger door and let himself in, sitting as casually as if we'd made plans to go somewhere. For a second, I thought I was going crazy. I was even crazier than my mother.

"What are you doing here?" I asked. "School's over."

"I get tutored in chemistry," he said.

It was hard to imagine Jim Wiley bent over a Bunsen burner, taking notes about temperatures and oxidation.

"So I hear you're, like, the worst driver ever."

"Oh, yeah, says the guy who bulldozed his house."

Instead of being offended, Jim laughed. I made Jim Wiley laugh. "Yeah, good point. Have you ever driven right through a house?"

I imagined my own home, a pile of rubble. "Not yet."

"Well, I guess you don't totally suck, then. Yet." He didn't say anything for a second, and I wondered what I would do if he asked for a ride home. But instead he said, "Looks like you're having some trouble."

I chuckled. "Yeah, I guess."

"First thing," he said, "that's the steering wheel. It steers things."

At first I wasn't sure if he was making fun of me again. But his voice was even and encouraging, something he might have picked up while getting tutored himself. He went on to talk about the pedals—an accelerator, a brake—and the mirrors, which I adjusted so I could see all sides around us. When I was ready, he said, I could press on the brake and shift the car into drive. And then slowly I could move my foot from the brake to the accelerator, and we'd drift across the parking lot. I tried to repeat everything he said in my mind but could only remember every other word.

"If we die," I said, gripping the steering wheel, "you can't blame me."

He laughed. "Fine, I'll take all responsibility for our horrific deaths."

The chorus was practicing scales now. I forced myself to breathe in time with them. *It's just a car,* I reminded myself. Wheel, pedals, speedometer—they all worked together neatly and efficiently—or at least they were supposed to. I ached for one thing to work perfectly that afternoon. If I could just do this one simple thing.

I touched the gas pedal, and the car inched forward. My stomach twisted, but Jim said, "Hey, that's it." I didn't dare turn to see his expression, but his voice was soft and enthusiastic, so I imagined he was actually enjoying this three-mile-an-hour trip across the parking lot.

After a second, I was, too. We were coasting along effort-
lessly, toward the darkness at the end of the parking lot and the
fields beyond. Jim rolled down his window, resting his arm on
the edge. Air drifted in and out of the car. The steering wheel
didn't rattle under my hands. As long as I held the wheel and
knew where the brake was, we wouldn't hit anything. I could
breathe again.

At the end of the parking lot, I pressed the brake and put
the car into park. I wasn't ready for turning yet. Even so, I
thought that if Jim hadn't been there, I would have danced like
an idiot. "Oh, my God!" I said. "I didn't hit anything!"

He laughed. "Yeah. Mr. Kane can sleep easy now."

I wondered if I could repeat this experience in class. It
would be more difficult with Mr. Kane and his clipboard, classmates in the backseat, and orange cones all lined up. Maybe
this was a fluke.

Jim must have seen my face fall, because he said, "We could
try this again sometime. I promise I won't teach you how to
demolish your house."

Let's do this again sometime — it was something I'd have
expected to hear on a date, even though I knew driving around
the parking lot with Jim Wiley didn't exactly qualify. Still, it was
something. And maybe eventually I would be able to guide the
car out of the parking lot, away from the high school, across
town and onto the highway.

"A little demolition would be all right," I said.

Chapter Six

*Obviously I faced the possibility of not returning when I first
considered going.*

—Amelia Earhart

Since my driving skills were still limited to a straight line, Jim
drove me home. After he'd crashed into his house, his license
had been suspended for six months. He told me he missed
being behind the wheel and didn't mind chauffeuring. All my
mom's radio stations were set to light rock, so I had to fiddle
around with the dial, trying to find something that didn't suck
too much. We drove by the houses I passed every day, windows
glowing warmly.

"So what's the driving fear about?" Jim asked. "Were you in
a bad crash or something when you were a kid?"

I tapped a finger against my seat belt. I hadn't talked about
this with anyone else—not Theresa, not Mr. Kane, not even

my parents. But Jim had helped me actually drive, so I thought he might understand. "Sort of," I said. "I mean, nothing happened. I was like four and ran after a ball into the street—you know, like kids do—and this car stopped just in time."

It was one of my earliest memories. Katy was a baby, and Mom was doing tummy time with her in the yard. I threw my ball into the air and caught it over and over; then I missed and raced after it, even though I knew I wasn't supposed to. I didn't want it to roll down the street and away forever. I don't remember the car approaching, but I remember the screech of the brakes and my mom screaming, "Alex, no!" Then she was screaming at the driver, who got out of the car in a panic. He tried to apologize, but Mom kept shouting, "You could have killed her!" She held me so fiercely, I thought she was yelling at me, too, which made me start crying.

"I was okay and everything," I told Jim. "But I keep thinking I could do that to someone. I didn't even know I'd be like this until driver's ed. I mean, I'm fine if I'm a passenger. Right now I don't care if you go a hundred miles an hour." Then I remembered this was the guy who broke part of his house. "Not that I want you to."

Jim laughed; it was a good laugh, a throaty tenor. "All right, no drag racing until your third time out."

"Thanks so much. But, yeah, I don't know what the deal is. Driving's not something I've ever really looked forward to, like everyone else. I used to think I'd like it once I started, but I never thought I'd get so freaked out by it."

"And that's where the football field comes in." He grinned. "You should've kept going, right from one end zone to the other."

"Maybe next time," I said. "If Mr. Kane lets me drive again." That reminded me of the disastrous meeting between Mom and Mr. Kane. Between the successful drive across the school parking lot and actually being in a car with Jim Wiley, I'd kind of forgotten. Now my stomach clenched as I realized we were getting closer to home. I didn't know what I'd find there. Given the choice, I would rather have been back in driver's ed, with Mr. Kane and the Volvo.

"He will," Jim said. "Mr. Kane loves the underdog. He didn't look at me like I was a crack addict when I came back this year."

I was surprised Jim brought it up. We didn't exactly hang out a lot, but I never heard him brag about driving into his house. "So where were you, anyway?" I said, tugging at a stray thread on my shirt.

"Well, with the crashing into the house thing, my parents got the idea I was not really doing anything with my life—and I guess that was true—so they sent me to stay with my grandparents in Indiana, way out in the boonies. Like even more than here."

"Fun."

He shrugged. "When I was a kid, I liked going to see them a lot. They have this soybean farm, so there was a lot of space to run around. I was kind of into it." I imagined Jim in a pair of overalls and a trucker hat, and I tried not to laugh. "And my grandparents are okay, so I went." He turned down my street. "It was kind of good to get away for a while."

Maybe Mom needed to get away for a little while, too. Except instead of going somewhere, she'd decided to be Amelia Earhart.

"It's the yellow one on the right," I told Jim as we approached my house. "You can just pull right in the driveway." Inside, several lights were on—more than just Katy's and my room and Teddy's room. Dad and Mom must have gotten home already.

Jim turned off the engine and the headlights. "How are you going to get home?" I asked. I hadn't thought that far in advance. If he wanted a ride, my dad would have to give it to him. And I wasn't sure I wanted Jim coming inside the house yet, depending on what we'd find.

"I'll walk," he said. "I don't live too far." I wanted to say that I knew, that I had seen his house before, and I had even seen when the front corner had been smashed off, when he drove his parents' car straight into their bedroom—their closet, actually. I was walking Jackson early one Sunday morning when I saw the cluster of police officers, firefighters, Wileys, and a few neighbors with coats over their pajamas. Steering Jackson in that direction, I could see the hole at the front left corner of the Wiley house. Mrs. Wiley's quilted slippers and winter boots poked out, and a couple of her long skirts fluttered in the breeze. Mrs. Wiley herself stood on the lawn in a nightgown and a George Mason University sweatshirt, talking to an officer. She explained, "We felt it before we knew what it was." Mr. Wiley kept touching the broken edges of brick and plaster, as though he could understand what had happened if only he could gather the pieces together. From what I could see, Jim wasn't there. Maybe they'd already taken him to the police station or the hospital. I didn't tell anyone about seeing the accident — not my friends, not the girls on the soccer team, no one. It was all anyone was talking about, but for some reason it felt like my own secret. And even after the driving lesson with Jim, it felt like too much to admit.

Dad's silhouette passed in front of the living room, then retreated again. I didn't see Mom with him. Maybe she was better, like Dad had promised, but if she wasn't, I didn't want to go inside and find out. I didn't even unbuckle my seat belt.

"Your parents are going to be okay with me driving?" Jim asked. "Sometimes people get protective about their cars."

"Insurance and everything," I said.

"Right."

I shook my head. "No, it's fine." I wanted to stay there and talk about anything, even car insurance, but my father passed by the window again and I could tell he was waiting for me. "Thanks. For driving and helping me drive and everything."

"No problem," Jim said. "You're really not that bad."

We swung out of the car, Jim tossing me the keys as he rounded the trunk. "See you tomorrow," he said, and I waved good-bye. He shoved his hands into his pockets and strode down the driveway and across the street, moving through the cold glow of the streetlights. I watched him until he cut through a neighbor's yard and disappeared.

Inside, someone had left the TV on. Usually I would have shouted hello, but now I just stood in the kitchen, listening for footsteps elsewhere in the house. But my father must have heard the door close, because he walked in from the living room.

Before he could say anything, I told him, "I brought the car back. We had to leave it at school today."

"Yeah," he said. His face was drawn, and he absently rubbed the shoulder he'd pulled the day before. "I saw."

On the table was a stack of mail. I began sifting through it, trying to find something with my name, but everything was addressed to my parents: *Mr. and Mrs. Winchester; David Winchester; Mrs. Janet Winchester*. I turned over the envelopes so I wouldn't have to see the names.

"I didn't drive," I said. "It was a friend."

"Yeah, I saw that, too." He glanced toward the door as if to find Jim standing there. "That wasn't Josh, was it?"

"No, it was Jim. Jim Wiley. It was the only way to get home. And he drove carefully. I don't know how you guys are about that, other people driving your cars." I wanted him to yell at me. At least it would have been a conversation about something else. Not the conversation I knew was coming.

"Alex, that's fine," he said. "I don't care about the car. Let's sit down, all right?" He guided me into the living room, where the news was still on. A tornado had ripped through a small town in Oklahoma; they were interviewing people in front of shredded homes and piles of wreckage.

"Good thing we don't live out there, right?" I said, sitting on the couch, next to Jackson. I scratched around his ears, so he put his head on my lap. "They say the sky goes green before it happens."

Dad switched off the TV. "So I took your mom to the hospital."

"I know," I said. "It's Lyme disease, right? That's what you said it would be." Lyme disease was better than a brain tumor. Mom had gotten a tick bite and didn't notice. She'd end up on antibiotics. Everything would be fine in a week.

Dad leaned forward in his chair, forearms resting on his knees. "They did some tests, and that's probably not the case."

"Well," I said, "what is it?"

"They're not really sure right now."

"What do you mean, 'they're not sure'?" I could hear my voice getting louder. "They're doctors. It's their job to know these things. They didn't just let her leave like that, did they?"

Dad shook his head. "She's still at the hospital and now she refuses to respond to any name except Amelia Earhart. They—they're not sure if it's medical. They recommended a psychiatrist—"

"So they can't do anything for her?" I wanted the doctors to provide a simple explanation and give Mom a week's worth of medication, erasing anything unhinged in her brain.

Otherwise, she would go on thinking that she was Amelia Earhart. What were we supposed to do with her like that? She wouldn't even know who we were.

"Hey, calm down." Dad glanced briefly over his shoulder. "I haven't told your brother or sister yet."

"They don't know Mom's nuts?"

"She's not nuts, Alex. And I don't think they have to know until it's absolutely necessary."

I thought of Teddy and Katy upstairs, maybe worried that Mom had Lyme disease or pneumonia or malaria or whatever. Maybe they were even thinking about when she wouldn't get out of bed for a week. But they didn't know that Mom wasn't Mom anymore, that she was Amelia Earhart. That maybe she would drive off a cliff in the car, thinking she was flying a plane. I wished I could have been upstairs, too, unaware of all the cracks in Mom's mental state.

"So where is she? In the psych ward?" I didn't like the thought of my mom around people who heard voices and tried to claw out their own eyeballs.

"It's not like an asylum," Dad said. "They're just keeping an eye on her."

I pulled Jackson onto my lap. He licked my neck. "When is she coming back?"

Dad sighed and scratched his beard. "Once they have an idea about what's going on, I guess. Probably in a few days. Honestly, Alex, we can't really afford to keep her in there forever."

But what if she wasn't better? How were we supposed to talk to her at breakfast? Somebody would have to take care of her. What if people found out? They'd have to, eventually, if she were just around, calling herself a famous pilot. That's who I'd be at school — not even the girl who was death on wheels, but the girl with the crazy mom. We couldn't let her come home until she was better again. They had to make her better again.

Before I could tell Dad any of this, he said, "And please don't mention anything to your brother or sister, all right?"

"Then why are you telling me?"

Dad leaned forward, hands clasped together. "I'm going to need your help, Alex. We're not in a great situation, and I'll need you to do things around here and help with your mom when she comes back."

I looked away, my throat tightening.

"And besides," Dad said, taking my hand, "you were right there today. Wouldn't you be upset if I'd lied to you instead?"

No, I thought. I wanted him to lie. To tell me Mom had the bubonic plague or leprosy or whatever. I would have believed him. But I still would have been wondering. "Fine," I said. "I've got homework to do, so . . ."

"All right." Jackson jumped down from my lap and went to sit by Dad's feet. Dad didn't seem to notice.

Katy was in our room, doing math homework on her bed. She glanced up when I came in but immediately turned back to long division. Katy's fingers ticked as she counted out her answers. She sighed and erased something in her notebook. I grabbed a pillow from my bed and threw it at her, hitting her in the side of the head.

"Hey!" Katy hurled the pillow back at me, but I caught it. "What's your problem?"

"Nothing." I sat on the edge of my bed, tapping my sneakers against the floor. Katy was trying to figure out her math homework again. "I drove tonight," I told her, tossing my pillow from hand to hand. "Jim Wiley taught me."

"Congrats."

"He's the one who drove into his house."

Katy looked up. "What'd he get you to do, take down the school gym?"

I grinned. "Not yet."

"So you're giving up driver's ed at school to take lessons from Jim or something?" she asked. "I don't think you'll get your license that way."

"I don't know yet." Katy knew that Mom and Dad were supposed to meet with Mr. Kane that afternoon. And presumably, she knew that something was wrong with Mom. Even though Katy had justified the maps to herself, I wondered what she thought about Mom being in the hospital.

"So Mom's sick," I said.

"I know," she said, flipping through her textbook. "Dad said they were running some tests. Do you know how to make a fraction into a percent?"

"She probably won't be back for a few days," I said.

Now Katy was comparing two different pages. "I think

it has something to do with decimals. You did this, like, four years ago and you can't remember?"

I threw the pillow at her again, this time hitting her book. "Ask someone on the bus tomorrow."

I didn't expect to see Katy's face so distorted with anger. Her eyebrows were furrowed and her lips were twisted as she shouted, "Stop throwing things at me," and hurled the pillow back, catching me in the head.

"I'm trying to talk to you," I said. "You always get all upset when I ignore you, and now you're just ignoring me."

"You're not talking about anything," Katy said. She closed the book, but her finger marked her place. "Dad already told me all of that, and I really need to get my homework done already."

"What if Dad didn't tell you everything?" I didn't want to be the only one who knew. I promised myself that if Katy outright asked, I'd tell her. That was fair enough.

Katy opened her mouth, then closed it again. She looked at me hard. "Like what?"

"Like how Mom freaked out at the meeting with my driver's ed teacher today." Katy's face furrowed as she thought about whether or not she wanted to know more. I felt bad but I couldn't stop myself. If Dad wasn't going to talk about it, maybe Katy would. "Like how she's having some kind of mental breakdown."

"Like how—" She stopped herself and stood, like a marionette being jerked up. Grabbing her backpack, she pulled out everything—books, notebooks, a few broken pencils—and chucked it onto her bedspread. "You know what? No. I'm busy. I've got work to do. Dad told us that he brought her to the hospital because she's not feeling well, so that's what happened. If she had a breakdown like before, we'd know."

"What about the maps—?"

"I don't care!" She sat in the middle of the mess on her bed. "Stop talking to me."

I was about to throw the pillow again, but as Katy opened her history book and tried to focus on a page, I saw that her face was red and her eyes were glossy with tears. Which was probably what Dad had been expecting when he asked me not to talk about Mom's mental health with my younger brother and sister. Even though Katy and I had our share of fights, I felt bad seeing her curled up in a pile of textbooks and handouts.

"Sorry," I said, collapsing onto my bed and staring at the ceiling.

"Sure," I heard Katy sniffle.

I counted the glow-in-the-dark stars Katy and I had stuck there when I was in middle school. "I didn't mean anything," I said. "It'll be fine." Saying that, I reminded myself of Dad.

The next morning, I found Teddy pouring Cheerios into our largest mixing bowl. "What are you doing? I said. "That's like half the box."

"I know. I'm hungry."

Dad had already left for work, which wasn't a surprise. Last night he intercepted me on my way to brush my teeth, whispering so Katy and Teddy wouldn't overhear. He told me he felt bad but he couldn't take another day off now, when there really wasn't anything he could do. He'd given the hospital his cell number and the number at the post office, so they could contact him in case anything happened during the day. And he'd be back a little later than usual tonight, since he was going to stop by the hospital to see how Mom was doing. Otherwise, I was in charge of things at home — to see that everyone got off to school all right, that we had lunches, and that Katy and Teddy did their homework when they got home from school. "Don't go mad with power, all right?" Dad told me, messing up my hair. He was even going to add a cell phone to his plan and give it to me. "For emergencies," he said.

Now Teddy was rummaging through the refrigerator. While he was distracted, I put some cereal back in the box.

Teddy placed a carton of milk and a bottle of Hershey's syrup next to his giant bowl of cereal. I thought he was going to make chocolate milk to go with it, but instead he started to drizzle chocolate on the Cheerios.

"What are you doing?"

"Making breakfast," he said. "Mom doesn't let us get the good cereal with marshmallows and chocolate, so I wanted to make it myself."

I gazed into the bowl. "Inventive." It wasn't much worse than letting him have chocolate milk. I searched for something less sugary for myself.

"I'm a pretty good cook," Teddy said as he stirred his mixture together. "I can make it for you, too." I thanked him and said I felt like yogurt. He munched on cereal as he told me about playing soccer at recess with the other second-graders. "I did that thing you taught me, that thing where you hit the ball with the side of your foot instead of your toe."

"Good job." I smiled. "Did it help?"

He nodded solemnly. "It helped a lot."

When Katy came downstairs, she grabbed an apple and a bowl of cereal and joined us at the table without saying anything. Even Teddy didn't talk much. It was strange to be together in the morning, minus our mother. Usually she would be quizzing Katy on the categories of biological classifications or signing a permission slip for Teddy or telling me where I could find the shirt I wanted to wear. This morning felt like one of those dual images in the comics section of the paper—two pictures that were almost identical, except for small differences, like an empty cup of coffee instead of a full one, or a flower missing a petal. Everything else was the same except for one thing.

"What are we having for lunch?" Teddy asked.

Dad didn't leave me any money, so we'd all have to make something. "I don't know," I said, getting up from the table. I didn't even know what we had. Had Mom gone grocery shopping that week? "We can make peanut-butter sandwiches."

Katy wrinkled her nose. "I'm sick of peanut butter."

"Fine," I said, closing the refrigerator. "Make your own. You're old enough."

"Who said I wasn't?" She brushed past me and began rifling through cupboards. Since I'd tried to tell her about Mom, she'd barely talked to me.

"No crusts," Teddy shouted to me.

I considered not even going to school at all. Who would know except for the school? Dad would be too distracted to find out. I shouldn't have even had to go. My mom was in the hospital. How could I focus on physics or Spanish with that on my mind? Last year, a freshman girl's dad had had cancer, and she was always out of school, since she went with him to treatments and doctor appointments. In the hall, teachers would ask how she was doing, not yell at her for having missed a few classes. This wasn't really any different, I told myself. I could stay behind while Teddy and Katy caught the bus, claiming I'd walk. Who'd know the difference?

But then I remembered Jim was at school. It would be worth suffering through classes to see him again. Not that I knew how things were between us. He'd stood up for me and helped me learn the very basics of driving, but that didn't necessarily mean we were going to have lunch together. Even so, the possibility of something happening was better than the idea of staying home.

"Come on," I said, handing Teddy his lunch. "We're going to be late."

Walking through the front doors at school, I hoped no one would remember that my mom had freaked out at school.

Hopefully there had been a bigger scandal that morning, like some freshman got pregnant or busted for selling pot out of her locker.

"Hey, Winchester!" Nick Gillan was standing with a few members of the football team. "Can I get a ride after school? I'm feeling kind of suicidal."

They laughed and I muttered, "Screw you." When I tried to push past them, it seemed like the hall was suddenly full of jerseys.

"Hey, Winchester," Nick said, "can your *mom* give me a ride?"

I froze, fists clenched. Until I'd messed up the football field, no one had bothered me at school. When I was on the soccer team, I'd been almost popular. Now all people did was bother me and I was sick of it. But before I could say anything, someone else called my name.

"Alex?" Mr. Kane was standing nearby, arms folded over his chest. "A minute?"

"Sure," I said. The football players were still chuckling to themselves but had turned back to their lockers. I didn't feel a rush of gratitude toward Mr. Kane. After all, he was the one who had brought my mom to school. If he hadn't insisted on meeting with her, she would never have been here for people to see in the first place.

Mr. Kane led me to the door of the teachers' lounge. Inside, my math teacher was stirring creamer into her coffee. I could hear the copier spitting out pages, one by one.

"I just wanted to see if everything was all right. With your mom, I mean," Mr. Kane said. Usually he looked at me like I was sent from a special hell, specifically to frustrate him, but now his face and eyes were soft. I bristled. I didn't want his pity.

"Yeah, my mom wasn't really feeling well," I said. "Lyme disease or something. My dad had to take her to the hospital."

He nodded. "So she's doing better?"

"Oh, yeah," I said. "Yeah, a lot."

Mr. Kane looked at me unblinkingly for a moment, and I wasn't sure if he believed me. I wasn't even sure if I believed me. I stared back.

"Great," he finally said. "I hope she's a hundred percent soon. Until then, maybe your dad can come in for that talk?"

"Right. Absolutely." I wasn't sure how Dad would be able to take time off from work for a parent-teacher conference, much less for anything else.

He smiled. "Until then, how about you observe in class but don't participate? Best I can do."

"Really fair," I said. "Can't wait." Mr. Kane smiled again, and I had to stop myself from glaring at him as he retreated into the teachers' lounge. Granted, being restricted from driver's ed was the best news I'd had since Jim told me I didn't suck too much at driving. But I hated that Mr. Kane now felt sorry for me because my mom had gotten so upset in his office. Out of all the people in the world, he was one of the top five I didn't want to have seen that. And to make everything worse, he was being nice about it. He probably thought we had this secret bond now—children bearing the burden of their ill parents. I didn't want to be a member of that club. Mr. Kane wasn't going to make me one.

I didn't see Jim until our only class together: physical education—fantastic. 'Cause everyone looks so much better in mesh jerseys from the eighties. Since the weather was still good, we were outside for tennis, which I actually didn't mind. I was pretty good at sports, and now PE was the closest I got to playing anything. At least it came with less pressure. Mom said I'd get into a better college with an athletic scholarship, but I didn't think her lectures and so-called helpful suggestions after every game were worth it when I decided to quit last year. Sometimes I wondered if I'd made the right choice.

We had more students than courts, and anyone who didn't have basic tennis skills had to line up and take turns serving. Jim rushed in late with a couple of senior guys and stood at the back of the line. I glanced around, pretending I hadn't seen him, until I turned and he was looking right at me. We smiled; he nodded a hello, and I waved before I realized how lame my wave was.

Maddie nudged me. "You and Jim?"

I thought about telling her what had happened last night. But that would also mean talking about my mom and why I was even at school to get her car in the first place. "Not really. I mean, I've talked to him a couple times, but that's really it."

"He's totally into you," she said.

"All right, everyone," our PE teacher, Mrs. Harriott, called out. "Look at Amanda's serve. It's a nice, fluid motion."

Amanda Baxter tossed a tennis ball into the air and swung her racket, sending the ball neatly across the net and into her would-be opponent's court. When she smiled, it was kind of smug.

"She's on the tennis *team*," Maddie said.

"I think she's team captain," I said.

"That's like cheating." She leaned against the chain-link fence. "Is it too late to say I've got cramps?"

Ponytail swinging, Amanda Baxter ran over to the next court to play a real match with another tennis-team girl. "Alex," Mrs. Harriott said, "you're up."

I shuffled over to her. Although I was okay with playing tennis, I didn't exactly want to go after star-player Amanda Baxter. Mrs. Harriott handed me a racket and a ball, telling me to toss it straight into the air. "Remember, one fluid motion." The racket made contact with a satisfying twang, but instead of sailing into the other half of the court, like Amanda's ball had, mine slapped the net.

"Not bad," Mrs. Harriott said. "But you're hitting it down. Try again."

The ball had just left my hand when I remembered something I'd read in elementary school: Amelia Earhart was sporty. That's one thing I liked about her when we learned about famous women in fourth grade. She had been a tomboy growing up, and she had made her own makeshift roller coaster.

I couldn't remember much else, aside from the mysterious death. The ball came down again without me even swinging at it.

"Awesome serve!" someone from the fence yelled.

"All right, all right," Mrs. Harriott said, "one more try."

I managed to hit the ball this time, although it was into the net again, so Mrs. Harriott let me go to the end of the line, saying I'd get it next time. I barely heard her. I was still thinking of Amelia Earhart. My mom was becoming this person, and all I had of her were these little facts I'd learned in class. What was Mom thinking about in the hospital? Was she imagining herself as a young Amelia Earhart, playing tennis and pounding together a homemade roller coaster? Was she sitting in her hospital bed, thinking she was flying? Could she see the sky right now, bright blue and dotted with clouds? Did she see it the way she'd always seen it, or did she know what it felt like to fly through those clouds? And how could she? Was it just her imagination, or had she searched for the answers without any of us knowing what she was doing?

A hand waved in front of my face — Jim's. "A little spaced-out?" he asked.

"Oh, no," I said, sliding my fingers through one of the links in the fence. "Just one of those days, I guess."

Now Maddie was serving. Her racket sent the ball flying with a twang into the next court. I lifted my face to the sun, closing my eyes and listening to the thunk of the ball bounce, and then another thwack of the racket.

Next to me, I heard Jim shift his feet. "So were your parents okay about the car?"

I wished the talk with my dad had been that simple. "Oh, totally. But my sister was worried that we'd destroyed the school gym or something."

He laughed. "I wish. That could have gotten us out of class today."

When I opened my eyes, Jim was glimpsing me from the side. God, he was cute. I couldn't help smiling. "More time to practice driving." I liked the thought of Jim and me practicing anything together, preferably just the two of us in very close proximity.

But the clear skies and another thwap of a tennis racket reminded me of Amelia again. I wondered if my mother was practicing being a famous missing pilot.

Instead of going to the cafeteria for lunch that afternoon, I slipped into the library. With institutional bookcases and hard-backed wooden chairs, it wasn't exactly a place I usually hung out. Plus, the selection was pretty limited. (More money went to our football team, who apparently couldn't win unless they had a perfectly manicured field.)

At one table, a group of kids was playing chess. Two librarians were sorting books at the front. A handful of kids were on the computers, checking Facebook or doing research for papers on *Lord of the Flies*. The rest of the library was deserted, thankfully. I strolled through the science section and past the history books before stopping in front of the biographies. I ran my finger over the spines—John Adams, Robert Browning, Winston Churchill. For a minute, I didn't let my brain register what I was doing.

I just want to see if it's here, I thought.

I stopped at two slim volumes—basic biographies, like the ones I'd read for projects in middle school. The name stared back at me twice: *Amelia Earhart, Amelia Earhart.*

She was on both covers. One was a full-length picture of her standing by a plane, wearing baggy pants and a scarf, the uniform Mom had recently adopted. Amelia's face was a little tense, as though trying not to squint as she looked into the sun. The other photograph was closer up, of Amelia sitting in a plane, her hair covered by an aviator's cap and goggles. Her features were surprisingly soft. I'd imagined someone harsher, who'd survived near-death experiences and didn't have time for moisturizer. She looked so young. I wondered when it was taken. She was probably closer to my age than Mom's.

The back covers talked about the mystery of her disappearance, how she broke down barriers for female aviators, and how she was beloved the world over. It was all information I could have gotten from Wikipedia, but I didn't want to look up anything online in case someone saw me or saved the search history.

One of the librarians, the younger one, wheeled by with a cart. I clutched the books to my chest, feeling like I'd been caught with porn or *Mein Kampf.*

"Need any help?" the librarian asked.

"No, thanks, I'm fine," I said.

She smiled with her lips pressed together. "I'll be in History if you need me."

So will Mom, I thought, and laughed. But when the librarian raised her eyebrows, I tried to turn it into a cough. "Right. Thanks so much."

I waited until she wheeled over a few rows before looking at the biographies again. Thumbing through them, I caught sight of things Mom mentioned—a sister nicknamed Pidge, a husband named George (who was also her manager), and names of planes, like the Lockheed. How did she know? Had she learned about this kind of thing before, like when she was in high school, or did she pick up a book recently and everything snowballed from there? She could have been doing research for years without any of us noticing. It would have seemed so ordinary for her to pick up a biography.

In the middle of one book, there was a section of pictures— Amelia in a parade, Amelia standing beside dozens of different planes, Amelia with George Putnam, who was always in a suit. Turning the pages, my stomach twisted with anger.

It's not her fault, I told myself. She died in an ocean somewhere. It's not her fault that Mom's going crazy.

But after a while, I couldn't stand her face anymore—the smug smile, the steady gaze into the distance, the hands shoved in the pockets of her bomber jacket. She looked so daring. It was like a challenge to anyone else, including my mom. Who asked Amelia to come into my life? She was dead. Couldn't she stay that way?

The librarian cart squeaked its way to the front desk. Quickly, I tore a page out — part of the photograph section. Then another page, text about her first flight. Then two more. Blood pulsed in my neck. I crumpled the pages in my hand. If I could have, I would have lit them on fire right there in the library.

The first bell rang. I stuffed the pages into my pocket and replaced the books on the shelf, hoping that no one else would look at them until after I'd graduated. My heart was pounding, and not just because I had messed with school property. I felt the torn pages burn inside my pocket. Even though I'd just wanted to destroy them, I couldn't let them go quite yet. Although Dad said he'd take care of things, I thought I should be prepared — just in case. When I went past the librarian's desk, I was running.

"Slow down!" the young librarian called after me. But I didn't stop until I was out of the library and halfway down the hall.

CHAPTER SEVEN

I didn't realize it at the time, but the cooperation of one's
family and close friends is one of the greatest safety factors
a fledgling flyer can have.

—Amelia Earhart

Mom didn't come home the next day, or several days after. I kept making Teddy sandwiches and riding in the backseat during driver's ed. At night, when Dad would get home, I'd ask how Mom was doing. At first he sounded hopeful, saying that the doctors were sure it wasn't anything physical, like a brain tumor, so we should be grateful for that. But she was still calling herself Amelia Earhart. The hospital psychiatrist said it wasn't schizophrenia or multiple personality disorder, which Dad thought was good news. Even so, the doctor said it might take some time to work out.

When Dad told me, I asked, "What does 'some time' mean?" He just replied, "However long it takes." After another day or so, he could barely look at me when I asked about Mom.

Katy still didn't talk to me much, as if it was my fault Mom was gone. She started going to bed early just so she wouldn't have to see me across the room. Which was all right with me. If she didn't want to talk about anything, even when I basically asked her if she wanted to know the truth, fine. And it gave me some time alone to look at the pages from the Amelia Earhart book.

They were mostly about Amelia Earhart's first experiences flying. (I'd have to go back to the library if I wanted to learn about her mysterious last flight.) The pages even mentioned technical details about flying in those early days, which made me think about driving and how difficult it was to deal with mechanical things. When she first started flying, Amelia, like most other beginner pilots, had had a hard time making her plane fly level. One kind of plane in particular, the Canuck, tended to nose down on a right turn. I wondered if Mom knew any of this mechanical stuff.

It felt wrong, holding on to the torn pages like that. It was like an admission that I'd need to know about her, that Mom wasn't going to get better. But I still couldn't tear them up or throw them away. The stolen pages, which I could shove under my bed if Katy walked in, didn't feel real yet. They weren't a whole book. And even though I didn't want to, I kept wondering about why Mom would want to be Amelia.

Not that Amelia Earhart's life wasn't exciting. At first I thought it might just be that—Mom wanted something more thrilling. But there were lots of exciting, glamorous women:

Sacagawea, Annie Oakley, Frida Kahlo, Susan B. Anthony, Sally Ride, Katharine Hepburn, Lady Gaga, any of them. Why Amelia? Did Mom want to fly? Travel? It wasn't like she got out of Virginia very often, but she never talked about places she wanted to go. I felt like the pages I'd torn from the biographies might be a key. Like the answers were all there, between the lines—I just had to figure out the code.

At school, I kept thinking about the books in the library. The torn pages I kept in my backpack already felt thin and tattered. Maybe if I just knew a little more, I could make sense of what was going on. Of course, I could have known a lot more all at once if I just checked out the books or went online, but I didn't want the librarian asking me about Amelia Earhart like the books were for a school assignment. Individual pages were safer—just ripples of information at a time, not a whole wave. With enough of those glimpses, I thought I could get things back to the way they were.

One night about a week after Mom left, I was in the basement getting laundry out of the dryer and Dad came looking for me. He said, "How about you come with me to the hospital on Friday?"

I stopped looking for a striped sock's twin. "Come with you?" I said. "Like what, to visit?" *Please don't mean "to visit,"* I thought. I didn't want to sit in some stiff metal chair, talking to Mom who didn't know she was Mom and who would be in a hospital-issue bathrobe.

Dad leaned against the washing machine, which was rumbling with another load of my clothes. "No, Mom's coming home, actually. I thought —"

"So she's better?" I looked straight at him.

"Well," he said, "not exactly."

I chucked my pile of clothes in the laundry basket and got the ironing board out of the corner, jerking it open. Usually I didn't care about ironing, but at the moment, I felt like potentially burning something. "'Not exactly' is like 'almost,' right? Like how when you have the flu and you're in bed for a while and the next week you're still dragging but not contagious so they send you to school anyway?"

"She's not contagious." He chuckled. "They've figured out that much."

I attacked a shirt with the iron. "Oh, great. I was really worried about that. I mean, if there were two Amelia Earharts, we wouldn't know what to do. There'd probably be a duel or something. An air duel. But, hey" — I threw the shirt back into the laundry basket — "at least then we'd get rid of one." Anger smoldered in my lungs. I could practically taste it — like engine smoke.

Dad had been trying to smile but stopped. "She still thinks she's Amelia," he said.

"Isn't that kind of a problem? Like sending somebody home with a broken arm? What did they even say? 'Sorry, good luck with that'?"

"They suggested therapy —"

"Oh, *therapy*," I said. I grabbed another shirt, one of Katy's that had gotten mixed up in my laundry, and ironed it anyway. "Mental problems are always super easy to fix."

"Nobody said this was going to be a quick fix. It'd be great for your mom to stay in the hospital, get private treatment twenty-four hours a day, until she had all her issues sorted out, but that's not really an option right now, Alex. We just don't have the money for that, so she's coming home." The washing machine stopped rumbling, and we studied each other in silence for a second. Then Dad reached into the laundry basket and refolded the shirt I'd just ironed. "It's tough and it sucks, but we've just got to deal with it, all right?"

That was it, I thought—dealing with it. Whenever kids at school suffered personal tragedies—parents with cancer, car accidents, fires—people would say, "I don't know how they can deal with that." But there was no other option. People didn't deal because they rose above; they dealt because there was nothing else they could do.

Dad went on to say that he thought it would be better if there were two of us at the hospital—more people for her to recognize. (*Or not recognize*, I thought.) If she got familiar with us, maybe she would start to remember things.

I wondered if we would have to go through the house and reintroduce everything to Mom—this is the couch, these are the stairs, this is Jackson, this is water, this is a window. Although, I guessed she would already recognize all of the inanimate objects; Amelia Earhart would have had stairs. It

98

was the rest of us that she wouldn't know. Who would we have to be for her?

"I'm not going to make you," Dad said, "but if you want to come to the hospital, I'll write you a note to get you out of school for the day."

"For the emotional strain," I said.

"Something like that."

I unplugged the iron. Who was going to notice wrinkles now, anyway? Amelia Earhart probably didn't have time to iron. "Fine. Count me in. I'll make sure to get the straitjacket washed before then."

Dad smiled and put his arm around my shoulders, planting a kiss on the top of my head. "I'll iron it for you."

Friday was two days away. I kept thinking about what it would be like to have to go pick up Mom. After not having seen her for almost a week, it had all started to feel unreal, like I'd imagined the whole situation. But then I'd remember seeing her in the driver's seat, unable to figure out how to get home.

I went back to the library a couple of times a day. Just to look, I told myself. Maybe there would be some clue, some detail of Earhart's life that would tell me why my mother had gone crazy. That would help me when I had to live with her again. One of the biographies was actually by Amelia Earhart, which I hadn't noticed the first time around. I pulled it from the stacks and shifted it from hand to hand, as if I would catch whatever my mom had, just from being too close to the words.

She speaks directly to other young women, the back cover read, *urging them to test themselves, to go as far as they can — and beyond.*

What was "beyond"?

I slid the book back onto the shelf and took out the other biography, the one I'd torn pages from. Flipping to the index, I hoped to find some term that would stand out. *Friendship, flight across the Atlantic. Roosevelt, Eleanor. Putnam, George Palmer.* At least George was Amelia's husband. It would have been too confusing if Amelia had never married — Mom might not have gone anywhere with Dad if she thought he was a random guy.

I turned to one of the pages about George. Amelia had written him a letter before they got married, saying she wasn't exactly nuts about the idea, but she'd give it a try as long as he understood she couldn't be tied down: *On our life together I want you to understand I shall not hold you to any midaevil code of faithfulness to me nor shall I consider myself bound to you similarly. . . . I must exact a cruel promise and that is you will let me go in a year if we find no happiness together.*

Shit, I thought. *Did they break up?*

What would Dad do if Mom tried to leave him, thinking she was Amelia Earhart leaving George Putnam? Did Mom even know about this letter? I flipped ahead, trying to find some hint of marital problems. No section on divorce in the index. Maybe it had worked out all right for George and Amelia. Until she went missing, that is.

Even so, I didn't want to leave the page with the letter behind. I could quote it, or something, and see Mom's reaction. And then I thought I should take a few more pages, about George and Amelia's relationship, just in case. I looked around—a group of kids was at the far table, sharing math homework. A few others were going over Spanish vocabulary in the corner. The librarians were at their desk. I waited until I heard the chanting of verbs—*viajo, viajas, viaja*—and tore.

What the hell was my problem? I could just check it out, like a normal person. But having the entire book on me would have been like admitting that something was really wrong. Besides, in the grand scheme of things, I figured this wasn't so bad. If Mom could become another person altogether—a famous historical figure, at that—then I could become a vandal of school property.

I grabbed a random biography, just in case, and went to the librarians' desk. The young librarian I'd seen before put down her coffee. "Checking out?" she said, taking the book. "Curie is fascinating."

"What?" I said, then glanced down. I'd picked up a copy of Marie Curie's biography. "Oh, right. Yeah. She's great."

She stamped the back of the book. "Due on the sixteenth of November. Interested in chemistry? Or just some fun reading?"

I shoved the book into my bag, on top of the ripped pages from the Amelia Earhart book. "No," I said. "Research."

At lunch on Thursday, Josh complained about the SAT prep class his parents had signed him up for. "Last night it was like, 'Pass the chicken; here's your prep book,'" he said, drowning his fries in ketchup. "It's every Saturday morning. At eight. Who does that? They looked at me all happy, like I should throw myself on the floor and kiss their feet because now I'm going to get a perfect score."

Theresa was pulling apart her chicken enchilada. She wrinkled her nose. "Is that supposed to be guacamole?"

"Thanks for all the sympathy," Josh said.

"It's not like they signed you up for boot camp or one of the rehab clinics out in Montana. And if you get a good SAT score, you can get into college and out of here."

That was how Theresa saw a lot of our academic career at Oak Ridge—a means to an end. I hadn't even picked up one of those prep books. Mom might have mentioned it over the summer, but she definitely wasn't on my case now.

"And you've already memorized the SAT vocab list," Josh said.

Theresa looked kind of smug but didn't get a chance to answer, because Caroline Lavale appeared at our table. "Hey, y'all," she said, smiling so it looked like her lips hurt. "How's it going?"

"Hey, Caroline," Maddie said. "Do you need a place to sit?"

Caroline shook her head and laughed. "No, I just wanted to tell you about the pep rally and game this weekend. We're playing Franklin, and they're, like, the team to beat, so we're hoping to get a really good crowd."

"Sorry, we don't exactly do football. Or anything involving physical exertion and the accompanying cheering," Theresa said. She'd either forgotten that I'd been on the soccer team until recently or had chosen to ignore that fact. "Besides, why do you care what the football team does? They're not exactly good."

"I do color guard," Caroline said.

Theresa looked at Josh. "Another thing your parents could have done to you."

I remembered how Nick and the other football players stopped me in the hallway and talked about my mom. "Um, hello, you were there," I told Caroline. "I fucked up the football field. I'm the team's worst enemy. Pretty sure no one wants me at the game."

"They fixed it fine," Caroline said. "I'm sure if you apologized—"

"Apologized?" My eyes hardened.

"Anyway." Caroline kept smiling but the sunshine drained from her eyes. "I really hope you all show up. It would mean a lot to the players and all of us in color guard and cheerleading."

"Yeah, well, they'd better hope I don't do it again." I didn't really mean to snarl like that—usually Caroline was fine—but I couldn't help it. At my side, Theresa grinned. "See you in driver's ed," I told Caroline as she rushed to the next table.

After my last class, I shoved my way through the crowds to get to Jim's locker. He was there already, sifting through notebooks, and didn't notice me a few feet away. For a second, I wavered—what if Jim was okay with the occasional phys ed conversation but not with extended periods of time together?

Then I remembered the Amelia Earhart quote, about going to the edge and beyond. I was barely anywhere, let alone beyond.

"Hey, Jim," I said. "Remember when you said we should drive again? Can we try that? You teaching me how to drive?"

He raised his eyebrows. "Now?"

"No, not now." It would have to be soon, before I lost my nerve. "How about tonight? I can probably get my mom's car again." It wasn't like she'd be using it anytime soon. Even when she came home tomorrow, Dad probably wouldn't just let her drive off.

"Works for me," Jim said, closing his locker. "Are you still doing straight lines?"

I hadn't exactly practiced since that night in the parking lot. Whenever Dad wasn't at work or at the hospital, he passed out in the chair at home. "How can I get out of straight lines if you haven't taught me anything else?"

He laughed. "Fair enough. I'll come by your place. Around seven?"

"Sounds great. See you tonight," I said, walking away before I could talk myself out of it or say anything stupid. I wasn't sure how it would feel to get behind the wheel of a car again. But even if I threw up or passed out or otherwise made myself look ridiculous in front of Jim Wiley, it was something I needed to do. And not so I could get my license or pass driver's ed. Not even so I could stop being that dumb girl who couldn't drive. I just didn't need one more thing to be afraid of.

Teddy was at a friend's house and Katy had gymnastics that afternoon, so I holed up in our room with the freshly torn Amelia Earhart biography pages. For the last few days, I'd had to look at the pages in secret, hidden in another book or after Katy had gone to sleep. Now I had the chance to spread them out on my bed so I could see all of them at once. There were nine in all—two that were just photos, the rest all text. I felt like an archaeologist who had excavated bits of clay pots and pipes and was now trying to figure out how it all fit together within the context of my mother's own history.

One page was about Amelia's first ride in an airplane—how she went up in a plane with Frank Hawks, and that was when she knew what she wanted to do with her life. She said, *As soon as we left the ground, I knew I myself had to fly.* Another was about a flight around the world, which didn't work the first time she tried it. She and her navigator, Fred Noonan, couldn't get off the ground in Hawaii. The next time she tried the around-the-world thing, she disappeared.

There was one picture of her sitting in a cockpit, turning her head to look back. She wasn't looking at the camera, just at something or someone beside it. All the dials and knobs made me queasy, especially after reading about how Amelia probably died during her flight around the world.

I held up a page with a picture of Amelia and George. She was crouching on the wing of a plane and he stood in front of her, holding her hand up as if he were about to kiss it. The caption underneath said that they were saying good-bye in Miami, before her final flight. But neither of them would have known that about the "final" part. I wondered if the picture had been staged. Maybe they'd stood that way for fifteen minutes to get the right shot.

The door opened; Katy barged in. "What's that?" she asked, tossing her gym bag on her bed.

I shuffled the papers together and pulled them onto my lap. "Aren't you supposed to be at gymnastics?"

She kicked off her sneakers. "Amy had a dentist appointment, so we left early. What's that?"

"Nothing," I said. "Stuff for class."

She smirked. "Uh-huh. Then why are you hiding it like it's porn?"

"Geez, Katy, it's not porn. Just mind your own business, all right?"

"Then why won't you show me?" Katy lunged for the papers. I tried to hold her off, but she had stronger arms. (Stupid gymnastics.) She tugged hard and got a few pages, staring at them in confusion.

"These are just from a book," she said, turning them over in her hand. "What is this, Amelia Earhart?" She looked at me. "Did you steal these?"

"No," I said, standing and grabbing for them. If she threw them out or messed them up, I'd never have them to study again. "I found them like that."

She held me off with her hand. "Then why are you freaking out about them? What did you do, tear them out at a bookstore? And it's not even, like, a good book. That is so freaking weird, Alex. You are seriously mental."

It was that word. Katy was almost laughing; I couldn't help myself. "Maybe it runs in the family," I said, pushing her away. "Where do you think Mom is? She's not sick with pneumonia or exhausted or whatever Dad told you. She's crazy. She thinks she's Amelia Fucking Earhart. Now, just give me back those pages already!"

Katy handed them over. Her expression was numb—she might as well have been a mannequin—and it seemed like all the blood had drained from her face. In the next room, I could hear Teddy jumping on his bed, something Mom never let him do.

"What are you talking about?" Katy said, voice choked. "She's fine."

"No, she's not." I tucked the Amelia Earhart pages in one of my notebooks. Katy's face started to tense, but I kept going. "We're bringing her home because we have to, not because she's a whole lot better. Remember when we saw her with those map printouts in the kitchen? That was because she thought she was Amelia Earhart, not because she wanted to take us to Florida."

"She was tired."

"Oh, come on," I said. Katy's eyes and cheeks reddened. "You had to know. I basically told you—before, that first night she was gone."

Katy stumbled backward, meaning to sit on her bed but missing and collapsing on the floor instead. "Ow," she said, rubbing her tailbone. She looked up at me. "What do you mean, she thinks she's Amelia Earhart? That's, like, the stupidest thing I ever heard. You're making it up."

"I'm not. That's what she told Dad and me after she freaked out at my school." I slumped to the floor as well. "I was there. She's really gone crazy."

"You're such a bitch," Katy said, wiping her nose with her forearm.

My sister never swore. Usually I liked to do it to annoy her. Now it was strange to her hear call me a bitch. It didn't sound right, as if she weren't sure about using the word and was trying it out. For a second, I wished I could take it all back, shove the words back in my throat, even though she'd find out the truth soon enough. Even though I was relieved that I'd have some-one to talk with about Mom. But then we heard footsteps on the stairs. Katy bolted into the hall and threw herself at Dad.

"Why didn't you tell me?" she said, really crying now.

Dad pulled her into his room. I followed and closed the door behind me. He didn't even need to ask what Katy was talk-ing about, just looked at me, his face fallen behind his beard. "Alex—" he said.

"What?" I said. "You had to tell her today, anyway. It wasn't like you could keep it a secret for much longer. Mom's coming home tomorrow. What were you going to do, surprise them?" I felt like I could go careening off the walls with so much pent-up energy all coming out at once.

Dad's eyebrows lowered. "You told Teddy?"

"No," I said. "I'm not stupid. But someone's going to have to."

"Jesus, Alex, I told you I would take care of this," Dad said. "I asked you this one thing, not to tell your brother and sister." Katy kept wiping her face with her arm, so Dad went into the bathroom and got a few squares of toilet paper for her. "Sorry, Katydid, we're out of tissues."

Katy took the toilet paper and blew her nose. "Thank you." She sniffed and sat on the edge of Mom and Dad's bed. "Alex said Mom's crazy."

Dad sat beside her. "Mom's going through a really rough time right now. She's calling herself Amelia Earhart—"

"Told you," I muttered, but Dad cast me a look.

He kept talking about how the doctors thought it might be stress, and that Mom was going to see a psychiatrist, all the stuff he'd told me. This time, it sounded rehearsed. He promised things were going to get back to normal soon.

Katy rested her head against Dad's shoulder. "That is so messed up," she said.

"Look, Alex and I are going to pick Mom up from the hospital tomorrow," Dad said. "You can come if you want, but you don't have to. If you think it would be too much—"

Katy shook her head. "No," she said solemnly, "I want to go."

She looked so small and red and stoic—a little survivor. I kind of hated her for it, since I'd only agreed to go after Dad said I wouldn't have to go to school that day. And here Dad had been so afraid to tell Katy, because she was too young to handle things. He should have talked to her from the beginning and left me out of it.

"Can I use Mom's car?" I said suddenly. "I need to practice driving."

Dad frowned. "I can't really go driving right now, Alex—"

"No, you don't have to. There's a kid at school who's helping me. He took the same driving class last year."

"Don't you need to have an adult with you in the car if you don't have your license yet?" he asked.

"He's eighteen," I said, unblinking. "And I've had my learner's permit for way over nine months, so it's okay." That wasn't exactly true—technically, I was supposed to have my learner's permit and a certification from driver's ed (which obviously wasn't going to happen anytime soon) before I could be on the road without someone over twenty-one. But with everything that was going on, I didn't think Dad would remember Virginia's exact permit laws. "Jim's a good driver."

Katy scowled. "You mean that guy who drove through his parents' house."

Dad's eyebrows went up. "He drove through a *house*?"

"Not *through* a house," I said. "Just, you know, kind of into it. But whatever. I drove through a football field and you still make me drive. And he's the one who helped me actually stop freaking out about getting behind the wheel, so he's already better than my driver's ed teacher anyway."

"Alex, there's no chance in hell that I'm letting you take driving lessons from this kid. You want to practice, we'll pick a time."

"When?" I demanded. "Tomorrow? Mom sure can't stay home alone. And Katy can't take care of her. So when exactly are we going to have these fun driving jaunts around town? Hey, I have an idea. Maybe Mom can sit in the backseat and we'll pretend that she's on her first trip across the Atlantic. Did you know that Amelia Earhart didn't actually do any flying the first time? So this'll be perfect."

Dad stood, walked to the window, and rubbed his shoulder. He was very still for a minute. Outside, a car drove past and then the street was quiet again. I didn't like fighting with Dad, and mentioning Mom was kind of low, but I just wanted to get out of the house.

"All right," he finally said. "Let's meet this kid. Then we'll see about driving."

I was surprised he let it go so easily. I'd expected him to stand his ground, saying I should leave it up to Mr. Kane, or that he'd make time, or for him to at least argue a little more. But he looked tired — more than usual.

Dad turned to me. "But seriously, Alex, is this your biggest concern right now? Driving around?"

On the bed, Katy wadded up the used tissue paper. I remembered Mom lying under the covers, pieces of Kleenex scattered on the floor like dogwood blossoms. "It should be."

Chapter Eight

It is a skill attained through practice in order to master a vehicle under as varying conditions as are likely to be encountered. One can choose to drive only on deserted country roads and one can fly only on good days over regular airways. . . . But, to get from either craft its best performance and to be prepared for whatever may happen, both lessons should be learned.

—Amelia Earhart

I almost called Jim and canceled our driving lesson that night so he wouldn't have to come to my house, where everyone was mad at me, but then I realized that it would be worse to stay at home. Even if I drove into a ditch and the car exploded, at least Jim and I could have a normal conversation before we were crushed by tons of metal.

Jim showed up just after seven. I practically pounced on him before he could even ring the doorbell. "I'm really sorry," I said, throwing open the door.

He stopped. "You can't drive tonight?"

"No . . . I mean, yes," I said. "It's just that—my dad wants to meet you so he knows you're not going to show me how to drive through any houses. Except right now I kind of think you should show me that. It might come in handy later."

Jim shuffled from foot to foot. "Is your dad cleaning his shotgun or something?"

I shook my head and stepped aside so Jim could come in. "He should be grateful I'm driving at all. I always said no when he asked me to practice."

Dad was in the kitchen, waiting for us. His eyes were almost hooded; it was way more serious than I'd ever seen him look. Katy and Teddy sat at the kitchen table, pretending to do the newspaper word scramble and smiling smugly. Geez, Dad wasn't even going to make them leave. They were acting like this was a date—which it obviously wasn't. Jim just felt a kinship because we both liked to wreck things with cars. I was trying not to think about it as a date, and this wasn't helping.

"Hi," Jim said, trying to make eye contact with everyone. "I'm Jim Wiley."

"Hi there, Jim," Dad drawled, reaching out for Jim's hand and shaking it firmly.

"Well, here he is," I said. "We'd better go before it gets dark, so—"

Dad gave me a look like I'd told a funny but inappropriate joke. "How long have you had your license, Jim?"

"About a year." Jim pulled out his license and handed it to Dad. "I got almost a perfect score on my driving test—the written, too. And I haven't had an accident." He glanced at me. "Except for that whole thing with my house."

"Yeah, how about that?" Dad said.

"I already told you," I grumbled.

"No, it's okay," Jim said. "It was stupid—really stupid—and I've definitely learned my lesson. It was the first time anything like that had happened. I'd never even gotten a speeding ticket before then."

"Go big or go home," Katy said, and she and Teddy giggled. I glared at them, hoping they'd suddenly burst into flames.

Jim ignored them. "You can call my parents and ask. I've changed a lot in the last year." He glanced at me out of the corner of his eye. "Plus I know how much it sucks to have this driving thing hanging over you at school."

It was the best thing he could have said. Dad knew I was a freak not only because of the whole driver's ed debacle but because of Mom's recent public breakdown, too. And he hadn't been there to stop it. I had to keep myself from doing a happy dance. Although a little part of me deflated—it was just about the car thing for Jim. Chivalrous, maybe, but not exactly romantic. Even so, I'd take it.

"So can we get going?" I said. "I'd like to try that whole driving-a-mile-an-hour-in-a-straight-line thing again."

Dad eyed us both, then said, "All right," more to himself than to us. He tossed me the keys to Mom's car. "Be back by nine. Sharp." He held up his wrist. "This is the most accurate watch ever. I'll be checking it."

"Right, Dad. See you later," I said, moving toward the door and practically pulling Jim along with me. Behind me, I could hear Katy start to complain about how it was so unfair that I got to go out with a boy on a school night, especially after I'd been so mean to her.

We got in the car, Jim at the wheel. I'd assumed we'd just go back to the school parking lot, but Jim turned left on Grant, away from Oak Ridge.

"Hey, school's that way," I said.

Jim steered the car onto another street, also not in the direction of the high school. "We can't do the parking lot again. You've done that already. We need to mix it up. I mean, it's not like you're going to be driving in parking lots forever."

My stomach dropped. "No, it'll be great. I'll go from parking lot to parking lot."

"It won't be anything scary. It's all back roads. No one to hit and nothing to worry about. You don't even have to turn." When I dug my fingernails into the edges of the seat, he said, "We don't *have* to, you know. I can just take us back to the parking lot."

I didn't want Jim to think I was some complete failure already. I peeled my fingers away from the seat. "No, it's a good idea. Let's mix it up."

We drove through neighborhoods, down Archer Street, with its antique shops, past the post office and the gas station. He turned right and we headed out of town, past the movie theater and strip malls. While he drove, I kept stealing little glimpses at him. It was hard to believe that Jim Wiley, with his perfect lips and a conspiratorial laugh, was sitting next to me. He wanted to help me. It felt so natural to go driving together. I held that idea like a firefly, delicate and flashing against the night.

He veered off the main drag, onto the long road that led toward the reservoir. Out here, there weren't many cars and trees stretched up overhead. Then we drove farther down, where there were large stretches of land—some farms, some new developments. The road wound through the country.

"It's really pretty out here," I said. "Although, if this were a horror movie, you'd totally be taking me to a secluded place to kill me."

Jim laughed. "Yeah, that's it. I'm just lying about spending last semester with my grandparents. I was really in a mental institution."

I tensed. It was that word again. It made me think of lobotomies and padded walls and electroshock therapy.

"Hey, you don't have to be scared," Jim said. At first I thought he was reading my mind, but he kept going. "We're out in the middle of nowhere, with no one to hit, and we're going to drive two miles an hour. What's the worst that could happen?"

"Right," I said. "Simple."

He pulled over to the side of the road. "Let's do this."

I almost suggested that we skip the driving lesson and hang out somewhere instead. But Jim was already out of the car, coming around to the passenger side, so I got out and rounded the car. In front of the driver-side door, I felt my legs get heavy and numb. "Maybe I can just walk everywhere," I said.

"You can't walk to Mexico." Jim swung himself into the

passenger's seat, closing the door behind him. "Well, you could, but it would take a seriously long time."

I got into the car. "Mexico? Why Mexico?"

"Why not?" he said. "Wouldn't you want to go to Mexico? As opposed to, like, the Taco King on Harris Street?" I tried not to smile but mostly failed. "Okay, I figured we could practice driving on a real road. Just straight ahead. No U-turns, nothing scary."

The road didn't seem too menacing. I adjusted the mirrors and the seat. When I turned the key in the ignition, the car hummed awake. Suddenly my chest felt full, as if all the air in the car had rushed inside of me and I couldn't take another breath or I'd explode.

"It's okay," Jim said. "Man, you've really got a phobia about this."

"I just—" I was trying to breathe. "I don't know—"

"We're not going anywhere," he said. "Look, we're in park—see the *P*?—so we're totally fine. Just like the car was off. And you did it last time. Nothing to worry about."

I remembered when Mom couldn't remember how to drive after freaking out in front of Mr. Kane. I couldn't let myself end up like that.

"It's okay," I said, inhaling and exhaling again. "I'm all right."

"You sure?" Jim looked a little nervous.

"Yeah." I tapped my fingers against the steering wheel. "I didn't think it would be like this, you know? When I drive, I feel like I don't have any control. It's supposed to be all about freedom, but I don't feel like that at all. I keep waiting for something terrible to happen."

"Nothing terrible is going to happen," Jim said. "No one's here. Just us."

"I know," I said, even though I didn't. Terrible things could happen anytime. You could run after a ball and get hit by a car. Your mom could go crazy in the middle of a parent-teacher conference. Your baby sister could die before she even had the chance to see the sky.

But I couldn't talk about that with Jim yet. He was being so nice and looking at me with those beautiful eyes, as though he hoped I would be okay. I wanted to be okay. So I grabbed the gearshift. "Drive, right?"

I breathed in and out slowly, then rested my foot on the gas pedal. The car crept forward. Nothing exploded. My arms didn't feel like they were full of water. Someone could have passed us on foot, but it was all right. I was doing it again—driving and not dying.

"Hey, that's it," Jim said. "But we're still kind of in the breakdown lane."

I didn't dare take my eyes off the road. "And?"

"We sort of need to be over in the actual road." I opened my mouth to argue, but he said, "There might be glass or something around here." Dammit. "It's really easy. All you have to do is turn the wheel to the left a little. Like barely at all. And keep your foot like it is."

The words got all jumbled up in my mind. Foot—where? Left? I kept going straight.

"Anytime now," Jim said. When I didn't turn, he rested his left hand on top of my right, holding the steering wheel. The slight contact made me almost stop breathing, but in a good way. "Here we go," he said, helping me move the wheel just a little. The car veered back into the road, and Jim brought our hands back to their original position.

"Easy, right?" he said.

Inside my chest, my heart thudded. I had to keep from laughing like an idiot. "Yeah," I said. "Super easy."

He took his hand away from mine. "And look, you're on the actual road. This is way better than just some stupid parking lot. One lesson and already you're so much better than half the kids in Mr. Kane's class."

I laughed. "Right." I wished I could have glanced over at Jim, but I was afraid if I did, something would go wrong and we'd end up flipped upside down in a ditch. As it was, the driving wasn't so bad. It was so quiet around us, and the glow from distant houses was soft. The sun was just disappearing behind the horizon, making the sky purple and pink and orange and deep blue. My hand felt warm from where Jim had rested his on it. I wished he would touch me again, even something as small as that. Suddenly driving didn't feel like being trapped or compressed; instead, it was like the car had opened up and we were gliding above the ground without any aid at all.

"Check you out," Jim said. "Fifteen miles an hour!"

I glanced down and saw that he was right. For a second, I thought about slamming my foot on the brake—I could kill something at that speed—but I didn't want to look too scared again. But now I kept glancing down to make sure we didn't go too fast.

After a while, Jim asked if I wanted to try reversing. I stopped the car. "Oh, excuse me," I said. "I forgot I had eyes in the back of my head."

"You don't need superpowers," he said. "It's easy. We're not going to try to parallel park or anything. Just a little backing up. Like five feet. Just to get an idea of it." When I didn't say anything, he started talking about the little *R*, which meant reverse. And how it was the same as going forward; I just had to glance in my mirror and out the back window instead.

I gave it a try. At first, I wouldn't let my foot press the gas pedal. Then I hit it too hard and we jerked backward before I could slam down on the brake.

"That's okay. And look, you've already gone backward. Now, try again, only a little slower."

This time I applied pressure carefully. At first I wasn't sure if we were actually moving, it was so slow, but then I saw the ground retreat from under us. In the rearview mirror, the road came to meet the car. I hit the brake again. "I went backward!" I said.

"You can go two directions now," Jim said. "Crazy, huh? You can basically go anywhere you want. Canada or Mexico."

"I'm totally going to drive backward all the way to Canada. As long as it's at five miles an hour."

We drove around for a little while longer, mostly going forward. Jim even convinced me to try turning onto another street. It took me about ten minutes to get the courage to veer right — I didn't want to go careening into someone's fields — but I did it. By the time Jim and I traded places again so he could drive us home, I could practically feel little sparks shoot out of my skin. When I was finally allowed to drive in class again, I wouldn't suck so much — I hoped. (I didn't want to think about what driving would be like without Jim's calm encouragement.)

And even better, aside from the first anxiety attack, I hadn't thought about Mom or Amelia Earhart.

The next morning, I heard Dad waking Teddy up for school. Katy and I were allowed to sleep in, because we weren't going to the hospital until a little later in the day. Teddy whined that he was the only one up and that we should have to wake up, too. Dad offered toaster waffles to make up for it.

For a second, I thought about getting up, too, and following Teddy off to school. Let Katy and Dad deal with Mom on their own. But I stayed where I was. I'd already disappointed Dad by telling Katy everything, anyway. It was supposed to have been the two of us, Dad and me. I didn't want to see his face fall again, now that he was the only parent around who actually knew who I was.

When I fell back to sleep, I dreamed about being on the

ground, prop planes flying overhead. I waved at them and shouted for them to come pick me up, but they only circled a few times before disappearing into the clouds.

I'd been to the hospital a few times before—when I was eight and broke my arm falling off the monkey bars at school, when Katy was nine and got stung by a bunch of bees, when I rode in the ambulance with Mom, and when I saw the baby who was born too soon. This time, Dad parked in a short-term lot and guided us through a part of the hospital I'd never been to, the psychiatric ward.

Somewhere, there were girls going to visit their mothers in the cancer ward. For a second, I wished I could be doing that instead. Then I realized how messed up that was. Who wants their mom to have cancer? It's not like Mom was going to die. Unless she really wanted to emulate Amelia Earhart.

I'd expected patients running around in straitjackets, reenacting scenes from *One Flew Over the Cuckoo's Nest*. But it looked like any other part of the hospital. The waiting area had uncomfortable chairs, bad paintings of the ocean or a garden, and a nurse typing behind an old computer. The walls were shades of gray and yellow—cloudy or sunny, I thought.

Katy and I sat on opposite couches while Dad talked to the nurse. It was the first cool day of fall, so he was carrying an extra jacket for Mom, for when we took her home. When he came back from the nurses' station, he told us that he had to talk to the doctor for a minute, and then we could all see Mom. "Wait right here, okay?"

He disappeared around the corner. For a few minutes, Katy and I listened to the sound of the nurse's fingernails clicking against the keyboard. People walked by in jeans and T-shirts. I wondered if they were visitors or patients.

I glanced at the clock. If it had been any other day, I would have been in calc class, probably trying to convince my teacher that I'd done the homework. It was hard to tell which would have been preferable—public humiliation or sitting here under a watercolor of a rowboat. "Aren't you glad I got you out of school?" I asked Katy.

She was flipping through an old issue of *Good Housekeeping*. "Mom never lets us skip school."

"Amelia might."

Katy put down the magazine. "Stop talking about her like she's someone else. She's not—she's Mom and she's confused, but she's still Mom."

After looking at Amelia Earhart pictures the past few days, I kept seeing her face imprinted over Mom's in my mind. "I know that," I said. "I just think we should be prepared. Things are different."

"Duh," she said. "I'm not five."

A large group walked by, so we shut up. One woman hung back and sat beside Katy, yammering into the cell phone tucked under her neck. "No, I told you we couldn't," she said as she dug through her purse. She pulled out a pack of cigarettes and expertly lit one. "No, that's just not going to happen. We can't."

Katy frowned. "You're not supposed to smoke in here."

The woman blew smoke in my sister's direction. "My son tries to kill himself and you're trying to tell me what the fuck to do?" She turned her body away and went back to her conversation.

Katy looked like she wanted to shrink back into the cushions; her face was getting red, and she tried to shield herself with the magazine. At the desk, the nurse didn't seem to notice either my sister or the cigarette.

"Come on," I said, getting up and grabbing Katy's arm. She followed, magazine still in her hand.

Dad had gone down the hall. I pulled Katy along, glancing into rooms to see if he was in any of them. Once, I caught the eye of a patient—a woman with muscular arms and stringy hair—and rushed past as if I'd intruded. Down the hall, I heard two voices speaking low. As I got closer, I could distinguish one of them as Dad's.

". . . insurance will cover this?" he was saying.

"Dad," I said. Katy followed me into the room, practically hiding behind me. The doctor, a tall man with a beard and a clipboard hugged to his chest, had his mouth open to reply to Dad's question but closed it when he saw us. The room was like any other in the hospital—a couple of beds, flimsy blankets, venetian blinds, tiled floors. Everything smelled like stale popcorn and antibacterial hand cleaner. Mom was sitting on the bed closest to the door, smiling at us pleasantly. I stopped. All the air in my lungs seemed to vanish, so for a second, I thought I would cry, but I managed to take a breath instead. I wondered how she saw me—who was I? She was wearing her own clothes, at least—jeans and a sweater, and not some awful hospital gown. For a second, I hoped Mom would call me by name, even to say something disapproving, but her face remained unchanged.

"Can you girls wait in the hall?" Dad said. "We're just finishing up."

"Nonsense," Mom said, gesturing for us to come in. "You keep shoving girls out of the room and they'll never learn anything."

There she went again, acting like the champion of women's rights even though she didn't know who we were. She patted the bed beside her. Katy and I glanced at Dad, who shrugged and waved us in, so we walked stiffly to the bed. I sat next to Mom, while my sister perched beside me on the edge of the bed. Mom grabbed our hands and shook them enthusiastically. "Hello. Amelia Earhart. So glad you could come today."

"Yeah," I said, "me too." I leaned away from her.

The doctor studied Mom. "So," he said, his voice light but curious, "who do we have with us this afternoon?"

"Ninety-Nine business," she said, beaming at my sister and me. "Some of the best aviators working today. You should see them in the air—natural as you please."

Even though it wasn't real, for a second it was kind of nice to see Mom so enthusiastic about my nonexistent flying skills. If she couldn't say the same about my driving abilities, at least this was something. I didn't remove my hand from under hers; she gave it a squeeze. *It's Mom's hand,* I had to remind myself.

The doctor made a note on his clipboard. "That's encouraging. She feels comfortable with you."

"She should," Katy said. "She's only known us since we were born."

Mom's smile drooped a little. She looked across me, to Katy. "Well, at least it feels like that," she said.

CHAPTER NINE

*The more one does and sees and feels, the more one is able
to do, and the more genuine may be one's appreciation
of fundamental things like home, and love, and
understanding companionship.*

—Amelia Earhart

They called it a delusional disorder. I'd never heard that phrase
before. The bearded doctor, Dr. Cowan, told Dad about it while
Katy and I were supposed to be helping Mom gather her things.
It wasn't like schizophrenia, Dr. Cowan explained. Mom wasn't
hearing voices or experiencing hallucinations. She wasn't out-
wardly bizarre or impaired by her beliefs; a stranger could look
at her and think she was totally normal. Mom simply disre-
garded any logic that countered her idea that she was Amelia
Earhart. Most likely it had been caused by a great deal of emotional stress—some kind of trauma. With time, Dr. Cowan told
us, she could be treated with therapy and medication. When

Dad asked how much time, Dr. Cowan mentioned how psycho-therapy varied with patients, and it generally took a while to find the right balance of medications for a particular person's unique chemical imbalances.

"Why Earhart?" I asked.

Dad and Dr. Cowan turned to me, as if they'd forgotten I was in the room. In the bathroom, packing up her toiletries, Mom was talking to Katy about how excited she was to have us on board with the Ninety-Nines.

"I imagine it's because of the intrigue," Dr. Cowan said. "Earhart was an important figure in female aviation. She traveled all over the world. And then there's the matter of her disap-pearance. Even now, people are still fascinated by her story."

"But Mom's never talked about her before. She's never even talked about traveling anywhere."

Dr. Cowan coughed and said it was probably a combination of reasons for choosing Earhart. Then Dad asked him some-thing about therapists, so I had to go back to putting Mom's clothes in a duffel bag. But Dr. Cowan's answer left me empty. Anybody could have been interested in Amelia Earhart with reasons like that. But what about Mom specifically? If I could have become anyone, it wouldn't have been Amelia Earhart.

Dad got the names of a couple of therapists and shook Dr. Cowan's hand enthusiastically.

On the way home, Mom talked about how glad she was to have completed her solo flight across the Atlantic. "The northern winds were the problem," she said, gazing out the window and rubbing the car lock with her index finger. "The wings were getting iced over. I didn't take the same course that Lindbergh did, you know—I started from Newfoundland. I ended up landing in a field in Northern Ireland. A farmer asked me if I'd come far, and I said, 'From America.'" She laughed and looked around as if she expected us to be in on the joke.

We didn't respond. It was like Mom was talking about her sex life and we didn't know what polite answer we were supposed to have. I was sitting with her in the backseat. Presumably, if she had the idea to jump out in the middle of the street, I'd have to go after her. I didn't think Amelia Earhart ever had to bail out of a plane—until the very end, maybe, and Mom hadn't mentioned the disappearance so far.

"That's the high school on the right," Dad told Mom. I could see the parking lot full of cars. Farther back, kids in gym uniforms were running around the soccer field.

I slouched deep in my seat. "Oh, geez, Dad, let's just drive right by it. I'm skipping today, remember?"

He chuckled. "I called the school, Alex."

We were past the school now, so I sat up a little. "What did you tell them?"

Dad coughed. Katy and I both stared at him. "Well, I just mentioned that your mom still wasn't feeling well, so you were coming with me to the hospital."

"You didn't tell them the truth, did you?"

"Of course not."

I settled back into my seat. "Good. So we're not telling anyone for a while, right? Unless Mom, like, burns the house down or something."

Katy turned around in her seat and looked at me, eyebrows knit together. "Did Amelia Earhart burn her house down?"

"Probably not," I said, kind of smiling. "I haven't gotten that far in my reading."

Mom sat up a little straighter. "Of all the ridiculous ideas. Of course I've never burned a house down."

"Yeah, Amelia," I said, rolling my eyes. "Thanks for letting us know."

"We're going to keep things as quiet as possible," Dad assured us. The wheel shifted under his hands, straightening onto our street. "It's our business and no one else's."

I supposed Dad had called Forrester Family Dental to let them know that Mom wouldn't be coming into work for a while, but I didn't think he told them about Mom's stories of crossing the Atlantic. But they had to assume something was wrong. The only other time she'd missed work was when she lost the baby. We hadn't talked much about that, either.

At least no one would have to know at school, not the details anyway. I could put on my annoyed face and pretend my parents were still looking at report cards and bothering me about the SATs. It would be my secret.

Once we were home, Mom went right to the kitchen drawer where she had left her maps. From the look on Dad's face, I could tell he was wishing he'd hidden them somewhere. She spread them out on the kitchen table, sighing with satisfaction as the paper crinkled open.

"Now, Gip," she said, "what do you think about the trans-pacific route? I've made notes here."

"How about we look at that later?" Dad said.

Mom snorted a laugh. "Well, I'm surprised at you. Usually you're the one who's pushing more and more things onto my schedule. Now I'm trying to plan something and you want to wait until later. Think I'm too tired from that trip across the Atlantic?"

Dad and I glanced at each other. "Doesn't sound like that would have been an easy trip," he said cautiously.

"No, it wasn't, but I'm perfectly fine to discuss the next route. After we go on that lecture tour you've been talking about." She rested her hands on the table. "You know I get tired talking to so many people."

"We don't have to go anywhere," Dad said. He walked over to Mom and rubbed her back.

Mom shook off his hand. "No, no, I've got too much to do. And you'll be on me tomorrow, I'm sure. No rest for the weary." She picked up a pencil and started making notes beside Hawaii.

"Amelia, are you hungry?" I asked, grabbing a bowl from the cupboard.

She didn't look up from her map. "I'm fine, thank you."

I got out a box of Cocoa Puffs, which Teddy had convinced Dad to buy, and a carton of milk. "Dad, you want anything?"

131

"Thanks, Alex, no." Dad circled the counter to stand beside me as I poured. "You know, Dr. Cowan said we're not supposed to encourage her—"

"Katy!" I shouted up the stairs. "You want cereal?" After a second, I heard a distracted "No" come from our room, so I only poured one bowl.

Dad handed me a spoon. "You probably shouldn't call her Amelia."

I took a couple of bites, chewing slowly. "So what am I supposed to call her? Mom? I don't want her freaking out or bolting outside or something."

He sighed. "I don't know. I don't know, but that's what Dr. Cowan said. Not to agree with her, but be gentle about it."

"Well, that's really helpful," I said. "Should be easy. Just like a high-wire act." I held my arms out and mimicked balancing on a tightrope, using the lines of the tiled floor to guide me, and trilled a circusy tune as I walked. When we were little, Katy and I liked to try out different acrobatic moves—handstands in the yard, swinging around tree branches, balancing on the edge of the fence by the elementary school. Katy was always much better at it than I was. But I used to think that being a tightrope walker in the circus would be a good job. I could walk in a straight line, and I was good at not looking down. When I still took gymnastics, I would walk across the balance beam and imagine I was in a sparkly leotard, high above the crowd, and everyone was awed by my death-defying turns and steps. Sometimes—especially when I was failing something as lame as driver's ed—it still seemed like a good career choice. I twirled around and spread my arms in a kind of triumph.

Mom had torn her attention away from her maps and was looking at me. "That was very graceful," she said.

I wasn't sure if it was Mom or Amelia Earhart talking. "Thanks."

"You could even do some stunt flying."

"Yeah. I bet." I hated that she was right there, looking at me and talking to me, and yet she wasn't there at all. She didn't want to be there. Before this, my mom and I got into a lot of fights. I would have taken any of those instead of this compliment that meant nothing. "Sorry," I said. "I don't think I'd be a good stunt flyer after all."

I was pretending to do the homework I should have done for that morning when Theresa called. I'd already ignored a couple of her texts.

"Where were you today?" she asked. "Are you sick?"

"No," I said. I was hiding under my covers because Katy refused to leave, and I didn't want to try another room in case Dad or Mom was in there. "My mom was throwing up and stuff, and my dad wanted someone to stay with her while he was at work, so . . ."

"Lucky. We had this heinous pop quiz in English, and I'm not supposed to tell you about it, but study chapters five through seven of *Gatsby*. And get this—Maddie and Josh want to go to the football game."

I sat up, making a little tent out of my covers. "Like where guys hit each other and get points for it?"

"No good movies are out, and they think it'll be funny to go and make obnoxious comments. Of course, Josh will probably get his ass kicked later, but what are you going to do? So can you think of something better to do tonight, or are we going to the game?"

After everyone hated me for messing up the field, I wasn't exactly crazy about the thought of showing up at the football game. Even though the grass was fine again and all the lines were repainted, it was still like I'd shot the football coach. "I don't know, Theresa. Seriously?"

"Well, think of other ideas and then call Josh and Maddie. Maybe you can talk them out of this."

I hadn't even set the phone down when it chirped again. I expected Theresa, with an alternative idea for tonight, but an older woman's voice came from the other end of the line. "Hi, this is Barbara Ellis. Is this Alex? Sorry, I must have gotten your number mixed up with your dad's."

"Mrs. Ellis?" She was Mom's friend. Even though I had seen her a bunch of times, since she had watched us when Mom was in the hospital, my stomach always tightened when I heard her voice. "You want to talk to Dad?"

"If he's available."

I crawled out from under the covers and went to find Dad, passing by Mom, who was still in the kitchen poring over the maps. He was in the living room, with Patsy Cline on the stereo and Jackson at his feet. I handed him my phone and sat beside Jackson, who was chewing on his favorite stuffed duck. Absently petting Jackson, I listened to Dad's side of the conversation: "Uh-huh. . . . Any time you have. . . . That would be great. . . . For now, at least. . . . Uh-huh. Thanks so much, Barbara."

When he hung up, I frowned at him. "What did she want?"

Dad cleared his throat and started mumbling about how he'd have to get back to work soon, especially since Mom wasn't going to be working for the foreseeable future, and therapy would be a lot, even with whatever insurance would kick in. Mrs. Ellis had offered to stay with Mom for most of the day, in case anything happened. But he was avoiding something.

"Just say it," I said.

He pressed his palms together. "We've all got to give stuff up, Alex. I really need you to be here when you get out of school—"

"You're kidding me!" Jackson whimpered and moved away from me. "So, what, the bell rings and I've got to be here?"

"She's your mom, Alex."

"No, she's not. She doesn't think she is." When I marched into the kitchen, Dad followed me. We stopped, seeing Mom at the table. "What's your name again?" I asked.

Mom waved a hand at me, like I was telling a joke. "You know very well I'm Amelia."

Dad's frown deepened, and he positioned himself so Mom couldn't see his face. "Don't try to confuse her anymore, all right? She's your mom, underneath all the maps, and that's it. Now, I really need your help here if we're going to get her any better. I don't want to have to fight with you about this. Can I count on you or not?" The lines of his face sharpened in his seriousness, but I could barely look him in the eye because there was a sadness, too, and disappointment. As if I should have been the responsible older sister, rallying everyone in support of Mom. I didn't want to have to deal with this, either, and the fact that Dad thought I should made it worse. From driver's ed to the Mom situation, that's mostly what I felt like — this huge disappointment to everyone. Except Mom, who thought I was some fantastic girl pilot.

"Fine," I mumbled. "I'll be here. Except for driving practice. With Jim."

He nodded. "All right. As long as I'm home before you leave."

I tried to swallow the lump forming in my throat. "Should we put together a schedule? Like a chore wheel? Thursday: take out trash, hide maps from crazy Mom."

"Hey, if you want to take the trash out, too, be my guest."

He was trying to make me laugh, but I didn't want to, especially with Mom right in front of me. I felt like I usually did in the driver's seat, with the windows shut and the ceiling pressing down and all the air gone.

I didn't tell Dad when I left to meet Theresa and the others at the football game. Not that I told any of my friends I was coming, either. I just assumed that, without a better suggestion, that was where they'd be. Even if Theresa had convinced them to go somewhere else, I didn't really care. I just wanted to be out of the house, and the football game was probably the last place Dad would look for me.

Katy was the only one to see me go. When I pulled on a sweater, Katy looked up from her copy of *To Kill a Mockingbird*. It was practically the first time she'd acknowledged me since we got back from the hospital. She'd spent the afternoon tearing through her homework. She had probably gotten through everything due Monday and started working on stuff that wasn't due for weeks. "Where are you going?"

"Out." I grabbed my cell and some money, just in case. I didn't feel like coming back for a while. "And it's Friday. Stop doing your English homework, already."

"Does Dad know?"

"Does Dad know that you're a total nerd? Yeah, probably." I stopped at the door. "Don't tell him, all right? I just need a minute out of this house."

She stared at me for a second, then sighed, holding her book up again. "Fine. Just don't run away or anything."

I smiled at her. "If I decide to run away, I'll bring you with me."

I felt like running all the way to the football game. It was brisk out, but the air felt good against my skin, like I'd been stifled under bulky coats and wool sweaters all day. I passed kids playing basketball in their driveways, moms unloading groceries from cars, people standing by their mailboxes and flipping through their mail. Outside, it was any other Friday. None of these people knew that, at my house, we'd just brought Mom home even though she wasn't better yet. But I didn't want to think about that anymore. I tried to wipe the image of Mom and her maps out of my mind before a lump formed in my throat. Instead, I started walking faster, then jogging, and then I was running on the side of the road. It wasn't like running laps in gym. For a moment, I felt like I could run forever.

By the time I reached the school, the game had already started. The stands were pretty crowded—our team must have continued their winning streak. Everyone was a blur of maroon-and-gray sweatshirts. Girls huddled together like it was colder out than it actually was. On the sidelines, cheerleaders with sparkly makeup bounced around and chanted, "Let's go, Oak Ridge," over and over. I could see Caroline Lavale with the other color-guard kids. Even the marching band was waiting by the field. I didn't know we kept them around for anything other than the lame costumes and funny hats.

So far, no one had scored. I didn't really know the rules, so it was hard to tell who wasn't doing well and who might actually score at some point. But people kept getting excited whenever a player managed to catch the ball.

Near the stands, the Key Club had set up a card table with baked goods and hot chocolate and cider. I bought a cup of cider and stood beside the stands with it, sipping as I watched guys line up and run into each other.

"Alex!" I heard Theresa shout from overhead. When I

looked up, she was leaning out of the stands. "I didn't think you were coming."

I wished she hadn't shouted my name. Other people turned to look as well. It was like I was a spy for the other team. What did they think I'd do? Get a Mack truck and run over the whole defensive line?

"Come on. Sit up here," Theresa said.

I climbed my way through the crowd to get to my friends, smelling alcohol from most kids I passed. With the surprisingly good season, people celebrated harder. My friends squeezed together to make room for me. Everyone else glared like I was bad luck, and I started to think that coming to the game wasn't such a great idea. I hoped the players hadn't noticed. Dealing with them was bad enough already.

"So," I said, "are you having fun? Is it everything you dreamed it would be?"

Theresa rolled her eyes. "Oh, more."

"Psh, whatever," Josh said. "We got to see Nick Gillan get sacked. That was pretty satisfying."

"Too bad I missed that one," I said.

"Don't worry," Maddie said. "It's not even halftime yet. There are still plenty of chances for him to get his ass handed to him."

Even without the possibility of Nick Gillan getting his face mangled, I liked the brutality of it all. After feeling so awkward and helpless at home and in the hospital, it was kind of nice to see people slam into each other and throw one another to the ground. If I'd been a guy, that's what I would have signed up for. I even found myself cheering a few times. Theresa looked at me like I'd lost my mind — not such a stretch these days — but Josh and Maddie got into it, too.

By the second half, Franklin had scored two touchdowns, while we were still stuck at zero. The Franklin cheerleaders were mocking our players, and the Oak Ridge cheerleaders were making obnoxious rhymed comments back.

"Now, this is the Oak Ridge team I know," Josh said. "No skills to back up their asshole behavior."

"Might as well stick with what you're good at," Maddie said.

Behind me, I thought I heard someone say my name. I almost turned around, but then I heard it again: "It's because Winchester's here." I sipped the rest of my cider, pretending I didn't notice. The voice came again. "You're killing us, Winchester!" I glanced over my shoulder to see a group of JV football players at the top of the stands, some jerk sophomore in the middle looking right at me. He had acne and a squarish head. I couldn't remember his name.

"Fuck off. You didn't even make the team," Theresa said.

"Go drive away, Winchester," the sophomore said. "Drive off a cliff."

At that moment, if my dad had suggested that I homeschool myself so I could stay with Mom full-time, I would have taken him up on it. "I'm gonna go," I told Theresa. "I'll talk to you later."

Theresa frowned. "Come on. Don't listen to him."

"It's not just him," I said, standing up. Behind me, the sophomore and his friends started hooting. "I don't care. It's fine. I should get home anyway." Before Theresa could persuade me to stay, I shoved my way back through the crowd, down to the ground again. The sophomores applauded as I left.

I crumpled the empty cider cup and tossed it into the trash. One lousy moment—that was all I wanted. One moment that didn't make me worry about anything, and some dumbass sophomore had to attack me. His parents were probably sane and knew his name. Couldn't he go torture them and leave me alone?

I was bending down to tie my shoelace tighter, so I could run the whole way home again, when I heard footsteps behind me. It was Jim Wiley. He smiled, which made all my limbs soften. Then I remembered how frazzled I must have looked.

"Hey. I didn't know you were into this kind of thing," I said before he had the chance to ask me about why I was leaving.

"You either," he said. "Will and Everett talked me into coming."

"Same here," I said. "Not your friends, I mean. My friends." Shit. Couldn't I talk right? I felt like every inch of me was an exposed nerve.

"Yeah." He brushed his hand by his head, like he meant to push it through his hair but remembered too late that he'd cut most of it off. "You shouldn't let those assholes get to you," he said.

I tried to smile, but my face felt too tight. "Oh, right. I don't care about them. I just didn't feel like staying anymore."

"That's cool. Are you just headed home?"

On the field, the marching band took its place, along with the color guard. Over a loudspeaker, someone — it sounded like Simon Kelly, obnoxious honor student — said they were playing "I Feel Good" by James Brown. Horns blared and everyone cheered. Drums buzzed like the engine of a plane.

I'd just gotten out of my house; I didn't want to head back now, but what else was there? My friends were still here, clapping for Caroline Lavale as she swung a maroon flag around the field. In town, there were just useless little gift stores and restaurants, nowhere I'd want to hang out alone. Even hiding in the movie theater was out — the Cineplex was out by the strip malls, too far to walk. And, of course, I didn't have a car.

"What's with you, Jim?" I said suddenly. "We weren't friends before this year. Why are you teaching me how to drive, anyway? It's kind of hopeless, right?"

His eyebrows rose, and he looked like he wasn't sure if he should apologize or back away and let me rant by myself. "No, you're doing okay —"

"I'm like this freak who can't drive and messes up the football field. Why are you hanging out with me, anyway? What is it, pity? I've got enough of that, thanks, so I don't need you to do me any great favors."

"It's not pity," Jim said, a little harsher, like I'd offended him. "I like hanging out with you."

"Because we both broke stuff with cars?" A little voice in the back of my head kept screaming at me to just shut up already. Did I want to alienate the one guy who was actually being nice to me? The one guy who made me forget the current mess that was my life? But the anger fizzing in my veins kept me going. Dimly, I wondered if this was what it was like for Mom—a glimmer of logic overwhelmed by the sharp and buzzing frustration. And instead of stopping, I took a step toward Jim so we were almost touching. "Before this year, you never even said hello to me, and now you're giving me driving lessons and standing up for me in Spanish class. What's your deal?"

He didn't move away from me. Instead, he seemed to get closer. My heart pounded.

"Remember that time in the woods, when you saw me trying to graffiti the rock?" he asked. "You liked it. You said it looked kind of like a phoenix, which was really cool, and nobody else in this school would've gotten that, not even my friends."

I stopped. Inside, the buzzing frustration started to dim. I was glad I hadn't listened to Mom and decided to cut through the woods that day.

"In case you missed it," Jim said, "most of the people in our school suck. So it's nice when somebody comes along that you can just talk to and not feel weird around. Especially after driving into a house. So if you want to get mad at me some more, go ahead, but you wanted to know, and that's my deal."

For a second, I just stared at Jim. I still felt a kind of buzzing, but it was different now. On the field, the marching band started playing "I Heard It Through the Grapevine," and they were a little off the beat. The cheerleaders were encouraging the people in the stands to clap.

And I before I knew it, I was kissing Jim Wiley.

Before now, most of my kissing experience consisted of spin the bottle and being cornered by guys at parties. I didn't even really know what I was doing when I started kissing Jim. I hadn't exactly thought past that point, but then he started kissing me back and we were pressed together and his arms were around me, and I never wanted to stop kissing him. Suddenly everything was charged. I felt like all the atoms in my body were spinning and zipping through space.

Spinning and zipping were exactly what I was looking for.

The football game was over and most cars had disappeared from the parking lot by the time Jim and I stopped kissing. For the last hour or two, we'd been lying on a grassy hill behind the library, well hidden from everyone at the game. When car horns started blaring in the distance, I looked up.

"Does that mean we won?" I asked.

Jim kissed my neck. "I don't think they know the difference."

I tried not to giggle and mostly failed. "Either way, best football game ever."

In a way, the whole day felt unreal. A couple of weeks ago, I'd barely spoken to Jim before, and now I knew that he smelled like peppermint shampoo and had sensitive ears. I didn't feel awkward or inhibited with Jim at all; everything felt really right. All I had to think about was how kissing left me kind of dizzy and breathless and how he knew how good it felt to be touched on the small of the back. And he was just the right height so we could lie down next to each other and match almost perfectly. Overhead, stars were just becoming visible. Everything smelled like peppermint and grass and burning leaves. I wanted to stay there forever.

"Why didn't we do this sooner?" I asked.

We kissed and didn't break apart for so long that I thought he wasn't going to answer. "Because I had to win you over with my driving skills first."

"That's exactly what won me over."

Suddenly the voices coming from the football game sounded closer. Jim and I broke apart just as a group of freshmen stumbled around the corner. "Oops," one of them slurred, and they giggled but kept walking.

We sat up, brushing grass off ourselves. Suddenly it felt a lot colder and I shivered a little. "What time is it, anyway?" I asked. Jim pulled out his cell to check. It was later than I'd expected. Way later than I should have been out. "I should get back," I told Jim.

"You sure?" he said. "Will McNamee texted me. People are going over to his place if you want to come."

I didn't know if I wanted to share Jim with anyone yet. Instead of saying so, I claimed that my parents would probably be waiting up, since I hadn't told anyone I was going out. "You should go, though. We'll get together later."

Jim reached toward me and pulled a blade of grass from my hair. "Just so you don't get in trouble," he said, and kissed me again.

By the time I got home, most of the lights in the house were off, including the one in Mom and Dad's room. I wondered what Katy had told Dad.

Jackson, who was at the door when I opened it, trotted back to his pillow bed in the living room. I padded slowly into the kitchen, my sneakers squeaking against the tile floor. Mom was at the kitchen sink, gazing out over the darkness of the backyard. For a moment, I hoped she had given up the Amelia Earhart stuff and was just Mom again, even if Mom would yell at me for being out late and not letting anyone know where I was. Then I noticed she had a dozen index cards in her hands and that she was whispering to herself. "... *aviation, this young modern giant, exemplifies the possible relationships of women with the creations of science . . .*"

When I hit a creaky spot on the floor, she glanced up. "Hello there," she said, smiling. It wasn't Mom. "Just going over my lecture notes."

"Hey," I said. I backed away, thinking I'd leave her to whatever she thought she had to be doing, but my stomach rumbled. The hot cider had been a while ago. And Mom seemed pretty distracted anyway, so I looked in the refrigerator and found a slice of leftover pizza.

"Did they order out?" I asked. Even though Dad had said

we were supposed to remind her of real-life stuff, I wasn't sure where that line blurred.

"Oh, yes. They got Italian. Lovely country."

I didn't bother heating up the pizza. At first I considered taking it to my room, but I knew Katy would object—she had a thing about crumbs—and I didn't want to run into Dad in case he was still awake. Instead, I sat at the table. "Have you been there?" I said. I wasn't supposed to ask these kinds of questions, but with the rest of the house dark and quiet, it felt like Mom and I were just talking, like we sometimes did when neither of us could sleep. Even if she wouldn't talk to me like she was my mother, I thought it would be better than not talking to her at all.

Her smile was beatific. "I've been all over Europe. After my solo flight."

"Did you like it there?" I took a bite of pizza.

"Well, it was very exciting. Lots of talking to the press, that kind of thing. When I came back to New York, there was a ticker-tape parade. But mostly I just wanted to be flying. G.P. says that's all a part of it, the media side, but it's not quite the same, is it?"

"No, I guess not." I'd never been in a plane before. When we went to Florida for vacation a few years ago, we drove the whole way. Maybe it would be exciting—the sudden lift and push backward into your seat, seeing the ground disappear below, rising through the clouds and into the sky.

"So I kissed this guy tonight," I told her. "He's teaching me how to drive."

Mom's face fell a little. She leaned forward, resting her hand on top of mine. "Now, I know attention can be nice, but don't let romance stand in the way of your career. I told George about that before I agreed to marry him—he'd have to let me go if I wasn't happy after a year."

"Yeah," I said, "I know. And Jim and I aren't getting married or anything. I don't even know what we're doing. It was just nice." I couldn't help smiling. "Really nice."

She gave my hand a squeeze. "You'll make the right decision. And look how it's worked out for George and me so far."

I thought about Dad, upstairs, probably already asleep because he'd be working tomorrow and because he was exhausted. "You love him, though, right? Even though you said that he'd have to let you go if you asked him to. That was just in case. You're not still thinking about leaving him?"

Sighing, she drummed her fingernails against the back of my hand. "He pushes me—it's just so much sometimes. The tours, the lectures, everything. It's good for me, I know. But it's quieter in the air." She laughed. "Not with the engines, but a different kind of quiet. I suppose that's alone enough for now."

Chapter Ten

One of my favorite phobias is that girls, especially those whose tastes aren't routine, often don't get a fair break. . . . It has come down through the generations, an inheritance of age-old customs which produced the corollary that women are bred to timidity.

—Amelia Earhart

On Monday, it was my job to get Katy and Teddy ready for school. Katy was all right on her own; I had to practically drag Teddy out of bed and toss him into the bathroom. He kept collapsing against me like he'd lost all muscle control. "I don't feel well," he said. "I'm too tired." I told him that I didn't care, and he could go puke in the nurse's office at school if it came to that. After I took off Friday night, Dad wouldn't let me out for the rest of the weekend, which meant I hadn't seen Jim since the football game. It was the first time in a while that I was actually looking forward to school.

"Teddy!" I shouted from the kitchen as Katy and I made lunches. "Get your butt down here or I'll kick it down."

He clomped down the stairs and slumped against the kitchen table. "Hey there, sunshine," I said.

"Hi," he mumbled, starting to pick at the bagel Katy had set out for him. "What're you making?" When I told him ham and cheese, he groaned and held his head in his hands as if it weighed a thousand pounds. "I don't *want* that."

"Fine," I said. "Make it yourself. I'm just doing this to be nice."

"I don't want to make it *myself.* Just make me something *else.*"

I shoved the sandwich in a paper bag, along with a mini box of raisins and some baby carrots. "Oh, my God, Teddy, whine me a river."

He began to swing his legs, kicking the underside of the table. "*Mom* would make something else for me. Make me something *else.* Make Mom make lunch." When I turned, Teddy's face was red and scrunched, like he was about to cry.

"She's . . . sleeping," Katy said.

I knew Dad had talked to him about Mom, even though I wasn't exactly sure what Dad had told him. How was he supposed to explain a mental breakdown to a seven-year-old? At least when Mom was curled up, we could say she felt sick and achy, and he seemed to buy it. But now Mom was there but she wasn't Mom, not even in some quiet, distant way. She would pretend that Teddy was someone else—a nephew, the son of her sister, from what I could tell. So Dad was just trying to keep Teddy away from Mom as much as possible, and he asked us to do the same.

"We have peanut butter," I said. "And I think chicken. Do you want that?"

Teddy slid from his seat to the floor, disappearing under the table. "I'm not going to school today," he said. "You didn't have to go Friday, and I don't have to go today."

I rolled my eyes. "Teddy, get up. We were helping Mom. It wasn't a real day off."

His sneakers slapped the tile floor. Nearby, Jackson squeaked and moved into the living room. "Mom's pretending to be someone else and doesn't have to go to work. I can pretend to be someone else, too, and I won't have to go to school."

Katy and I looked at each other. "Teddy," I said. "Teddy, stop being stupid. You're fine."

"I'm not Teddy."

I didn't even want to ask who he'd be—some superhero, probably. For a second, I thought about saying I didn't care if he went to school or not, but then I imagined him standing at his window, thinking he was Spider-Man and could web himself to the next house. I knelt on the floor and grabbed his arm. "Yeah, you are. Now, get up." I pulled, and he screamed.

By the time I heard the knocking, it was more like banging. "Door," Katy said.

I'd wrestled Teddy from under the table and handed him to Katy. "Calm him down or something," I said, and rushed to the door.

It was Mrs. Ellis, here for her first shift. "Is everything all right?" she asked, trying to glimpse behind me.

"Yeah," I said, "it's just my stupid brother. Come on in."

She followed me into the kitchen. When Teddy saw her, he stopped struggling in Katy's arms, embarrassed. He started to wipe his nose on Katy's sleeve, and she yanked her arm away. "Ew, Teddy!"

Mrs. Ellis smiled with her lips pressed together. "Well," she said, "it looks like you've been having quite a morning."

Suddenly I felt like we were such a mess. The counter was covered in stuff for lunch, and boxes of cereal had been left out. In the corner, the trash can was overflowing. No one had bothered to vacuum in a while, so stray bits of leaves and dog hair gathered in the corners. Since I'd been doing a lot of the laundry, all of our clothes were wrinkled. I wasn't sure if Teddy had had a bath that weekend. We'd never been an obsessively neat family—even when Mom had all her mental capacities, she hated cleaning—but now everything felt out of order and dirty. I tugged at the ends of my hair. Even though I'd showered that morning, it felt gross and uncombed. In crisp khakis and a fisherman's sweater, Mrs. Ellis looked fresh, but then, she always did. She was around Mom's age, and probably Mom's closest friend in the neighborhood. She was nice enough, and she would do stuff like lead her daughter's Girl Scout troop and organize an egg hunt every year for Easter. Her kids—a boy and a girl, older than us—were off at college, or maybe they had even graduated by now. I wondered if they knew that their mom would be sitting with our crazy mom during the day.

"Mom's still asleep," I told her. "She stays up late."

"That's all right. It's better for her to get some rest. You kids better hurry or you'll be late for school." She kept smiling without her teeth. It was like Mr. Kane and how he got nice. Not that Mrs. Ellis ever hated me, but I didn't want her smiling like that, all patient and unblinking. I didn't want her waving good-bye like she was our mom.

I grabbed a bagel and pressed it into Teddy's hand. "You can eat this on the bus," I said. He didn't argue and kept holding my hand as we marched to the bus stop.

When I got off the bus, my insides were wringing themselves in anxiety. I wanted to see Jim—and I didn't want to see him. What if he thought us making out was a total joke? What if I saw him pressed up against a locker with some short-skirted freshman? What if he thought I was a loser, just like everybody else? But he was also the only person I felt calm around these days. In phys ed, Mrs. Harriott matched everyone up with a partner to practice backhands, and, of course, I got paired with Amanda Baxter, tennis champion, so I never got the chance to really talk to him.

A couple of hours later, when I was in line to get an iced tea at the cafeteria, Theresa and Maddie were talking about how their moms sucked, and I didn't even want to hear it. Jim was just paying for his lunch when I caught his eye.

"Hey," he said. "I was gonna eat outside. You want to come?"

I said yes without even looking at my friends or explaining to them what had happened.

We found an empty spot outside the gymnasium. It was sunny, and probably one of the last nice days we'd get to have lunch outside before the cold weather set in. Nearby, kids with sixth-period phys ed jogged around the edge of the soccer field. At the tennis courts, Mrs. Harriott blew her whistle, and the kids ran over to her, cutting down the white center line. Jim told me about Will's party—"A lot of random sophomores showed up; you didn't miss much"—and I told him about crashing senior parties when I was a freshman and on JV soccer.

"It was like we were these stupid little magpies, going after whatever was shiniest," I said. "We just stayed in a huge clump and giggled a lot."

"But you don't play anymore, right? Soccer, I mean."

I shook my head. "I decided not to this year."

"Why not?"

I rubbed my thumb against the label on my bottle of iced tea until the edge came unglued. "I was just sick of it. I mean, I really liked playing, but it was, like, a lot of pressure." I could almost hear my mom, telling me that I could do better.

"Like how?"

"It just was." My tone was harsher than I intended, and Jim blinked in surprise.

"Sorry," he said stiffly. "I just think if you like something, you shouldn't let stuff like that stop you."

I peeled the label off my bottle and took a breath. "So if you could be anyone, who would you be?"

Jim bit into an apple. "That sounds like the essay question on a college application." He grinned. "Are you trying to steal my answer? Because I'm definitely getting into Harvard with that one."

"Yeah," I said. "I think I'll have a better chance if I apply as you. Seriously, it's just a fun question."

"Anyone?" he asked.

I sipped my iced tea. "Anyone. Living, dead, imaginary, whoever. If you could just become them."

He leaned back against the brick wall of the gym. "I don't know. Let me think for a second — I have to remember everyone who's ever existed in the universe."

"Not everyone," I said. "Just the good ones. That cuts out, what, like fifty gazillion people? That's so easy."

He laughed; I loved that I could make Jim Wiley laugh.

"Time's up," I said. "Who would you pick?"

"Oh, thanks. Only the huge question of my future identity and you give me about a minute and a half." He exhaled sharply. "I don't know. Maybe Banksy."

"Banksy?"

"He's this street artist from England," Jim explained. "Graffiti artist, you know. But it's not just tags or whatever. He does these really cool stencil paintings and prints, with all these subversive messages. And of course his work is on regular building walls. You could walk down the street and see his work. In fact . . ." He pulled his phone out of his pocket, scanned through it for a second, and then handed it to me. I flipped through the images—a bird with a gasoline nozzle for a head, two kissing policemen, a wall labeled DESIGNATED PICNIC AREA.

I handed Jim back his phone. "That last one is stenciled writing. Does that count as art?"

"Why not? That's what I like about it. Plus, not many people know who Banksy actually is. You don't have to be some famous guy hanging art in famous galleries to be an artist. I think that's pretty cool."

I just stared at Jim for a second. Even though I'd seen him try to do graffiti art on the boulder, I didn't peg him as someone who would have thought much about what it meant to be an artist. "Is that like what you were doing at the rock?"

He laughed. "Trying to do. The rock's a good place to practice because people don't notice if it sucks."

"I think you'd make a good Banksy."

Jim's face reddened a little, and he nudged me with his knee. "Maybe he'll go crazy and cut his ear off, Van Gogh–style, and I'll have to pick someone else to be."

I stiffened at the word "crazy" but tried to smile. "You have nice ears. Don't get rid of them."

"Thanks. I kind of like them myself. Anyway, he's the first one I thought of," Jim said. "There's probably somebody better, but for now I'll say Banksy." He tapped my knee with his apple. "What about you?"

"I don't know," I said.

"Come on, it's your question," he said. "You have to know."

It seemed dangerous to even think about. "What about Amelia Earhart?"

Jim nodded. "She was pretty cool. Except for that whole thing where she died young. You lose points for that."

"Disappeared," I said. "No one actually knows what happened to her."

"I dunno, some people have some convincing theories. Like, I'm pretty sure aliens got her." He laughed and nudged my leg with his.

I wished aliens had abducted Amelia Earhart. Then Mom probably wouldn't have wanted to be her. "Yeah, she was just the first person who popped into my head anyway. I'd probably choose someone else." I tugged a blade of grass from the ground and began tearing it into tiny pieces. "Maybe Jane Eyre."

"Jane Eyre?" he said. "From the book?"

"Yeah. I had to read it for Heickman's class last year. Jane's smart and she holds her own even though everyone's a dick to her. And she and Mr. Rochester—that's her boss—are the only ones who get each other. Although Jane's life kind of sucks for a while. Well, the ending was happy. It was just getting there that was bad." In the distance, I could hear the electronic ring of the bell. "That's lunch," I said, starting to collect my things.

"How about driving tonight?" Jim said.

Dad wasn't exactly happy with me, and I was supposed to watch Mom until he got home. And now that Mom was back in the house, I wasn't sure what that meant for Jim coming over— especially after I basically told him about the Amelia Earhart thing. "I don't think I can tonight," I said. "I'm supposed to watch my little brother. Maybe later this week?"

"Sounds good. We can practice parallel parking." I froze, looking at Jim like he'd suggested we give Russian roulette a try, and Jim laughed. "Come on, I bet Jane Eyre would've loved it."

"Sure," I said. "Eighteenth-century governesses love parallel parking."

Theresa attacked me in the hall before driver's ed. "See, I'm a little confused," she said, linking my arm with hers so it looked like we were being best-friendy, but really she just didn't want me to escape. "If I were going to hook up with Jim Wiley during lunch, I'd give my friends a heads-up about it. Then we could all exchange high fives afterward."

"We don't have to exchange high fives," I said. "Jim and I just had lunch."

"Since when are you and Jim Wiley having lunch? I know he stood up for you and all, but I didn't think you exactly hung out."

"We didn't. Until now." I wasn't sure how to tell Theresa about what had been going on with Jim and me — or even what to tell her without making my mom a part of that. "He's been helping me drive."

Theresa's eyebrows disappeared under her bangs. "You're actually driving?"

"Mostly in straight lines," I said.

"So he's, like, your secret driving coach? Why would he do that?"

I rolled my eyes. "Because he wants hook up with me in the driver's ed car. That Volvo is a major turn-on." I eyed Theresa. "Actually, we kind of made out during the football game."

She stopped in her tracks. Since our arms were still linked, I jerked to a halt. "Are you kidding me? And you've been holding on to this since Friday? Who *are* you? This is why people invented texting, Winchester! Where were you guys, under the bleachers?"

"We're not freshmen," I said. "We went to that grassy hill behind the library."

"Are you guys together now?"

"No, that's basically been the extent of it. That and lunch today. So I don't even know what's going on." It should have bothered me, not knowing where Jim and I stood—were we going to hook up again, or were we dating, or were we just friends and the making out had been kind of accidental? But somehow I didn't want an explanation just yet. A boyfriend would expect to come over and hang out sometimes, meet my parents eventually. For now it was better to keep our relationship—whatever that might be—as far away from home as possible.

"You should invite him to Halloween," Theresa said. "It's coming up, and Josh wants to do something. Horror movies, maybe. Do you think your parents would let us stay over?"

"Um, my dad has to get up early—"

"Oh, right, the mail thing," she said. "Wherever, then. Invite Jim and see what he says. Then maybe you can tell what's going on between you guys."

"Right." Even without my mom, I wasn't sure if I wanted Jim and my friends to all hang out just yet. For now, being with him was like my own secret thing. I liked having a small part of my life that wasn't anyone else's and wasn't messed up in some way.

"Don't worry," Theresa said. "We'll figure something out."

I unlinked my arm. "Right. We'll figure it out."

Caroline Lavale was practicing reversing by a curb when Theresa sold me out. "Hey, Mr. Kane, you should let Alex try." She glanced at me with a little smile, like I should have thanked her when really I was wondering why she wanted to torture me.

On my left, Edward Baker grabbed for the door handle and made like he was going to roll out. "Oh, no," he said. "This time she's going to drive into a brick wall."

"Edward, stop being a drama queen," Mr. Kane said.

"She's been practicing," Theresa said.

"Just a little," I said. For a second, I was afraid she'd specify the person I'd been practicing with, whom Mr. Kane probably wouldn't consider a great driving instructor, but Theresa just kept glimpsing at me with those half smiles, like we had this great secret.

Mr. Kane looked at me through the rearview mirror. Caroline had stopped the car and put it in park, like she wasn't sure if she should let me have a turn. If this had been two weeks ago, before he met my mother, Mr. Kane would have been glaring. But now his eyes were softer and kind of hopeful. "Have you been practicing, Alex?"

I squirmed against the seat belt. "Kind of," I said. "Just forward and backward, mostly. Nothing really impressive." For the last couple of weeks, I'd been happy to sit in the backseat and watch everyone else pull off three-point turns and parallel parking and other magnificent feats of automobilery. And even though I'd managed to drive a few times without killing anyone, I was afraid I wouldn't be able to do the same thing here, in the driver's ed Volvo, with Mr. Kane feeding me instructions instead of Jim. But the idea of driving with Jim was that someday I'd be able to drive other places, with other people. On my own. I thought it might be nice to tell Jim that I'd successfully driven four feet without him in the passenger seat.

"I want to try," I told Mr. Kane, staring into the reflection of his eyes in the rearview mirror.

"All right. Caroline, you're out." Caroline turned off the engine so she and I could switch places. She gave me an encouraging smile as she slid into the backseat.

I hadn't been in the front of the driver's ed car since the day I drove onto the football field. For a second, I had trouble breathing—was it inhale and exhale or the other way around? I imagined everyone in seventh-period classes leaning against the rows of windows, waiting for me to screw up.

"Don't worry, we're not going to try anything fancy," Mr.

Kane said. "Just a little forward motion. Straight lines. Easy, right?"

I gripped the key and turned it. The engine whirred. I closed my eyes and tried to focus on everything Jim had told me. I was listening to his steady voice when Mr. Kane said, "With your eyes open, preferably."

In the back, Edward muttered, "You've got to be kidding me."

"I was just getting ready," I said. Beside me, Mr. Kane looked a little less hopeful, like he was about to suggest that maybe I should wait until the next class to try driving. I wanted to show him that I didn't need pity. With my hands grasping the wheel, I released the brake and pressed my foot against the gas.

It was a little too hard. The car jumped forward and I hit the brake again. "Sorry!" I said. "Sorry."

"That's all right, Alex," Mr. Kane said, his voice shaky. "Try again."

"You got this," Theresa said.

I breathed deeply and tried to imagine the back roads with Jim—the sunset, the stars, the breeze, the quiet. Maybe it was what Amelia Earhart had liked about flying solo. I touched the gas, gently this time, and the car rolled forward.

"There you go," Mr. Kane said. I didn't look, but his voice sounded like it came from a mouth that was just starting to smile. "There you go."

We drove in a straight line to the end of the parking lot. If anyone had been watching from their seventh-period class, they would have seen the driver's ed car go about five miles an hour but not hit anyone or anything. It would have looked like anyone scanning the parking lot for a good spot. When there wasn't anywhere else to go, I pressed my foot against the brake and put the car in park.

"Alex!" Mr. Kane said. For a minute, I thought he was going to hug me. "Look! You've progressed!"

In back, Caroline applauded, and Theresa, who was usually above that kind of thing, joined her. She didn't even look too smug that it had been her idea I drive. Edward rolled his eyes. "Great, she can go twenty feet. So exciting."

Mr. Kane ignored him, scribbling notes on his clipboard. "I can work with this."

After class, Mr. Kane asked me to stay behind. The way he was smiling, I thought he would start weeping with joy over the fact that I wasn't turning out to be his greatest academic disappointment. "I've got to say, Alex, I'm impressed. I really am." He hugged the clipboard to his chest. "I wasn't sure you were ever going to stay cool behind the wheel. It just takes a little practice, right? And I know it can be tough with all your classmates in the car—like stage fright."

What I'd felt was worse than stage fright; it was a crushing phobia. But I didn't tell him that. "Right."

He took a breath. "All right. I still don't think I can pass you for the semester. You just don't have the time to learn enough, especially when you consider I've got other students in the class to think about."

"Right." It was fair enough, but it sucked that my progress couldn't get me through the semester.

"But," he said, "*but* . . . if you pass a special exam at the end, I can give you an incomplete instead of a failing grade and let you take the class again." He made a note on his clipboard. "Unless, of course, you'd rather just pay for outside instruction."

I didn't think my dad would count Jim's teaching as outside instruction, and even though I wasn't sure I ever wanted to start a career racing stock cars, I didn't want my time driving to have been for nothing. I imagined holding a freshly laminated license in my hand, showing it to Jim.

"No, that sounds great," I told Mr. Kane.

"Keep studying the book and keep paying attention in class, and we'll make a driver out of you yet." I expected him to break into song about it, but instead he smiled broadly and strolled away.

Theresa had been waiting for me. When she saw Mr. Kane leave, she ran over. "Hey, what'd he say?"

I frowned and swung my backpack over my shoulder. "He's not going to fail me."

"Good thing," she said. "It would be the suckiest thing ever to fail driver's ed. That stuff goes on your record, too. Plus, you'd just look like the biggest loser ever." I started to walk away, but she kept talking about how great it was that I'd been able to pull it together and drive, and that I'd done a good job, and wasn't it great that she'd basically forced me into it so

Mr. Kane could see? "I knew you'd never do it yourself, but I knew you could if you just got behind the wheel already, so I went for it. I knew you'd be happy about it once it was over."

"Yeah, fine," I said. She followed me inside the school and we dove into the crowded hallway. "But how'd you know for sure I'd do it? What if I freaked out again and killed somebody?"

"If you killed somebody, hopefully it would have been Edward. And besides, you *just* told me you'd been practicing with Jim. So either you'd been using 'driving' as a euphemism for sex or you'd actually gotten yourself behind the wheel. And you totally would have told me if you guys had sex."

"But it could have been different with Jim. I'd never driven in front of other people until now." Theresa looked so smug about everything. I wanted to yell at her about it, but as we headed for the stairs, kids pushed by us on their way to last period.

"But you did it," she said matter-of-factly. She kind of laughed. "Look, it all worked out, so why worry? You can thank me when you get your report card and don't have a big F on it." Without waiting for my argument, she ran up the stairs, on her way to French.

That night, I told Mom about driver's ed. It was after I was sure that Katy had fallen asleep. Her breathing was deep and steady when I got out of bed and crept across the floor of our room, escaping into the hall. I didn't even question that Mom would be awake. And sure enough, there she was again, at the kitchen table, maps spread out around her. But this time they were real maps, not taped-together ones from the Internet, of what looked like the U.S. She must have found them in a drawer somewhere, from various car trips. And on top of the maps was an old clock radio, one that Katy and I used years ago and forgot to throw out once it broke. Mom was humming to herself and fiddling with the bottom of the clock when she saw me.

"Got to keep your instruments in top shape," she said solemnly, waving the screwdriver in my direction.

I perched on one of the kitchen chairs. "Do you know what you're doing?"

She stiffened. "Of course I do. As if I don't know how to keep my own plane in working order."

"Sure you do," I muttered. "But if you electrocute yourself, I'm the one who has to call an ambulance."

I didn't expect her to even respond, but she let her screwdriver drop, clattering against the table. She stared at me, eyes hard. "What kind of a thing is that to say? We are just fine here. When have I ever let someone get electrocuted? No one is getting hurt, and I am in complete control of everything." She gripped the edge of the table, the maps crinkling under her fingers.

"All right," I said. "I didn't mean anything by it."

She drew a few deep breaths, and her face relaxed. Satisfied, she returned to her work. For a few minutes, I watched as she turned the clock over in her hands, shaking it every so often as she tried to figure out how to remove the bottom. I didn't want to upset her more by pointing out that it was just a clock radio, not a special aeronautic instrument. And maybe it would help her if she learned how to do things. Maybe she just needed to figure out enough stuff as Amelia Earhart to become Mom again. And I remembered how nice it was to drive that first time, with Jim—how gratifying to glide across the parking lot and have conquered one stupid little thing.

"Aha," she said, pulling the plastic shield off the bottom of the clock. Her face brightened.

"Can I see that?" I said. She handed it over, and I weighed it in my hands. I didn't want her to stick the screwdriver anywhere she might get shocked. But it wasn't plugged in, and there didn't seem to be any batteries, so I thought it would be safe enough. I handed it back. "Looks good."

She sighed and picked up the screwdriver again. "We'll see."

"I drove today." She looked up from the clock radio, her face patient and hopeful. "In front of other people. It was a class. I did pretty well, too."

"That's wonderful," she said. "Where were you headed?"

"Nowhere far. But my teacher doesn't think I'm such a spaz anymore." I shrugged. "It's nice not to feel so stupid in front of everybody."

She put her hand on mine and squeezed. "It's hard, isn't it?" For a moment, I thought she might be Mom again, who knew I was having trouble in driver's ed, but she kept going. "People think just because women wear skirts that we're incapable of working with any kind of machinery. As though all we can do is make a home and have children." She drew a deep breath and didn't exhale for a moment. I wasn't sure if she was thinking about the baby who died. I waited for Mom to cry or say more, but she shook her head and smiled with her lips tight. "It's nice to prove them wrong, isn't it?"

"Right," I whispered.

"And I'm sure you'll come up against a lot more opposition in your career," she said, her voice filled with gravity. "But you keep working. Just keep flying. You're all alone up there, anyway."

"Right." I slipped my hand away from hers. "I mean, I just want my license."

"Don't sell yourself short."

I shook my head. "My teacher says I need to take a test at the end of the semester and prove that I know things."

She sighed. "More hoops to jump through."

"No," I said, "he's being all right about it. Probably because he feels kind of bad for me, but I don't care. At least I don't fail this way." I picked up the screwdriver and twirled it between my fingers. "My friend Theresa basically made me drive, even though I didn't want to. And even though it all worked out okay, she didn't have to be such a bitch about it, you know? Like she knows what's best for me and I'm such an idiot that I can't do things for myself."

She laid her hands on the clock radio. "It's not all camara-derie out there, even among women," she said. "Some pilots are jealous of the attention we get."

"It's not that. And it worked out all right, but she didn't have to make it her idea."

"Some people don't like me, either," she said. She stared at me hard. "They think I'm all talk and no aeronautic ability. You just keep flying and show them what you can do."

Sure, I thought, *except you disappear in the end*. The idea startled me. Mom didn't seem to recognize that this would be the end of the Amelia Earhart story. Maybe she'd just go on being Amelia forever. Or maybe she'd disappear some-where. I'd walk through the front door someday and she wouldn't be there. I'd never see her again. I stopped twirling the screwdriver, letting it fall to the table.

Mom picked it up. "You don't have to throw the tools around," she said. "Not everyone's awake at this hour."

"Right," I said, a lump forming in my throat. Mom began to work at the clock radio again, humming to herself and occa-sionally muttering aeronautical terms I didn't quite under-stand. The hairs on my arms stood up; watching Mom was like watching a ghost. I sat at the table with her for another two hours as she took apart the clock and tried to reconstruct it. I was afraid that if I left, when I looked for her again, she would be gone.

CHAPTER ELEVEN

Ours is the commencement of a flying age.

—Amelia Earhart

Mom's first appointment with her psychiatrist was later that week. Dad arranged it so it was after school, when I could go, too. When I asked why, he said it was so I could tell the psychiatrist about what I'd seen of Mom's behavior, which had been more than either Katy or Teddy had seen so far. I didn't have to go every week unless I wanted to. The way he looked at me, eyes bright but a little sad, I could tell that he wanted me to be a regular feature at these meetings. I told him I'd have to think about it, especially since I needed to study for Mr. Kane's special exam.

Dad ate lunch in his mail truck that day to get the time off in the afternoon. The post office was being really great, he claimed, because he'd been such a dedicated carrier all these years. Even so, he didn't look at me when he said this, and I knew he was worried about what would happen if he took too much time off work. A lot of carriers would offer to take over his routes if he couldn't make it in. Dad was still in his postal uniform when he drove us to the psychiatrist's office.

"Maybe you should bring the psychiatrist's mail with us," I said. "She'd probably knock a few dollars off the price. For the convenience."

"Couldn't hurt. Too bad I left the mail sack in my truck." He glanced along Waverly Avenue, which was lined with old houses and new brick office buildings. "It's Dr. McGlynn. Number four-seven-five. There should be a sign out front."

In the backseat, Mom asked, "How many of these do I have to do today?" She had put on a long brown skirt and khaki blazer for the occasion—with the usual linen scarf, of course. That morning I'd been surprised to see her iron her clothes and brush her hair in the mirror. At first I wondered if she was Mom again, but she caught me watching and talked about how important it was to keep up appearances when talking to the media. She didn't love giving interviews and speeches, but it was all part of the job. The reporters liked to see that she was feminine, too. "G.P. taught me that," she said, patting me on the cheek as she passed.

"Just the one appointment today," Dad said. "It shouldn't be too bad."

She nodded. "That's a pleasant surprise. Usually you have me scheduled for about eight interviews in a row."

"Nope," Dad said. "This'll be the first." His voice was calm but his fingers tightened around the steering wheel.

Mom laughed, light and cheery. "Oh, yes, George. Maybe later I'll take a nap and have tea with the ladies' society."

"Why not?" Now his voice was tighter, like it was whenever he got mad at me for talking back. "Take a nap every day. You need the rest."

I turned around and could see the lines in Mom's face deepen as she started to argue. Before she could say anything, I said, "Hey, how about that Ninety-Nine meeting? That was a great time, right?"

She smiled at me. "Exciting, wasn't it?" She chattered about the air derbies, the solid group of aviatrixes we'd gotten, and how the world would *have* to start paying attention to female pilots. I thought I'd done a good job getting her to calm down, so I was surprised when Dad's fingers still clenched the steering wheel. "What?" I asked.

He didn't say anything for a second and then muttered, "Damn, we must have passed it. Keep a lookout, all right?"

My eyes didn't quite catch the house numbers. "I was just trying—"

"She's not—" He glanced in the rearview mirror at Mom, whose fingers rested against the car window, and dropped his voice. "She's Janet, your mom, and playing along might seem like it helps, but it doesn't." He stopped the car abruptly by the curb. "We're here."

It was one of the old houses—white, with a wraparound

porch and a bed of chrysanthemums out front. The sign didn't just name Dr. McGlynn—she shared the building with a chiropractor, a Kaplan SAT prep center, a nutritionist, and a law office. "She can't afford her own place?" I asked.

"How much space does she need?" Dad said brusquely.

Great. Now he was mad at me before our psychiatrist appointment. Dr. McGlynn would probably be able to sense the tension before we even told her anything. She'd probably ask about my relationship with my parents, and I'd have to tell her about fighting with my mom most of the time—until she became Amelia Earhart and thought I was some ace girl aviator—and how lately Dad, whom usually I got along with, had been disappointed in me about everything.

Inside, we climbed a tall staircase to the second floor, thick red carpeting muffling our footsteps. Offices split off a long hallway. From a distance I could hear voices and the tapping of fingers on a computer keyboard. Dad led us down the hall, to a door marked with DR. MARY MCGLYNN, MD in bronze letters.

The office was brighter than I'd imagined, with startlingly white walls and framed posters of tropical flowers. Behind a massive receptionist desk, a woman with frizzy red hair cradled a phone to her neck as she wrote on a huge calendar.

"Yes, Thursday at noon. We'll see you then." She looked at us. "Can I help you?"

Dad introduced us. The receptionist told us that Dr. McGlynn would be with us in a minute and to have a seat. She gave Dad a clipboard with forms to fill out. Glimpsing over his shoulder, I read the various questions—our address, insurance information, if Mom had ever been on other medication or had been hospitalized at any point.

An older woman with clipped white hair and a crisp pink blouse approached us. "Mr. and Mrs. Winchester? I'm Dr. McGlynn."

Dad stood to shake Dr. McGlynn's hand and introduced himself. "And this is my daughter Alex," he said. His eyes rested on Mom for a second. "And this is my wife."

We followed Dr. McGlynn into her office, which was smaller than I'd thought it would be and lined with bookcases. My eyes scanned the titles—*Trauma and the Mind; A History of Psychotherapy; Weathering the Storm: Mental Illness and Its Long-Term Effects.* A few medical textbooks were mixed in as well. Her desk was painstakingly tidy, and it looked like dust never settled on it. In the corner of the office was a small, leafy plant; I couldn't decide if it was fake or not.

"Thanks so much for taking us on such short notice," Dad said to her as we sat down—Mom and Dad on a small couch, Dr. McGlynn and I in a couple of armchairs.

Dr. McGlynn shook her head. "Dr. Cowan's a good friend." She picked up a set of folders from her desk and scanned through them, then set them on her lap. "He's sent along your paperwork from the hospital, but why don't you tell me a little about what's been going on?"

Dad talked about how Mom had seemed a little off for a while—distant and distracted—and he'd assumed it was because she was tired or stressed, but whenever he asked, she'd say she was fine and brush him off. Beside him, Mom sat up straight, hands folded neatly in her lap. Everything about her was tight. I was afraid she'd run out, the way she had with Mr. Kane, so I kept watching her. When Dad mentioned that meeting at school, he paused, waiting for me to pick up the thread, and I missed it.

"Alex?" Dad said. "The conference?"

He and Dr. McGlynn were looking at me; Mom was staring at a row of books, frowning. I glanced at Dr. McGlynn to see if she had any cues as to how I should answer, but her face was blankly concerned.

"It was about driver's ed," I said, and explained how Mom and Dad were supposed to meet with Mr. Kane, and how Mom had gotten upset when Mr. Kane had called her Mrs. Winchester.

"Rude man," Mom muttered to her hands.

I paused, not sure if I should keep going, but Dr. McGlynn's eyes were still on me. "She couldn't answer his questions. Or wouldn't, I guess. So she took off."

Mom stood up suddenly, like a windup toy jerking to life. "This interview is a waste of time," she said. "I need to plan my trip. George?"

For a second, I wanted to agree with her, just go home and give her her maps and let her be happy. Who cared if she wanted to be Amelia Earhart? It was a kind of contentedness, and even if she wasn't my mom, I could still tell her things. I wanted to believe it was better than having her on the brink of frenzy. I was ready to grab my parents and run when Dr. McGlynn spoke up.

"Please, we'll get to that," Dr. McGlynn said, voice steady. She looked at my dad. "How about you two wait in the other room while Alex tells me the rest?"

Dad nodded slowly and guided Mom into the next room. As he left, I could hear him making excuses—they'd have to wait just a little longer. I could hear him call her Amelia. Hypocrite.

"That's kind of what happened before," I told Dr. McGlynn. "Mom getting all upset, I mean."

"It must have been very upsetting for you," she said. I wondered if having a soothing voice was a requirement for getting an MD in psychiatry.

I shrugged and stared at the plant in the corner, trying to find any indication of life—bugs, dying leaves, damp spots of soil.

"So this was the first time you'd seen her like that?"

I told her about the little things we'd noticed before then, and how that day at school seemed to be the final straw. She hadn't been Mom since then, at least not so any of us had noticed. "Your job is to make her Mom again, right?" I said. "She gets to talk this out and get medication, and then she'll forget about being Amelia Earhart?"

"The aim is to work through whatever caused your mother's delusions, yes."

"What if she doesn't want to?"

Dr. McGlynn told me a little about trauma and coping

mechanisms and how the brain tries to take care of itself, but I didn't hear many of the details. Instead I imagined the inside of Mom's head, how she was like a tiny plane in a storm, not knowing which way was up and hoping all her instruments held together. She was calling, "Mayday! Mayday!" and the person on the other end of the radio was Amelia Earhart.

Dad and Mom switched with me. When they went back into Dr. McGlynn's office, Mom was calm again. I waited for them under the tropical flowers, pretending to read whatever magazines were on the coffee table. When they came out, Dad looked like he'd run a couple of marathons. He talked to the receptionist and made a standing appointment for Thursdays.

Just as we left the building, I heard someone say, "Alex?"

It felt like the porch under me was coming apart splinter by splinter. *Shit*, I thought. Theresa appeared on the porch beside me. *Shit, shit, shit.*

"What are you doing here?" I asked, a little too quickly. Mom and Dad paused on the front steps, and I wished I had psychic powers so I could tell them to get in the car before Theresa said hello.

"Hi to you, too," she said. "I'm just dropping off my SAT prep test." She glanced at my parents. "Hey, Mr. and Mrs. Winchester."

Mom frowned and opened her mouth, but Dad spoke over her. "Hi there, Theresa. Good luck with the SATs."

"Thanks." Theresa looked back at me. "You okay?"

I nodded, feeling like all the blood in my head had surged to my stomach. Every muscle in me, from my legs to my fingers, tensed. Dad guided Mom away from the porch, toward the car, and I tried to breathe a little.

"Did you just fail a prep test or something?" Theresa asked.

"Oh, yeah," I said, trying to laugh but it came out more choked. "No, I mean, I didn't fail, but my parents thought I'd do better. So they're all on me to practice and are signing me up for classes and whatever."

"That sucks," she said. "Let me know if you want to go over stuff. Sometimes Josh and I practice during study hall. We can all be miserable together." She glanced at the car. "Hey, can I get a ride home? I walked here—my parents are happy for me to take the classes until it means they have to drive me to the test center. Awesome, huh?"

"We can't." My breathing was sharp and shallow. "Sorry. Dad's got to get back to work."

"I don't mind if you drop him off first."

"My mom probably wants to yell at me some more. It's not a great time."

Theresa didn't seem entirely convinced but she said, "All right. I guess I'll see you tomorrow."

"Yeah. Sorry again." Without saying good-bye, I raced to the car before Theresa could get a good look at my mom, who was sulking in the backseat. When I swung myself inside the car, I said, "Drive. Just drive."

"You all ri—?" Dad started to say.

"Fine, just go."

We pulled away from the curb. I glanced at Mom in the visor mirror. She looked so pissed, I thought she might be herself again. I almost expected her to start lecturing me about how I should be preparing for the SATs like Theresa, but she snapped at Dad instead. "Why do you keep setting me up with these useless interviews? It's a waste of everyone's time."

"Dr. McGlynn—"

"I don't need a doctor." Mom folded her arms over her chest. "George, I swear I don't know what you're after here."

Dad braked at a stop sign and stayed there. "You're tired and upset. She's trying to help you feel better. Don't you want that?"

Mom didn't respond for a second. Another car drove up behind us and we had to pull forward, so I'm not sure Dad heard Mom say, "I'm fine. I'm fine, I am. I just have so much to do." She stroked her arms as if she were cold.

"This is what you have to do: get better," I insisted. "You don't have any other plans."

I was sure Mom's face would tense, but I knew she wouldn't listen anyway. In a minute, she'd be telling us about her first time in an airplane. It would be like she hadn't heard me at all.

That night, Mom was back in the kitchen, making charts or fiddling with broken appliances or something. Around midnight I got out of bed and walked to the top of the stairs, where I stopped and listened to her as she worked on something

179

Amelia-related. Instead of going downstairs to join her, I sat on the top stair and listened. At the top of the stairs I inhaled deeply, trying not to cry. If I only kind of listened to Mom downstairs, she could have been Mom again, muttering her frustration about the electric bill instead of weather patterns. I missed her so much that it felt like a real burning in my chest. It felt like smoke and ash filling my lungs, making it impossible to breathe. When I went back to bed a little while later, I had fitful dreams about burning and drowning at once.

Halloween was less than a week away. At lunch, Theresa and Josh and Maddie talked about what we were going to do. Josh was holding out for a horror-movie marathon and was slowly wearing Maddie down. Originally she'd claimed there was no way she'd watch some brainless movie about hot teens getting hacked up, but Josh promised to find something worthwhile. Soon she was making conditions about how much gore there could be, and I knew she'd cave.

"How about something old?" Josh suggested. "Like *Psycho*?"

Maddie cringed and dipped a fry in a pool of ketchup. "Thanks, but I'd like to shower sometime next week."

Josh nudged me. "Any ideas?"

I shook my head. "Not my genre." Earlier, I'd tried to avoid my friends' table. Theresa was being kind of weird around me ever since I'd brushed her off at Dr. McGlynn's office, and I still wasn't thrilled with her since driver's ed. Plus, I'd been hoping to catch Jim alone. At first I'd glanced around for him, but Maddie came up to me and practically dragged me to their table.

"You're not going to ditch us for Jim Wiley, are you?" Theresa asked.

Suddenly everyone was looking at me. "What does Jim have to do with anything?" I asked, tearing a napkin into little pieces.

Theresa rolled her eyes. "Hello, it's like a miracle you're having lunch with us today. You're always hanging out with him now. I mean, that's fine, but just don't be all distant now and disappear on us on Halloween, too."

I thought of that word, *disappear*. If the most famous female pilot in the world could go missing over the Pacific, could I go missing in the middle of school, with my friends around? And if I could, who would send out the search planes?

"Jim and I are not even a thing," I said sharply. "I just don't have any opinions on horror movies. Pick out what you want and I'll be there."

Theresa and Josh exchanged a skeptical glance. Maddie half smiled at me. "You and I can hide during the scary parts."

At the end of classes, I went to the library. By then, I'd gone over the torn pages so many times, I'd almost memorized them. Mom kept talking about her plans for her next flight, but which one was that? I was afraid it was the final one, the around-the-world one. If I was going to figure out what was going on with

Mom, I'd need the complete history. And this was the most discrete way to find it.

By that time, there weren't too many students in the library, just a few kids doing homework or on Facebook while they waited for rides home. I walked straight back to the biography section and pulled the Earhart books off the shelf.

Just check them out like a normal person, I told myself. *You should have done that to begin with.*

But checking the books out would make it all real. It would be like getting a book about mental illnesses or bookmarking a site about delusional disorders, which maybe Dad was already doing. I wanted to keep everything hidden in some small way. Plus, if I tried to check them out now, the librarian would notice that someone had torn out pages. She'd probably apologize and say she'd order another copy, and then I'd have to argue with her that it didn't matter to me, that I wanted them anyway. And then maybe she'd be suspicious of me.

"Hey," a voice said through the stacks. Jim strode around the shelves, hands shoved in his pockets.

Shit. I clutched the biographies to my chest. "Hey, what are you doing here?"

"I get tutored in chemistry, remember? Just waiting for Mrs. Frasier to get here. She had to give a makeup test or something." He nodded to my arms—more precisely, to the books. "What about you?"

"Not much," I said. "Just, you know, history project."

He tilted his head, trying to read the spines. "Earhart? Isn't she one of your favorites?"

I forced laugh. "Right, I mean, I have this paper about her and she's kind of interesting. I don't know if she's a favorite, exactly." I wished he'd forgotten about that. What had I been thinking, bringing her up in the first place? Now if he ever found out about my mom, he'd think that I was some nutcase, too. And what if that was the truth? That it was just waiting somewhere in the crevices of my brain?

But I still wanted the books.

"Well, I need to go," I said. "Gotta pick up my little brother. Driving tomorrow night?"

"Sure," Jim said. "And if you're not busy this weekend, there's this haunted hayride thing people are going to. It sounds cheesy, but a bunch of us went last year and it ended up being kind of fun."

I imagined trying to make conversation with Jim's friends, none of whom knew me that well. They'd have to ask about driver's ed, and maybe they'd heard about my mom showing up at school. "Scary stuff isn't really my thing."

"Trust me, it's not that scary," he said. "Last year we spent pretty much the whole time laughing."

"What if we did something else instead? Just us?" I suggested. I didn't want to blow Jim off entirely, but I couldn't handle being around a lot of other people.

"We could do both," he said. "The hayride thing one night

and just us another? It's not that scary, I promise, and my friends won't be dicks about it."

"No, I'm sure," I said, "but I'd rather do just us." I suddenly realized I was pushing Jim into a real date, and why couldn't I act normal for five seconds? Maybe he wasn't into that just yet and I'd inadvertently ruined whatever we had going.

But he studied me for a second, then nodded. "Just us works, too. We could see a movie, or there's the bowling place —"

"Let's do bowling. Fair warning — I used to dominate the bowling birthday party games."

"I'll make sure to bring my A-game. Or, you know, at least my B-game," he said. At the library door, Mrs. Frasier appeared with chemistry book in hand. "That's my cue. Enjoy Earhart."

I nodded. "Yeah, thanks." I made a mental note to keep the Amelia references to myself from then on — especially when we went out this weekend. Even though I accidentally made it happen, I felt a sudden rush of excitement for my first non-driving-related date with Jim. "Good luck with the chemistry and all."

When he went back to his table to meet Mrs. Frasier, I stuffed the books in my bag. I took a breath and strode to the door, hoping Jim wasn't watching me, because if he was, he would have seen me leave without checking anything out.

How did she know it all? After going through the books, I would try to get Mom to slip up. I'd ask her about specifics from Amelia Earhart's life—the name of the town where she was born, how long she'd been at Columbia and what classes she took. Maybe if I found something she didn't know about, I would get a glimpse of Mom again without her Amelia mask. But Mom always knew the answers. And she was always so happy to tell me.

"Women need practical clothing," she insisted. She was sitting cross-legged in the middle of her bed, half her wardrobe spread across the room and a large sketchbook in her lap. At first I thought she was actively trying to give me more laundry to do (it was piling up in the basement), but she looked so proud of herself. "It'll be a whole fashion line—my designs and my name."

I almost laughed. She had to be making this up. "So like, what, goggles and bomber jackets?"

"Dresses, blouses, hats. Clothing any woman could wear." She passed me her sketchbook. I flipped through pages of poorly drawn models in boxy outfits.

I handed the notebook back. "Who's going to sell it?"

"Macy's in New York and Marshall Field's in Chicago. We're hoping to have the line in stores within the next year."

"Which would be . . ."

"Oh, 1934 or so."

I wondered how the span of her life matched the span of Amelia's life. Was a day for Mom the same as a day for Amelia Earhart? Did it matter if today was a Thursday or a day in October? Or could Mom decide she wanted to live a certain part of Amelia's life and it became real, even if it didn't match up with Amelia's real timeline?

"You must be busy," I said.

She nodded and began scribbling in her sketchbook. "Which is why I can't waste a moment." I returned a skirt to her closet when she wasn't looking; I'd have to do the rest when she moved on to another activity.

It was like she'd been studying for a test and felt so pleased at knowing all the answers. I almost didn't want to stumble across an answer she didn't know.

If I had my license, I would have told Jim I'd meet him at the bowling alley. As it was, he had to pick me up at home, which meant I kept vigil by the living-room window and waited to see his car turn onto our street.

"So is this like a date?" Katy asked, perching on the arm of a nearby chair.

"Kind of," I said.

"When you go driving, is that a date?"

"No, that's just driving."

"So is Jim your boyfriend or your driving instructor?"

I frowned at her. "Don't you have homework to do or Jackson to walk?"

Katy opened her mouth to ask what was sure to be another obnoxious question when something crashed in the next room. "Everything under control!" Mom called, but I rushed into the kitchen anyway.

She was on her knees, half in one of the cabinets, pushing aside pots and pans. "Trying to find the right equipment," she said.

"Well, it's not in there," I told her. "Just, please, don't make so much noise at least. Jim'll be here any minute and—"

Dad rushed downstairs. "Alex, I got it," he said, bending down to where Mom was still rifling through the cabinet. "These are all pans, cooking equipment."

"Gip, I think I know what I'm doing," she snapped.

"Alex!" Katy called from the living room. "He's here."

Shit. "I'll be back later," I shouted to Dad as I ran for the front door. He tried to ask if I had money, but Mom was still trying to argue with him and I didn't stay to hear what else he had to say.

I met Jim halfway to the driveway, slightly out of breath. "Hey," I said, passing him on the way to his car. "Let's go."

He stopped and turned sharply to me. "Are you okay?"

"Yeah," I said, "I'm great. Just really excited about bowling."

"You sure?" He glanced back at the house.

"Yes, let's just go."

He took a couple steps forward, then stopped. "Are your parents not okay with us going out or something?"

"No," I said, a little louder than I meant to. "They're fine. Seriously. It's nothing, I promise."

He didn't seem convinced, but he didn't argue anymore. In the car, Arcade Fire filled in the space that would have otherwise been an awkward silence. I cursed myself for not handling things better and potentially ruining our maybe-first-date before it started.

"You look really nice," Jim said suddenly.

"Thanks," I said. I'd changed a few times before settling on skinny jeans and a cute top, which Katy assured me looked cute but would still let me bowl well. Jim was wearing a plaid shirt that made his eyes glow even bluer than usual. "So do you."

"Thanks," he said. "I figure my excellent fashion skills might distract you from bowling and maybe give me a chance to win."

I smiled. "Not a prayer."

I hadn't been to the bowling alley in years, but it looked just like I remembered it. The fluorescent sign above the door was supposed to say LEWIS AND CLARK LANES but only illuminated LEW AND LARK LANE. Inside, they had the same spiral-patterned carpet and the air smelled like French fries and shoe disinfectant.

We rented shoes and took a spot at our assigned lane. "This looks like a good one," I said. "Lucky lane seven."

"I called ahead," Jim said, and nudged me a little. We were both bent forward to slip on our rental shoes, heads almost touching. I smelled his peppermint shampoo and felt a little dizzy remembering how we'd kissed behind the library.

"I'm really glad we're doing this," I told him.

"Me too," he said. We leaned a little closer to kiss; it was brief but I felt it down to my rental shoes.

"Of course, that doesn't mean I'm going to take it easy on you," I said.

I was up first and threw a gutter ball. Behind me, I heard Jim laugh. "Where's all that big talk now?" he asked.

"I'm lulling you into a false sense of security." I picked up my second ball and took a breath, trying to remember how to step and swing my arm with the right speed and force and timing. The ball rolled steadily down the lane and knocked over nine pins.

"All right, I'm sufficiently nervous again," Jim said. "Any tips?"

"Try to time your steps with your arms, like this." I demonstrated the action I meant. "And don't try to twist your body or arm around."

"Try to move like I know what I'm doing. Got it." Jim knocked over four pins on his first try. "You're good at this sports thing," he said. "It's like your body naturally knows how to do it. In gym, you seem to get things, too."

I shrugged. "It's not hard to look that capable in Mrs. Harriott's class."

He threw another ball and hit two more pins. "No, you're good. Trust me, I know—I'm always flailing around after some stupid ball, and you never flail."

I wondered how long Jim had been noticing me in class and hid a smile. "I flail sometimes. But I guess it's just something I like doing. You don't need to stop and think about every little thing—you just go. And when you're on a team and the other people know what they're doing, too, it's like you're all part of this one motion. You get each other without having to talk about it. For a little while, at least."

"Do you miss it?"

I stood and picked up another ball, balancing it in my hand. "Sometimes. It's, like, the first season I haven't played since I was six, and it already feels like it was part of some different life." The ball hurdled down the lane and smacked directly into middle pins, sending all the others flying. I did a mini victory dance on my way back to the bench. Jim laughed and the sound made me feel effervescent.

"Okay, if you win," Jim said, "I'm blaming it on the unfair advantage of you having athletic talent."

We played three games, and I won all of them. By the last game, Jim caught up so that he just missed winning by two points. "That was really close," I said. "I almost got worried." When he raised an eyebrow at me, I laughed. "Almost."

"Next time, I think we should combine forces and get people to put money on a game," he said. "Will McNamee would totally take that bet."

I stiffened a little at the mention of Jim's friends. "Maybe."

"They're pretty cool — Will and everybody," Jim said, his voice a little sharper than I'd expected. "No pressure or anything, but I think you guys would get along."

"I know." I untied my shoes slower than necessary. Jim's friends seemed fine, but I was worried about being around them and having to keep track of the lies I'd have to tell. It was hard enough with just Jim. "It's just that I don't get a lot of free nights, with having to babysit my brother, and I'd rather it be us than a big group of people." It wasn't the exact truth, but it was the closest I could get. "And besides, we've got to practice a lot if we're going to destroy everyone else at bowling."

"You can show me all your secrets," Jim said.

I half smiled. "One or two."

Chapter Twelve

*An individual's life on the ground or in the air may depend
on a split second.*

—Amelia Earhart

"What's the legal parking distance from a traffic light?" Jim
was flipping through a copy of the DMV driving manual, which
Mr. Kane had lent me. "I don't even remember that, which
shows that you just need to know all of this for one test."

"All right, give me a minute," I said. We were sprawled in
the backseat of my mom's car, leaning against opposite doors
with our legs crowding the middle of the seat. We'd been practicing actual driving for an hour—again around the back roads.
(This time, however, Jim had me drive most of the way there. It
was the first time I saw an oncoming car. When I saw the headlights, I hit the brake even though the other car was safely in its
lane.) After doing the road practice, I suggested we go over the
manual, which meant we made out in the backseat for a while.

It was like that first time behind the library—just Jim, me, and the stars, everything exactly right. Finally we agreed we should do at least a little studying before I had to be home. Even with our shirts back on, it was kind of hard to concentrate on laws about distances and speeds. I kept remembering the pressure of his lips against mine and how good he looked without a shirt.

"Ten feet?"

"Close. Thirty."

"Oh, come on, that's way too much. Who needs all that room to turn?"

Jim raised an eyebrow. "Have you seen your turns?"

"Really funny." I kicked his shin a little. "I don't know what you're talking about. I'm an awesome driver. I take those hairpin turns like a pro."

"Sure, once you pass driver's ed you'll be ready for the Indy 500." He grinned. "Maybe in class you should practice going from 0 to 120 in under four seconds. Mr. Kane would love that."

I laughed. "I don't think the driver's ed Volvo could take it."

"It'll go out in a blaze of glory." He flipped through the manual. "All right, how about this one: What does a single broken line on the road mean?"

"You can pass cars, if there's no traffic coming from the opposite lane." In the backseat, on the side of the road, it felt like our own little world. I leaned against the door and the cool glass of the window. "Give me another one," I said.

Jim paged through the manual. "You know this pretty well."

"I already took the permit exam. You had to pass that to get into driver's ed."

"I failed it my first time—the permit exam. By three points."

I tugged at a loose thread on my shirt. "How about that time you drove into a house?"

Jim reached back and rubbed his head. "Yeah, how about that?" He paused, and I wasn't sure if I had gone too far. I was about to tell him never mind, but he said, "So Will McNamee and I've been friends since first grade—even our parents are friends. Barbecues in the summer, trips to D.C., that kind of thing. He's the one who always knows who's having a party, so I'd go out a lot with him, to people's houses or to some random field if somebody's brother could get a keg. Or we'd smoke up in his basement. It wasn't a *problem*, but I wasn't exactly doing a lot else with my time. And one night we raided his parents' liquor cabinet, which wasn't anything new, and then I drove home. I wasn't even crazy drunk, just a little buzzed." He drummed his fingertips on the front of the driving manual. "Plus, I'm kind of on epilepsy medication—"

"You're epileptic?" I said.

"Yeah, sort of. I get petit mal seizures—not the big stuff, jerking around on the floor. I kind of zone out for maybe half a minute. And that night I didn't take my medication because I wanted to drink with Will. I didn't want to have to deal with it, you know? Which was really dumb of me because that's actually what did it. I had a seizure, and by the time I came to I was face-first in an air bag."

"Did you get hurt?"

"A broken arm from how the hood crunched in, and some cuts and bruises. Otherwise I was fine. I had the seat belt on." He laughed grimly. "Safety first, right? And it was, like, all of a sudden, my parents were right there—my mom crying and yelling at me, and my dad not saying anything, which was worse, because usually he's the first person to yell at me."

I remembered seeing Jim's home that cold morning, with the neighbors crowding the driveway, the tow truck pulling the car out of the Wileys' yard, and the chunk of brick and plaster missing, exposing part of the Wileys' house. I remembered Jim's dad reaching out to touch the broken pieces.

"He was so pissed at me," Jim said. "My dad. He didn't talk to me for days. Then when he did, he said, 'You could have killed us.' Which was true. So I wasn't too upset when they sent me to my grandparents."

I wasn't sure Mom would notice if I drove a car into the house. Or maybe she would, but she would make an excuse for it, call it a malfunctioning plane. Blame faulty equipment. "Is your dad still mad at you?"

Jim shrugged. "Not as much as before. But sometimes he just looks at me and it's like he can still see the house all smashed up."

"My mom never lets anything drop," I said. It wasn't exactly true anymore, but saying it made me feel like it was real. "If I do one thing even a little wrong she's all over it."

"And we're supposed to mess up, right? It makes us learn from our mistakes so we're better and stronger for it."

"Obviously we're going to be really strong people." I reached across the seat and brushed his hand. "So do you still get seizures?"

He paged through the driver's manual. "Sometimes. Not that often. I got new medication and I'm better about taking it. That was, like, the third time I've had a seizure that even did anything. The first time anyone noticed was when I was in second grade and I was playing Little League. I was awful anyway, like, could not hit a ball, and in the middle of the game I'm at bat and not hitting anything and I collapse on home plate. Little League was too stressful for me, apparently."

"That's so scary."

"I was passed out, so I don't remember much. My parents were freaking out. The next year was a lot of testing to make sure my brain was okay, which it is. As far as I know."

"Good," I said. "I like your brain. I like all your parts."

Jim laughed and looked pleased. "I like all your parts, too." He tapped me with the driver's manual. "We should keep our parts safe. No more driving into houses."

I inched forward until our faces were almost touching. I liked getting to know the curve of Jim's face and the pressure of his hands, and I didn't want him to cause any other accidents. "Here's to keeping each other safe," I said, and kissed him until we couldn't breathe.

Halloween was on Sunday, which was the worst day for it because there was school the next day, so you could never be totally happy about trick-or-treating or watching horror movies. Teddy saw the upside; he'd gotten to wear his costume to school on Friday, for the elementary-school Halloween carnival, and then on Sunday he wore it around the house all day long and spent the day fighting aliens. This year he was an astronaut. Dad had helped him make the costume—his helmet was a white bucket with a square cut out for his face, with NASA stickers stuck on the side. His rocket pack was a couple of milk cartons painted white and superglued together.

"You're going to mess up your costume," I warned Teddy while he flung himself around the living room.

"No, I'm not," he said.

"Dad's not going to make you another one."

Dad was going to take Teddy trick-or-treating that night. I was supposed to stay home and hand out candy until Dad and Teddy got back, and then I could go to Maddie's house for scary movies. But it didn't feel like Halloween, and not just because it was Sunday. Usually the house was decorated with plastic pumpkins, pipe-cleaner spiders, and ghost stickers. Mom was really into decorating for holidays. A few weeks before, she'd get us together and cover the house in anything festive. She'd even dress up to hand out candy on Halloween. One year, when I was really little, she was a witch and cackled so well that I got scared. It was hard to see her under the makeup and fake warts. When I'd started to cry, she'd washed it off and said, "See, it's just me." But this year we forgot all about decorating until the last minute. As it was, the only decoration we'd gotten up was a life-size paper skeleton hanging on the front door.

I hadn't mentioned the scary movie thing to Jim. If it came up, I figured I could tell my friends he was busy.

In our room, Katy was getting her own costume ready. For a while, Katy wasn't sure if she wanted to dress up this year, but a group of girls from her gymnastics studio talked her into dressing up with them as *The Wizard of Oz* characters. Katy was the Tin Man and had stolen all the tinfoil and duct tape in the house.

"Do we have a funnel?" Katy asked. "For the hat." When I suggested she check the kitchen, she frowned at her piles of tinfoil. "Maybe later."

Since Mom had gotten back from the hospital, Katy had been avoiding her. Before Amelia Earhart, Katy would tell Mom everything. Now, when she wasn't obsessively doing her homework, Katy spent a lot of time at Amy White's house. Dad told Mrs. White that Mom wasn't feeling well, so she'd taken over gymnastics pickup entirely and invited Katy over for dinner a lot. Amy was fine, Katy told me once, but mostly she just liked pretending that she was part of a normal family.

"Maybe Mom's already taken the funnel," I said. "She could have decided to mix it up and be someone else for Halloween."

Katy almost smiled. "The Tin Man wouldn't be so bad."

"Unless she tried to drag the rest of us on some road trip to Oz," I said.

That was how the It Could Be Worse game started. We sat on Katy's bed, tossing ideas back and forth about what would suck more than our current family situation: Mom could have decided to be Hitler; Mom could have had leprosy; Mom could have been a cannibal; Mom could have decided to be Joan Crawford; Mom could have grown a second head; Mom could have thought she was a beluga whale. By the time we got to the whale, we were bent over laughing.

Teddy banged on the door. "What's so funny?"

Katy brushed the tears out of her eyes and tried to swallow her laughter. "Costume ideas," she said.

Trick-or-treaters started coming before dinner, when the sun was still out. The first time the doorbell rang, Mom went to answer it, but Dad stopped her, claiming they were reporters and he would handle the situation. Teddy kept getting up from the table and trailing behind Dad to hand out candy. Teddy's face got increasingly more worried every time it happened.

"We need to go now," Teddy said. He was still in his astronaut costume, which was looking a little dented around the rocket pack. "There won't be any candy left by the time we go. *Everybody*'s already out."

"Of course there'll be candy," Dad said. "You'll get so much, it'll end up in the refrigerator until Easter."

Dad had to take Katy over to Amy's house, so I was in charge at home. In the living room, Mom was curled up on the couch with Jackson, trying to write a letter to her imaginary sister Grace Muriel Earhart, aka Pidge. She was on a new medication, and so far all it did was put her in a haze. Beside her, Jackson gnawed at a tennis ball. Teddy waited at the door as Dad's car pulled out of the driveway, slowly because of the young trick-or-treaters on the street.

"We could go now," Teddy said. "You take me, Alex. You don't even have to dress up."

"Sorry, Buzz Lightyear," I said. "I'm on Mom watch. Dad'll be back in, like, half an hour, tops." I glanced into the living room. "You okay in there?"

Mom waved a hand at me. "Perfectly fine." She sighed.

When I offered to play soccer or a computer game with Teddy instead, he refused. "Let's just go," he insisted. "Mom can come with us. We can all go."

I folded my arms across my chest. "No way. Stop being a brat, already. Go play space invader until Dad gets home."

He started stomping on the tiles of the kitchen floor and yelling, "Now, now, now, now!"

"Teddy, stop it." I grasped him by the shoulders, and he struggled to pull away from me. In the other room, I could see

Mom stir. "If you calm down, I'll let you play the games on my cell phone."

He quieted and sniffled. I never let him use my cell. "Maybe."

Of course my phone was somewhere in the mess that was my side of my bedroom. I left Teddy in the kitchen, instructing him to hand out candy if any trick-or-treaters came to the door while I searched for the cell.

It wasn't in my backpack, or in the pockets of the jacket I'd worn that day. I checked under the bed, where I'd stashed the Amelia Earhart book I'd stolen from the library. I'd replaced some of the pages I'd torn out, taping them back in their correct places. It looked like I'd dropped it off the roof a few times, but at least now it was whole again. This one was written by Amelia Earhart, too—*in her own words*, the cover said. I flipped it open to a random passage.

> *A shadow of light played around the horizon and suddenly the stars were gone. Dawn is a fearful thing to see from the air. . . . It seemed to me I should be flying much more in its direction than I was. . . . I checked my charts and I checked my compass and everything seemed to be as it should—so I could only conclude that the sun was wrong and I was right!*

We were like that, telling Mom she was wrong while she insisted she was right.

I put the book back and shifted through papers on my desk. My cell was hidden under a stack of calc homework I'd set aside. I saw that Josh had texted me to ask if I wanted a ride to Maddie's that night. I figured I'd reply after Teddy was done playing.

The doorbell rang again, and I darted downstairs in case Mom decided to answer the door and confront the "reporters" herself. When Teddy didn't fling himself at the door with me, I was a little surprised. Behind the door were a couple of princesses and one ninja. I handed out the candy, complimenting their costumes, and watched as they ran down the driveway.

I glanced into the living room—no Mom, no Teddy. On the kitchen table, the maps had been left out, partially folded. Suddenly the house felt cavernous. My voice could have echoed when I called for them. "Mom . . . Amelia? Teddy! Come on, you can download a new game. And we'll raid the candy bowl."

No one answered. I dashed upstairs, checking Mom's and Teddy's rooms. Empty. No one in the bathrooms.

I even checked the basement, dark and full of random stuff we'd forgotten about. No one.

My heart started to race. Where would my mother have gone with Teddy in tow? She usually thought of him as Pidge's son, her nephew, David, so it wouldn't have seemed unusual to her to take him someplace. Immediately I thought of her car and ran outside, sure that it would be missing from the driveway, but it was still there. Since Dad and Katy had left, it had gotten dark out and the streetlights were just coming on. In the

street, parents followed groups of children dressed as super-
heroes and black cats.

Dammit, Teddy, I thought. *I am going to kill you.*

Either way I looked, there were tiny witches or cowboys or
Sesame Street characters. No astronauts. No moms dressed as
Amelia Earhart.

If Dad came home and found out that Mom had left with
Teddy, he'd flip out. And what could I tell him? That I had been
upstairs, reading about Amelia Earhart and ignoring Mom
downstairs? Dad would give me that look—his eyes squinty
and his jaw tightening up underneath his beard—and say
something like, "All I asked you to do was look after things for
a few minutes." Plus, I wasn't sure what Mom would do. It's
not like she would hurt Teddy, but she might not think about
him. She could get distracted and leave him somewhere, or not
notice if he got hit by a car. And even if Teddy was fine, people
would see her and come up to her and say hello, as if she were
the same woman they'd seen in the grocery store or at youth
soccer games when I was a kid. They'd stare at her when she
talked about how she was so tired these days, after the lecture
circuit she'd been on and that Pacific flight. They'd talk about it
with their spouses and children at home that night. Or worse,
she could try to take herself somewhere—the airport, Hawaii,
wherever. She could disappear forever.

I ran.

Considering they were on foot and probably not rushing anywhere, I thought I'd find them right away. But our

neighborhood connected with others in a small maze, so there were dozens of directions in which they could have headed. Plus, there were dozens of parents with kids on the street that night; even with Teddy's astronaut costume, it would be hard to spot them.

I rushed down the street and back, eyeing every house to see if Teddy was ringing any doorbells. Nothing. No astronauts or aviatrixes anywhere.

Waves of anxiety washed over me. My head felt cloudy, as if it weren't part of my body anymore—like it was floating thousands of feet above the ground. I felt like my body was going to fall apart, piece by piece, until I was a jumble of limbs in the street.

Someone else needed to be there, to help me stay in one piece. Someone who knew about pieces.

I ran all the way to Jim's house. By the time I got there, I was out of breath and shaking. His mom answered the door, a bowl of candy in her arms. Her smile didn't fade, but her eyes were shaded with confusion when she saw me.

"Can I help you?" she said.

"Is Jim home?"

She turned her head to shout for her son, but he was already in the hallway. "Alex?" He stuck his head past his mom, out the door frame. "Were we supposed to drive tonight? I thought—"

"No, you're right," I said. "We didn't have plans—"

"You want to come—?"

"No, not now." I was so on edge. I probably looked like a

freak in front of his mom, who was still at the door like a nice, normal mom, holding the candy and glancing at Jim to gauge his reaction. "Can you give me a ride?"

I calmed down enough to get out a few details—that my brother and mother left and I needed to find them, that Teddy was dressed as an astronaut and my mom was in baggy khakis with the ankles pegged and a long linen scarf wrapped around her neck. We took Jim's mom's car, a minivan, and drove off, stalking the streets and not going very fast because of all the trick-or-treaters.

"Oh, my God, it's like preschool rush hour out here," I said, straining against the seat belt to see out the window.

Jim turned onto another street. "So are they, like, trick-or-treating? Your mom and little brother?"

I didn't look at him. "No, Teddy was supposed to go with my dad later, after he got home. But I guess Teddy just couldn't wait."

"But if he's with your mom, isn't that okay?"

"My mom's not really feeling well."

"So maybe we should call your dad or something."

"No," I snapped. "We just need to find them, all right? That's why I got you. So let's just find them."

Jim tightened his grip on the wheel and didn't ask any more questions. Even though he'd told me about crashing the car and having epilepsy, I didn't know what to tell him about my mom, or even where to start. With that day at school—with the reason Mom's car was in the parking lot and why Jim first taught me how to drive? With the missing wedding picture? With the baby who died? And here I was, acting crazed myself. If I could just keep all the pieces of my life in place, not crashing into one another, I thought things might be all right.

The sight of a milk-carton rocket pack on someone's front porch caught my eye. "Stop, stop," I told Jim.

The minivan's wheels screeched. I was out the door before we came to a full stop and rushed toward Mom and Teddy, who were thanking a bemused man for his candy. When my brother saw me, his smile vanished. He clutched his jack-o'-lantern bucket—half full of candy now—and tried to hide behind Mom.

"Why, hello there!" Mom greeted me, her eyes clouded. "Were we meeting you here?"

Behind her, Teddy squeaked, "It's not me."

"What the hell were you thinking?" I hissed, almost swearing worse but remembering at the last second that there were families around. Once I saw that Teddy was fine, all relief vanished, and I was furious now. Reaching behind Mom, I gripped Teddy's arm and started pulling him toward the van. "Dad is going to be so mad at you, taking off like that. What the hell, Teddy? You could have gotten hurt."

"What seems to be the problem?" Mom said, following us.

"We're going home."

Teddy struggled against my grip. "It's not me. Blast off!"

On the sidewalk, a group of vampires and their pirate dad

watched us. So did Jim, still in the driver's seat. I wanted to disappear.

"I'm an astronaut," Teddy said. "Astronauts can go anywhere. Teddy didn't do anything. I'm going to Jupiter."

I grabbed his shoulders. "Stop it. Just stop it, all right?" Teddy's face was red and he started to sniffle; I was surprised to feel my own throat tighten. "It was really selfish of you to use Mom like that. Like she'd know that you're not supposed to go trick-or-treating until Dad got home. You took her out here, where people could see her or where she could wander off. You're such a brat, Teddy, I swear."

He grabbed for my hand. I almost couldn't hear him when he said, "Amelia Earhart would. . . . She'd like astronauts."

I took a breath and gripped his hand back. "We all like astronauts. But astronauts have to be safe, too, or they get in big trouble. You just can't do stuff like this, Teddy."

The minivan's sliding door opened; Jim had gotten out of the car and joined us on the lawn. "Everybody in?" he asked.

It would have been great to have superpowers at that moment—to become invisible, to teleport my family back home. But as it was, I either had to walk Teddy and Mom home, and risk running into more people, or get a ride from Jim.

Mom and Teddy climbed in the backseat.

Silently, I pleaded with Mom: *Don't talk. Don't say anything about flying or meeting the president or the Ninety-Nines.* Just let us get home with minimal damage.

Jim slid into the driver's seat again and started the car. Pulling away from the curb, he waved to the backseat. "I'm Jim," he said.

Teddy wiped his nose with his sleeve. "You drove through your house."

"*Into* his house," I said. "Not *through*."

"That's terrible," Mom said, her words a little slurred. "But you know, sometimes you have to crash before you can fully learn something. Part of the training, really. Are you taking lessons?"

Jim glanced at me. "I'm actually the one helping Alex learn how to drive."

"I wouldn't think you'd need lessons by now," Mom said to me.

"No, no, I still kind of suck," I said, then glanced at Jim. "Well, not as much. I don't crash into things as much anymore." Mom opened her mouth again, but I cut her off, talking about how Jim and I went out a couple of nights a week, which had made a huge difference in my skills. And not only that, he didn't get upset with me like Mr. Kane used to. I kept talking, bringing up anything—how I'd taken a left-hand turn the other day, how I'd remembered to use my blinker, how I turned on the headlights when it got dark out. As long as I was speaking, Mom couldn't. Or at the very least, Jim wouldn't be able to hear her if she got bored with what I was saying and started talking to herself. Jim didn't try to interrupt, either, just focused on the road as he guided the van back to my house.

By the time I got Mom and Teddy inside, I felt exhausted, like all my veins had been sapped dry. I'd texted Theresa to let her know that I couldn't make it to Maddie's and didn't look when I heard the ping of her response.

"Thanks," I told Jim, meaning a lot more but not knowing how to phrase it. "For helping me find them. And you didn't even run over any little kids."

"Anytime," Jim said.

I expected him to ask about Mom—why she and Teddy couldn't have just gone trick-or-treating on their own, or why I'd been so frantic to find them, or what I'd meant about Mom not knowing that Teddy was supposed to wait for Dad. Or why Teddy had claimed he hadn't been the one to break the rules, or why my eyes were rimmed with red and I couldn't really look at him without the fear that I might start crying in the passenger seat of his mom's minivan.

But he didn't ask me any of that. Instead he said, "Should I stay with you guys until your dad gets home? If your mom's not okay."

I shook my head. "No, we're fine. You can go." He probably thought Mom was an alcoholic, and that's why she'd been so out of it. I couldn't explain how the truth was much stranger. "I'll see you tomorrow."

He stared at me for a second and shrugged. "See you."

I watched the van pull out of the driveway and turn onto the street. For a moment, I waited on the lawn, hugging my arms to my chest. If the young skeletons and fairies noticed me, they probably thought I was just cold and waiting for someone.

That night, Dad lectured at Teddy about leaving without telling anyone—and Mom didn't count as "anyone." It was the first time Teddy had gotten in major trouble, and afterward I heard him smashing his Halloween costume to bits.

I tapped on his door and entered without waiting for permission. Teddy stood in the middle of torn cardboard and smashed plastic, cheeks flushed with fury, guilt, and sadness.

"It's gonna be hard to get to Jupiter now," I said.

Teddy thumped onto his carpet. "Dad was really mad at me. I didn't mean to."

I sat beside him and he curled up against me, warm like a puppy. "I know. It's okay." Sniffling beside me, he seemed much younger than seven. I thought of Katy, dressed as the Tin Man and out with her friends, pretending everything was fine. She and Teddy shouldn't have had to deal with this. But I was glad to have them around, as selfish as that was. They were the only two people who actually could relate to what I was going through.

"It's going to be okay," I whispered to Teddy, and wanted it to be true. I let him play on my cell phone and quietly threw away the pieces of his costume while he wasn't looking.

Chapter Thirteen

Over a mapped territory the pilot without much trouble can clock his speed with the landmarks he can recognize. When landmarks aren't available, different types of indicators are used to make the calculation.

—Amelia Earhart

The Monday after Halloween was the first day I wasn't looking forward to seeing Jim at school. It was my fault, of course — I'd given him a glimpse into the craziness at home and now I wished I could erase it all. I wanted to keep going like we had been, with driving lessons and laughing during lunch and furious kissing. Anything else would just complicate things.

I was intentionally late to homeroom so he couldn't find me beforehand, but it was impossible to avoid him during gym. Maddie had started talking with a couple of girls from her English class, so I was alone when class began. Jim stood beside me as Mrs. Harriott was breaking up the class into flag football teams.

"Hey, you okay?" he whispered. "I didn't see you this morning, so I thought—"

"Oh, I'm fine. We're all fine. Thanks for helping me out last night."

"It's cool," he said, taking a red flag football belt from the bag and handing it to me. "If you ever need a chauffeur, I'm your guy."

For a second, I thought that maybe I could tell him. He looked at me so solidly. Every other part of my life felt unsteady, but around Jim I was centered. When everyone else had thought I was a loser who couldn't drive, Jim had stood up for me. If I could tell anyone about Mom, it was Jim. But if he did get freaked out, I'd lose the one good thing I had right now. It was too much to risk.

I took the belt from him and forced a smile. "Just when you thought they couldn't make gym uniforms any more repulsive."

Jim shrugged. "I think you look good."

Now my smile wasn't forced. Mrs. Harriott yelled at us to line up—perfect timing, of course. As she went over the rules, I decided I wouldn't tell Jim about my mom. It was definitely too much to risk.

November was raw—cold and wet, but never snowing. The trees lost all their leaves, so the world looked brown and gray for days on end. I counted the sunny days we'd had since Halloween—about four, in a span of more than two weeks. On the morning news, meteorologists always mentioned that temperatures were below average for this time of year. They claimed it was going to be a long, hard winter.

Even after several weeks, it was still weird seeing Mrs. Ellis at our house. Usually she would be doing something productive—paying bills or knitting or starting her Christmas card list—while Mom rhapsodized about her first transatlantic solo flight. Sometimes they walked around the neighborhood, which usually put my mother in a good mood. Most of the time, Mom called Mrs. Ellis "Pidge." Mrs. Ellis's expression was always placid.

"Hi there, Alex," Mrs. Ellis said before she even saw me, having heard the front door open. I shuffled into the kitchen, where Mom and Mrs. Ellis were sitting at the table. No maps today.

"Come in, come in," Mom said. "I was just telling Pidge about the Pacific flight I've got planned. I'd like to hear your thoughts on the route."

I tossed my backpack aside and got a glass of water. "Right, the Pacific flight. Exciting."

Mrs. Ellis gathered her knitting—a lopsided sweater with snowflakes around the neckline—and smiled at me. "Not a bad day today," she told me. "I think the new medication she's on is helping. She doesn't get as upset if I remind her I'm not Pidge."

"Just kind of ignores you, right?"

She cleared her throat. "Well, yes. But it's better than when she used to get mad and refuse to talk for an hour. I think it's progress."

Mom had been going to therapy for about a month now. I hadn't been since the first time, but Dad went with her every week. I didn't ask what they talked about, but I could get the gist from Dad's attitude when they got back. Sometimes he'd be quiet and continually reach for his beard, stroking it thoughtfully. Other times he'd put on Patsy Cline as he made dinner, chopping vegetables in time with the bass. Mom had been on a few different medications at this point; one shelf in Mom and Dad's bathroom was lined with tiny orange bottles, all with scientific-sounding names. Even so, I didn't see a lot of progress. Mom still thought she was Amelia Earhart; she still thought Katy and I were in the Ninety-Nines and that Teddy was her nephew; we still lived with her maps, notebooks of lecture notes, and linen scarf.

But I didn't say that to Mrs. Ellis. "Great. That's awesome."

She got her coat from the closet. Pulling it on, she asked, "How was your day?"

"Fine." I gulped my water.

"Any big tests coming up? Julia and Ryan were always stressing out this time of the year, just counting the days until winter break."

"Nothing too bad."

"Your dad mentioned you were studying for a driving test. That must be exiting." She pulled mittens out of her coat pockets and tugged them on. "Julia couldn't *wait* to get behind the wheel."

I set my glass on the counter. "Well, the test is because I'm the worst one in my class, and my teacher's just being nice and giving me this test so I don't totally fail."

From the table, Mom said, "Don't be so modest. There's no way you're the worst one. In fact, I'd love your advice about the wind patterns." She stood and rubbed her hands together as if she were cold. "Let me get my notes."

Mrs. Ellis and I watched Mom rush up the stairs. For a second, we listened to her footsteps above us, in her bedroom. Mrs. Ellis sighed softly. "In any case, good luck with the test. Driving isn't as hard as it looks."

She left without saying good-bye. I felt a twinge of guilt when I heard the door close. I'd been a bitch, and Mrs. Ellis had been a big help to us. But I didn't like her asking about my day, as if she felt bad for me because my own mom wouldn't do that. And she was so hopeful about everything, even something little like the fact that Mom just decided to ignore her when she wouldn't play along with Mom's delusions. I didn't care about little shifts. Only something huge would impress me.

Mom came back with an armful of maps and notebooks. I kept noticing new ones, with images of Europe, Africa, or Australia. Ones that she couldn't have picked up around the house. She unfolded them on the table. "I think for the starting position—"

"How about later?" I said, grabbing my backpack. "Lots of homework."

Her face fell a little. "All right. I'll make some notes for you."

Listening to the scratch of her pencil as I walked away, I wondered about all the details she knew. So far, they seemed to line up with what I'd read in my stolen book and ripped pages.

I stepped carefully into Mom and Dad's room, even though there wasn't a huge reason to be cautious with Mom occupied downstairs. The bed had been made that morning, albeit messily. I wondered if that was Mom's or Dad's work. Everything else seemed ordinary—a pair of Dad's pants cast over a chair, a watch sitting on a nightstand. I wasn't even sure what I was looking for, exactly. Something that explained how Mom knew so much about Amelia Earhart. It wasn't like she'd come up a lot before October.

Kneeling, I checked under the bed—nothing. Nothing under the mattress, either. I opened the drawers of her nightstand: a random collection of forgotten paperback novels, hairpins, and travel packages of Kleenex.

Geez, I thought. *What if she's possessed by the ghost of Amelia Earhart?*

I opened the closet door and peeked in. Nothing looked unusual among the blouses and khakis. On the floor, shoes overflowed shoe boxes.

Then I saw it, under a pair of brown boots—Amelia's face.

I opened the shoe box and found two biographies hidden there. There were eight other boxes. In each one, I found the same thing—biographies, autobiographies, biographies written for children, books about the various disappearance theories, books about aviation, a Lindbergh biography, a DVD of a

PBS special about Earhart, several printouts from various web-sites, even a few novels featuring Earhart as a main character. More maps and charts. Receipts from orders from an aeronautical map website. A couple of other linen scarves, although not as nice as the one she usually wore.

Mom's stockpile spread on the floor around me, I felt breathless. How long had she been squirreling it away? It must have been months; the oldest receipt I could find was from last summer. How hadn't any of us noticed? Did she even need to look at these anymore, or did she refer back to them a lot to make sure she had gotten all her facts straight? Did she take out a book when the rest of us were in bed, reading until she had nearly every detail memorized? I shivered, imagining Mom sitting at the kitchen table at three a.m. with Amelia Earhart, until she couldn't tell the difference between Amelia and herself.

It was like seeing a virus under a microscope, one that had caused a serious illness. Sitting among the Earhart paraphernalia, I worried that I could be infected, too.

Stuck in one of the biographies, like a bookmark, was a folded piece of paper that I expected to be another map or more aeronautical information, but at the top it read HISTOPATHOLOGY REPORT and listed Mom's name as the patient. I scanned through sections like GROSS DESCRIPTION and MICROSCOPIC DESCRIPTION without understanding much of it until I found the word I was waiting for: *benign.*

"What . . . ? What . . . ?"

I hadn't heard Mom's footsteps on the stairs. Now she was standing in the doorway, gaping at me like a goldfish and unable to make a full sentence. I shoved the pathology report back into its book.

"I'm sorry," I said, trying to shove books back into their shoe boxes.

Her face crumpled. "What are you doing?" She pressed her fingertips to her temples as though afraid her brain might explode in her skull.

"I'm putting it back," I said. "I didn't mean—"

She practically fell on the floor beside me and snatched a biography out of my hands. "You're not doing it right!" Her voice was choked, and she was on the verge of shouting. It reminded me of that horrible day with Mr. Kane, when I had been in the car with her and she didn't remember how the car worked. "Stop it!"

I backed off. "All right, you do it." A couple of tears rolled down her flushed cheeks, but she didn't bother to wipe them away as she replaced everything in the closet.

"You had no right," she said, staring into her closet as if it were a great void. "I'm trying very hard. I do everything I can, and these are my things. *Mine.* No one is supposed to see them or talk about them." When she looked at me, her face was drawn and empty. Suddenly I felt very cold. "I can't have you around me."

"I'm sorry," I whispered, but her face didn't change. I was used to Mom being frustrated or disappointed with me, but this was something different. I'd been trying to help, and now she thought I'd messed up everything.

"I was trying to help," I said, but my voice cracked on the last word. My face burned and throbbed as I struggled not to cry—not while she was staring at me so coldly, not like when we used to argue. *It's not her*, I tried to remind myself, but a small part of me wanted her to wrap her arms around me so I could finally cry.

But that wasn't going to happen. Instead, I rushed out of the room, thinking maybe she'd at least ask me to stay and look over maps, but she didn't seem to notice that I'd gone. In the hall, I could hear her voice get calm and steady. I was sure she wasn't talking to me.

Although I considered calling Dad at the post office, I waited until he got home to tell him about the stuff in Mom's closet. After Halloween, it seemed like Dad was just waiting for me to mess up with Mom again. He had to leave me in charge when he wasn't home, but afterward he would ask how things went, like he expected to find the house burned down or Mom having escaped in a prop plane. So I wasn't even sure if I wanted to tell him about Mom's stuff. But I figured he would probably have to know that kind of thing for therapy. ("Where did your wife learn about Earhart?" "Beats me, probably picked it up on the street.") I waited until after dinner, when he had settled into his chair in the living room with the newspaper in his hand and Jackson at his feet.

He didn't say anything at first, just stared at a spot on the carpet. I wasn't sure he'd heard me until he said, "Do you think that was all of it?"

"I didn't exactly get a chance to look around. She was really mad at me." Mad seemed like the wrong word, but I didn't know how else to describe how panicked and lost she'd been.

Jackson stretched and yawned, and Dad reached down to rub his ears. "I guess we know now," he said.

"I guess." I wanted him to thank me or say that it had been a helpful find, but he didn't. "There was something else there, too. It was, like, test results."

Dad looked at me and I knew I didn't have to explain. "Your mom had some tests done a few months ago," he said. "She's fine. It was just something her doctor wanted to check on."

"They thought she had cancer."

He took a breath. "They wanted to make sure that she didn't have cancer. Your grandma died of ovarian cancer, so they were just being cautious. Seriously. We didn't want to worry you guys for no reason."

I wondered how long Mom had to wait for the results. I didn't even know what day she went in for testing. Maybe we'd fought that morning. Maybe she pretended to listen to Teddy repeat some joke he'd heard on TV while thinking about how something dangerous might have been growing inside her. But instead of asking Dad when it happened, I said, "What are you going to do? About the books and stuff."

He jostled the paper. "Ask Dr. McGlynn about it."

"But that's not until the end of the week. Should we get rid of them? Or just leave them there? Do you think she looks at them a lot?"

"Alex, I don't know. It can't do any more harm to leave them there for a few more days, so that's what I'm going to do. I think it'll be worse if we try to move them—she's probably worried about that, now that she knows that you know about them."

The idea made me want to see if the stash was still in her closet. "But what if it just makes things worse?"

"I told you: I don't know," he said sharply. "I'm trying here, Alex, I really am, but I don't have any of the answers hidden away. I'm trying as hard as I can to make the right calls. You're just gonna have to trust me on this."

I stood. "Fine."

"Hey." Dad set his newspaper aside. "You want to go over stuff for Mr. Kane's test? That's coming up."

I paused at the door. "That's all right. I got it." When I was little, Dad would go over multiplication tables or spelling lists with me. And I really needed to ace this test. But now it seemed like he and I were fighting all the time, instead of Mom and me—a kind of trade. Trudging up the stairs to my room, I felt a thick emptiness in my stomach, like homesickness. Like I missed them both.

In gym class, we started the volleyball unit—the one sport that I couldn't do. Whenever I hit the ball, it went in the opposite direction I'd meant for it to go. Since I was tall, Mrs. Harriott thought I'd be a star, even though I'd had the same problem for the past two years. After a few days of "Come on, Winchester, focus!" I wanted to send the ball at her head. Too bad I lacked control.

Maddie shared my frustration. She'd tried to get out of it on the first day, with a fake doctor's note saying she had weak wrists and shouldn't use them to hit anything. Too bad Mrs. Harriott recognized that Maddie's "doctor" had the same signature as her "mom," who wrote to excuse Maddie when she had her period.

"I think Edward Baker's going bald," Maddie told me as we lined up on the volleyball court. "Yesterday I was following him down the staircase from the English hall, and you could totally see it—bald spot. What is he, like, sixteen?"

I smirked. "By graduation he'll have a comb-over."

Maddie gagged. "Oh, God, at least we'll have those funny hats to wear. He can cover it up so the rest of us don't vomit."

"Richards! Are you paying attention?" Mrs. Harriott was midcourt. She'd been demonstrating the proper technique for a good serve, but now she was giving us a death stare.

"Yeah, of course," Maddie said.

Mrs. Harriott frowned. "We'll see when it's your turn. Now, everybody, if you keep your arm straight . . ."

When Mrs. Harriott's attention was back on the game, Maddie rolled her eyes at me. "Want to go to the Cloverleaf after school? Josh got his first paycheck from the drugstore and wants to spend all of it in one go."

Cloverleaf was the closest mall, half an hour away. Sometimes when we were in ninth or tenth grade, our parents would drop us off there on weekends and we'd walk around for a few hours, trying all the different scented moisturizers in Bath and Body Works, or sitting in the massage chairs at Brookstone, or pooling our money and getting huge pretzels covered in cinnamon sugar, which always smelled like heaven but were really disappointing once you actually took a bite. We hadn't gone in a while, since Josh and Theresa were taking SAT prep and Maddie usually babysat for her neighbors on Saturday mornings. Or maybe I hadn't been invited in a while. I didn't remember that Josh had gotten a part-time job. It must have been mentioned at some lunch when I was with Jim, but I didn't want to admit that to Maddie.

"After school?" I said. "Today?"

"Yeah, he can give us a ride. His mom's actually letting him use her car. He says it's because she's happy with his SAT prep test scores."

"I can't today," I said. Mrs. Ellis would be waiting for me to take over at two thirty.

"Winchester, Richards!" Mrs. Harriott was really glaring at us now. "If you know you've got the perfect serve, that's great. Run a few laps and think about how you're going to dominate today's game."

Maddie and I left the line and started jogging around the gymnasium. It was supposed to be a punishment, but I didn't mind running, especially if Mrs. Harriott forgot about us and we didn't have to play volleyball that day.

Maddie wasn't as happy. "She's such a bitch," she muttered. "So what about tomorrow? Maybe Josh can rearrange stuff. I feel like I haven't seen you outside of school in forever."

"I don't think I can this week," I said. "I've got to pick up Teddy from school. Mom's working overtime at the dentist's office."

"That sucks. We could go after your Mom gets back. That wouldn't be too late, right? And we could get food-court food for dinner."

Even without the need to be home that afternoon, I wasn't so sure. Josh would have to drop me off. What if they wanted to come inside and hang out for a little while? It wasn't exactly a rational fear, but the possibility made my head dizzy. "No, that's okay. You guys go. I'll join next time."

She glanced over at Jim, who was still in line, watching Max Olsen's pathetic serve. "Sure. Sometime." She picked up her pace and we ran without talking, feet hitting the floor in time with each other, until Mrs. Harriott called us back to the group.

Later that week, after having lunch with Jim, I stopped in the bathroom to wash my hands before class. It was the girls' room on the second floor, with the bad hand dryer, but it also had a huge window ledge, where three people could sit and hide out during class. So I didn't think much when, opening the door, I heard laughter. Then I saw it was Theresa and Maddie perched on the ledge, cracking up over something. When they saw me, they took deep breaths and stared at me for a second.

"Hey," Theresa said absently.

"Hey, guys," I said. For a minute, I felt like I'd stumbled into a room of giggling cheerleaders who'd been laughing about me. But these were my friends. I strode to the sinks. "What's up?"

Theresa shrugged. "Not much."

"We were talking about tourniquets," Maddie said, "and if you didn't have arms . . ." She and Theresa started to laugh again, mouths wide open and eyes almost closed. I kept washing my hands, moving slowly and methodically, until the water started to burn. After a minute, Maddie breathed deeply again and sighed. "I don't know. It's kind of hard to explain."

"I don't even know how it started," Theresa said. "Something at lunch."

"Right." I punched the air-dryer button and held my hands under its nozzle for a second, even though the air was cold and did nothing in terms of drying.

"You had lunch with Jim?" Theresa asked, looking at her chipped nail polish instead of me.

"Yeah. We ate outside the library."

She looked up. "So he doesn't let you hang out with *his*

friends, either?" She hopped down from the ledge. Maddie followed.

The air dryer stopped. I wiped my hands on my jeans. "Come on," I said, trying to sound exasperated rather than guilty. "It's not like I'm hiding him from you. Sometimes I have lunch with him, and sometimes I have lunch with you."

Theresa shrugged. "Whatever, it's not a big deal. I just didn't think you'd be that girl who ditches her friends for her boyfriend."

"He's not my boyfriend."

"Oh, I'm sorry," she said, almost laughing. "That's a *huge* difference. I feel a whole lot better now."

"I'll have lunch with you guys tomorrow."

Theresa slung her backpack over her shoulder. "Gosh, thanks so much. Can't wait." She brushed past me and fled into the halls. Maddie hung behind, fiddling with the strap of her backpack.

I hugged my arms around my chest. "What's her problem?"

"Alex, you're like the disappearing girl this semester," Maddie said. "It's like you're spending all your time with Jim. And if it's not Jim, you make some excuse about babysitting Teddy or whatever."

"I'm not. I don't." Even though I could have asked Jim to join our table at lunch—he probably would have been fine with it—I didn't want to, especially now that he knew there was something weird going on at home. Theresa was always pushing things—she needed to know everything about Jim, about my driving. If she thought anything was going on at home, she might push for answers there, too, and I wasn't ready to explain it to anyone yet. I could barely explain it to myself.

"Come on," Maddie said. "When's the last time we really hung out?"

"I've been busy," I said. Maddie crossed her arms and waited for me to go on. For a second, I thought it might be okay to tell her. "See, my mom—"

The door swung open, and I thought it would be Theresa, but it was a cluster of freshman girls, chattering in loud, high-pitched voices. They slid by us and stood in front of the mirror, reapplying their fruit-flavored lip glosses.

"Latin," Maddie said, moving for the door. "I'll talk to you later." I watched her go, feeling like a balloon slowly deflating. It was something I'd heard her say a million times before, but now it sounded like a brush-off instead of a promise.

I didn't want to rush home after school and babysit Mom, so I wasted time in the library, wandering through the stacks. Remembering Mom's stash at home, I didn't go to the biography section. The chess team was practicing at a large table in the corner, whispering insults at each other's moves. Through the window, I could see the gymnasium. Behind it, the soccer teams were probably warming up. I wished I could have been there instead. When I was on the field, I had such a sense of purpose. It didn't matter how good the other team was or how tired I was. All I had to do was get the ball where it needed to be, and no one could stop me. And even if I felt cornered, there was always someone to pass to. Together we were unbeatable, greater than the sum of our parts. I missed feeling unbeatable. Maybe if I'd stayed on the team, Dad wouldn't have made me stay home with Mom after school.

The librarians had hung some student artwork on the walls. Apparently the new art teacher was really enthusiastic about student work and petitioned to have a place to showcase it. In the library, with the librarians always around, there was less of a risk of portraits being defaced.

I strolled along the wall of artwork as if I were in a museum. Mostly they were watercolors or oil paintings of fruit or some-one's backyard, and most of them were all right—the occasional lopsided apple or weird perspective or shadow coming from nowhere. Not that I could have done a lot better; I quit art after freshman year. But a few were actually pretty good. Someone had painted a close-up of a bird. From a distance, you couldn't tell what it was, but up close you could see the curve of a wing and a smooth head. You could almost feel the texture of the feathers.

In the corner was the scrawl of a name: *J Wiley*.

I stopped and looked around, as if he might have been there. Jim was the only Wiley in school. How was he so good at this? Aside from that one time with the spray paint and the mention of Banksy, he hadn't talked about art. At least not mak-ing it himself. I didn't even know that he was in art class. I studied the name again to make sure I'd seen it right. There it was: *J Wiley*.

One of the librarians, the young one, strolled by with an armful of books and caught me staring. "That one's my favorite," she said, smiling.

"Yeah, it's really good." I felt a little guilty about destroying and stealing her books. "I know the guy who made it."

"Do you?" she said. "Well, you can let him know he's got a fan."

"Sure." She walked away, her flat shoes padding softly on the carpet. I kept looking at the painting. It was as if Jim had this secret thing inside him. How much did I really know about him? I wasn't the only one with secrets. I thought about everyone—Jim, Theresa, Mr. Kane, the librarian, the chess club—all existing on this one level that everyone saw. But underneath that there was a lot more, most of which you never got to see. I felt like the universe was something I could touch; it was all around me and humming with potential.

CHAPTER FOURTEEN

As soon as we left the ground, I knew I myself had to fly.

—Amelia Earhart

That night, I told Mom about Jim's painting. It was close to one a.m., but I hadn't slept before going downstairs. It was like I was waiting to talk to her. I don't know why I couldn't have had this conversation during the day, but with all the noise and activity of everyone else, it seemed like too much to deal with at once. During the day, I couldn't look at her without thinking that she should have been acting differently. I knew I'd be exhausted the next day, but talking to her at night felt safer. I felt like a little kid sneaking into her parents' room to assure herself that she was okay.

"I didn't even know Jim could do that," I said. "He was really good. His picture was a thousand times better than most of the other people's paintings."

Mom was trying to jimmy off the top of an old computer keyboard. In front of her were several other gadgets — a kitchen timer, a stopwatch, a CD player, an old handheld video game. I didn't ask how all these things were supposed to come together, but she worked as if she had some idea of what she wanted. She didn't look up at me when she spoke.

"I'm not much of a painter myself. I tried photography for a while, and, of course, I have my clothing line for active women."

Since I found her collection, she'd been trying harder to drop Amelia references, as though she had to prove something to me. Mostly I ignored her. "Well, Jim is, apparently — a painter, I mean."

"Is that something you're interested in?"

"No, it's not that." I flipped the stopwatch between my fingers. "It's like there's a lot left I don't know about him. Or anyone. You see people every day, but you don't know much about them at all. It's not bad, necessarily. But you only know this small part of them that they let you see. It's like we're all these icebergs, floating and passing one another."

Mom was quiet now. She set aside her screwdriver and studied me, her eyes slick and her lips pressed together. For a moment, I thought she might actually recognize me. I froze, wanting her to say my name.

"We all have secrets," she said. Then she swallowed and took the stopwatch from me. "I need to maintain a certain persona. G.P. says it's part of the job."

I slumped back in my chair. She was Amelia revived again, immortal and fearless. So I asked, "What's with all the equipment?"

She looked up. "Didn't I tell you? We're going to be using radio equipment for the Pacific flight. George is keeping everything very quiet—all those reporters, you know—but I think having a two-way will be quite helpful."

"In case you get into trouble."

"Heaven forbid." She sighed. "But yes . . . just in case."

It was the first day of Thanksgiving break when I got to see inside Jim's house. We were practicing driving, and by now I was feeling much more confident. I still refused to try parallel parking—"If I have to find a spot a mile away to avoid parallel parking, I guess that's what I'll have to do"—but I didn't have to talk myself out of a panic attack every time I got behind the wheel. I was even hitting speeds above ten miles an hour on roads I shared with other cars.

Gray clouds spread across the sky, but that didn't bother me. It had been overcast for days. Then, when I took a left turn onto Belmont, the first drops of rain splattered against the windshield. My hands gripped the wheel as I told myself that it was just a couple of raindrops, nothing to freak out about.

But then there were five more, then a dozen, and then it was pouring. Water streaked across the glass.

"Shit, shit," I said.

"Nothing to worry about," Jim said. "Just flip the wind-shield wipers."

I'd left the turn signal on, and now a tiny arrow on the dashboard was flashing green at me. I smacked at it.

"Right, the wiper switch should be right there. Turn it."

"Turn *what*?" I said. Rain smeared across the windshield, and my hands wouldn't release themselves from the steering wheel. The rain seemed like pebbles instead of water; I was afraid the windows would shatter. My foot meant to hit the brake, but I pressed the gas instead and we zipped along the street.

Jim reached across and flipped the wipers on. They splashed the water away, and I could see again.

I stopped the car, breathing quickly and brokenly. "How are you supposed to drive and put on windshield wipers at the same time? Especially when you're blinded by rain!"

Jim was trying not to laugh. "You get used to it. Want to try it again? Now that the rain can't take you by surprise."

"Shut up. It's not funny."

His smile fell. "I was just kidding."

My heart was still pounding. From the driving manual, I'd memorized the term "hydroplaning," when water gets between the wheels and the road, making it difficult to drive. I imag-ined us sliding off the road, flipping the car, and careering into someone. "It's like you never think bad things could happen."

"No, I just don't think *only* bad things are going to happen."

I leaned my head against the seat and tried to calm my

breathing. Rain pattered against the windshield. "It's like driving is all about control, and it always seems like I'm always out of control. Like no matter what, something bad is going to happen. I'm always waiting for the hit."

Jim reached over and placed his hand on top of mine. "It's okay. Really."

Even with the pressure of his hand and his steady voice, it didn't feel like enough. Just saying that things would be okay didn't make it true. But my heart was steadying and I didn't want to argue the point. I told Jim that I'd rather quit practicing for the afternoon. He suggested that we go to his house, since we were nearby, and maybe go over the manual instead. We switched seats.

At Jim's house, his mom was already preparing for Thanksgiving dinner. A bowl of peeled potatoes sat on the table, and I inhaled the scent of a fruit pastry in the oven. At my house, we weren't making a big deal out of Thanksgiving. (Except for Teddy, who decided that we all needed hand-shaped turkey name cards and Pilgrim-style hats made out of newspaper.) Dad was determined to cook a turkey, but since his culinary skills seemed limited to hamburgers and frozen pizza, Katy and I weren't expecting much.

Mrs. Wiley wiped her hands on a dish towel, smiling at me without showing her teeth. "Alex, right?"

I hadn't seen Jim's mom since Halloween, when I was a little hysterical on their doorstep. "Yeah. Hi, Mrs. Wiley."

I gestured to the oven. "Whatever you have in there smells great."

She waved a hand at me. "Just a cobbler. I got the recipe from Martha Stewart's website." Resting her palms on the counter, she looked from Jim to me and back to Jim again. "So. What are you kids up to? If you're looking for entertainment, I've got a few onions that need chopping."

For a second, I thought we should say okay, so Jim's mom might get a chance to realize I wasn't such an unstable mess, but Jim said we had driver's ed stuff to go over and we escaped to the basement. At my house, our basement was a dank, concrete cave filled with old toys, wedding presents my parents never used, and battered sports equipment. For a couple years, I even convinced Katy that cannibal trolls lived under the basement stairs. The Wileys' basement had been done over with carpeting, fake wood paneling, and leftover pieces of furniture. A model train set, complete with tiny trees and a small conductor, was displayed on a huge folding table in the corner. On the wall, a clock had different species of birds instead of numbers.

It was strange to think of Jim as a kid here. He and I had gone through the public school system together since we were little, but being—until this year—a grade apart, I didn't know anything about him as a kid. I wondered if he'd had birthday parties here, with piñatas and pizza, or spin the bottle when he was a little older.

Against the wall, a bookcase overflowed with hardcover

biographies and paperback novels. I glanced at the titles and noticed a row of thick photo albums. I pulled one out of its place.

"You're kidding me," Jim said. "Five seconds and you find the family pictures."

He tried to grab the book away from me, but I shielded it with my body. "No way!" I said, laughing. "You should've thought of this before we came down here." In the album, someone had written the title CHRISTMAS PAGEANT 5RST GRADE and neatly arranged photographs of small children in dresses and ties, all looking a little dazed and uncertain. I recognized the setting—the Sherman Elementary School stage, with its faded blue curtain and a dark-haired music teacher in front, probably leading the kids in a rendition of "Rudolph the Red-Nosed Reindeer" or "Santa Claus Is Coming to Town."

"Okay, which one are you?" I asked.

Jim shook his head. "You want to look at pictures, you have to guess."

I studied the photograph, trying to remember what Jim looked like in elementary school, back when boys were just kids we played soccer with. "This one?" I said, pointing to a little blond-haired boy in a green bow tie.

"Nice try, but not me. That's an awesome tie, though; thanks for thinking it's my style."

This time I tried a boy with a reindeer sweater, whose hair was a little curlier than the first boy's. "Him?"

Jim scratched his scalp. "I thought it'd take you longer than that."

"Oh, make fun of the kid with the bow tie, but you had reindeer sweaters? Now you need to wear one to school on Monday." I flipped the pages, seeing more pictures of Jim's first-grade class onstage, then pictures from his third-grade birthday party, and of his youth soccer team. One photograph was of Jim in his soccer uniform with an old man and woman, each with an arm around Jim.

"Those are my grandparents," he told me, tapping a finger against the picture. I asked if they were the ones he'd stayed with last year and he nodded. I studied the picture. Jim didn't resemble either of his grandparents, who were short and stocky and wore glasses with thick lenses. But in the picture Jim had a wide, gap-toothed smile, and he leaned his head against his grandfather's torso. They all looked right together, like family.

"They look nice," I told Jim.

"Yeah, they are," he said. "My grandma won't bullshit you at all—she tells it like it is, but doesn't make you feel stupid about anything, which was kind of what I needed. Plus, she still smokes and drinks, and, of course, she's healthier than people half her age. Doctors totally hate her. She's hysterical."

He turned a page and found another picture of his grand-parents, in the kitchen at Jim's house. From the way every-one was dressed and the glasses of lemonade on the table, it looked like summer. "Granddad's kind of a hard-ass—it's where Mom gets it from—and when I first got there, I hated him because he'd make me get up at five and help him do chores or whatever. But then one day he had me repaint the bathroom and, of course, started giving pointers. I was like, 'Granddad, I'm fine,' but he kept telling me what to do, until I was like, 'I know as much as you do about painting a room,' and he said, 'I went to art school—I know paint.' That, like, blew my mind."

"That's where you get it from," I said. "I mean, I saw your painting. The one in the library. It was really good."

Jim shifted his feet. "Right, thanks. Yeah, I guess that'd be where I get it. Apparently Granddad was really talented and took art classes for a while but had to give it up when his dad got hurt and needed him to take over the farm. He had never talked about it before, but then I kept asking questions about it and he'd talk about light and technique the way he would normally talk about how the rain would affect crop drainage. Art got to be our thing." He shrugged. "And it was nice to have something to do out there in the soybean fields."

"But you still do it here."

"Yeah. Actually, right here." He nodded toward a door off the main room. "My mom only lets me paint in that part of the basement, so I don't drip paint on anything."

I didn't wait for Jim to invite me to see it; I walked into the other room, which was unfinished, with concrete floors and exposed walls. All around were canvases in various states of work. Like the one in the library, there were several of birds, working out different textures.

"That was for a project," he said. "For class. We had to study something up close — Mr. Hall's into Georgia O'Keeffe — and I picked birds."

He must have gone through several paintings before settling on the one that hung in the library. Most of them looked like ordinary birds — pigeons, sparrows, crows — but there were a few exotic ones, like parrots and peacocks, in the mix. Like the one in the library, the texture was amazing. I reached out and touched one of the crow paintings, brushing my fingers along a feather and expecting it to feel like a real feather and not like dried paint.

"You're really good," I said, a little jealous that I couldn't do anything even close to this, but also proud of Jim, as if he was my actual boyfriend. "You could get into art school with that."

"I'm kind of thinking about that," he admitted. "Art is, like, the one class that I don't hate. Imagine getting to do that all day."

I nodded, although a small part of me felt worried — what if Jim went to school far away? — and then felt stupid for being worried. That was more than a year away, and I didn't have any major claims to Jim. "That sounds great. Just, you know, in your application essay, don't tell them you're just in it for the girls."

He smiled. "Hey, it got your attention, right? Jim for the win."

"Oh, right —" I started to say, but then Jim stepped toward me and suddenly we were kissing. *If he moves away to art school,*

I thought dimly, *I'm going to miss him.* I didn't have a lot of time to dwell on that, though. We moved over to the couch and got absolutely no driver's ed studying done.

It rained through Thanksgiving and the following day. By Saturday, we were kind of experiencing cabin fever. I would have called Theresa or Josh or Maddie, but I wasn't sure they were feeling especially affectionate toward me. Jim had gone to his aunt and uncle's in Chesapeake and wouldn't be back until Sunday night. And without a license, there wasn't much of a way for me to get around without getting soaked and frozen, so I stayed home and was in charge while Dad was at work. He told me I was a big help that week, and he didn't ask why I hadn't gone out with friends at all.

Even Mom seemed to feel it. Lately she'd been nervous, antsy, and kept pacing around the house, talking about the provisions she'd need and the problems she'd be bound to run into in the Pacific. Then she'd complain about being too old for this kind of thing. She wrote furious letters, tearing pages out of notebooks and searching the kitchen cupboards for envelopes. Aeronautical charts got tacked up on walls, and stray parts of old appliances appeared around the house. Once I caught her halfway out the front door, claiming she was late for a lecture. I told her it had been rescheduled and offered to go over the speech with her instead. When Dad was home, she'd pick fights with him about tours and his managerial experience and wouldn't listen when he tried to explain that he wasn't George Putman. In her bedroom, I could hear her pacing and saying people couldn't expect so much of her, that she was only one woman.

Katy was tearing through her homework. This year, she was getting better grades than ever. She'd always been a good student, but now her teachers were talking about magnet schools and college scholarships. She was putting together a diorama about natural selection when Mom came into our room.

"Anybody seen my goggles?" she asked, touching her pockets as if she'd find them there.

"How about you knock first?" Katy said.

Mom frowned at her. "I need my goggles. How am I supposed to fly anywhere if I can't even see properly? Do you want me to crash?"

Katy looked like she was about to say yes, so I suggested Mom check Teddy's room for the goggles. She went off without closing the door behind her.

Katy got up and shut it loudly. "She won't even leave us alone anymore."

"Better than her just leaving the house on her own," I said. "I'd rather her come in here without knocking than walk out the front door and wander off."

In the next room, Mom started yelling at Teddy for taking her goggles. "These aren't toys. They're serious instruments, and I don't appreciate you stealing them from me. Who knows what could have happened?"

I rushed over. Teddy was sitting on his bed and starting to cry. "I wanted—"

"You have to think more."

"Amelia, how about you get those charts out for me?" I asked. Anything to distract her. "For altitude checks. I'll handle things here."

She took a breath and looked at the goggles in her hand, still not quite satisfied. For a second, I thought she'd argue with me, but she walked out of the room without saying anything.

Teddy wiped away tears with his sleeve. "I hate her. I didn't steal her goggles. She left them out, and I was looking at them. I wasn't going to take them forever."

I grabbed a few Kleenex and sat on the bed. He snuggled up to me. "I know. It sucks."

"It totally sucks!"

Katy appeared at the door. "Sometimes when Alex and I are sick of Mom, we play a game." We taught Teddy the It Could Be Worse game and played it for a while: Mom could have thought she was Genghis Khan and try to conquer our rooms. Mom could have had elephantiasis. Mom could have thought she was a shark. Mom could have thought she was Marie Antoinette and made us bring her cake.

"Yeah," I said, "but then when we got fed up, we'd get to chop her head off. Definitely not worse than Amelia Earhart."

"She could try to steal a plane," Katy said. "That would definitely be worse."

That was true. I imagined Mom hitching a ride to Richmond or Dulles and walking onto the runway, pretending to inspect planes and getting attacked by airport security. At that point, I'd say let her suffer the consequences and get arrested. It's not always a blast being Fake Amelia Earhart. But if she managed to get in a plane, who knows where she'd try to take it? Most likely she'd crash it, not having any flight experience, and there would be little pieces of Mom on the tarmac. But what if she could get away? Where would she even try to go? Guam? Europe?

"Katy," I said, "you know when Mom has the maps out? And she's planning some flight?"

"Yeah." Katy looked a little annoyed that I'd stopped playing It Could Be Worse.

"It's not like she's planning one trip."

Katy shrugged. "So what? Amelia Earhart went all over, didn't she?"

What had Mom talked about? She told me about being in Europe, touring around and giving talks. And now she was talking about the Pacific trip. I remembered all of this from the books I'd stolen.

Mom was following Amelia's timeline. Even in her delusions, events for Mom happened in chronological order as they had for Amelia Earhart. Maybe things happened faster for

Mom than they had for Amelia—months didn't go by between flights or lectures, as they would have in real life—but Mom didn't pick out events randomly or mention anything out of order. It was like she felt she could only be Amelia Earhart if she mirrored her life exactly.

Then it hit me: she had three flights left. One between Hawaii and California. One from Los Angeles to Mexico to Newark.

I felt like I was going to fall off Teddy's bed and grasped the comforter to steady myself. And then the big one, the flight around the world that everyone knew. The one Amelia never came back from.

Mom was going to disappear. She'd have to, if she was going to keep following Amelia's timeline. I didn't know if that meant she'd stop being Amelia Earhart or if it was something worse. Something permanent. No one knew what happened to Amelia Earhart. What would Mom do with that?

It was like we were all in a plane—once we were on board, we had to keep going. We couldn't just step outside and end things partway through. We were thousands of feet above the ground, jostled by turbulence and headed for bad weather. Maybe we would make it safely to ground, but I worried that soon we'd all end up spiraling downward, weightless and vulnerable.

CHAPTER FIFTEEN

Please know I am quite aware of the hazards of the trip. I want to do it because I want to do it. Women must try to do things as men have tried. When they fail, their failure must be but a challenge to others.

—Amelia Earhart to George Putnam

I didn't tell Dad about the timeline. He hadn't seemed that interested when I talked to him about Mom's Amelia Earhart stash, so I could guess what his response would be to this idea: *We'll talk about it with Dr. McGlynn.* I couldn't see what good that would do. Mom wasn't getting better — she was getting worse. When was the last time she'd been Mom and not Amelia Earhart? But maybe it was the reverse — instead of having Amelia Earhart as a little voice inside her head, maybe now Mom was the small part of her, inside, that we didn't see. Maybe when she was silent, sitting on the couch and staring into the yard, she was thinking about her own life — Christmases in

Florida, her wedding day, putting us on the school bus for the first time. Every so often I would ask her what she was thinking about, but she'd just shake her head and laugh a little, telling me about her father in Kansas or how lovely her sister Muriel's wedding had been.

I wanted her to be lying. I wanted her to be thinking about us.

But that must have been part of the problem. Dr. McGlynn had said this was probably caused by extreme emotional distress, including the baby she lost. She wouldn't want to think about Katy or Teddy or me. We were the babies who had lived, and for some reason, we weren't enough for her.

Sometimes I couldn't think about her, either. Sometimes I would come in the house, taking over for Mrs. Ellis, and I couldn't even look at Mom. If she were in the kitchen, I'd be in the living room, throwing out honorary membership certificates she'd made for herself or hiding her goggles — anything to mess with her. Or I'd be absently watching TV and not really caring if she walked out the front door. I would curl my knees to my chest and think, *It'd be better for all of us if she just disappeared.*

But I didn't want that, either. It was like being in kindergarten again, when I released my mom's hand at the door and raced over to a bunch of kids making a block tower. When I looked up again and she was gone, my chest felt empty, as if the air had been sucked from the room, and I screamed for her to come back. Now that she was Amelia Earhart, at night I would sit with her and ask about the trips she'd taken. Sometimes I wouldn't even talk at all—I'd just watch her write notes to herself in her marbled notebook. Even being around her as Amelia Earhart was better than her not being around at all, at least for the moment.

I took Mr. Kane's test on the last day of classes before winter break. He told me I could take it during the History of Music exam, with the dozen seniors from his class. We all sat in the music room, the walls filled with posters of Mozart and Louis Armstrong and giant treble clefs. A few seniors glanced at me when I slid into a desk in the back.

"Are you in this class?" Tina, a girl with long brown hair, asked. "Alex, right?"

"Yeah," I said, trying to keep my driver's ed manual hidden. "I mean, yes, I'm Alex. No, I'm not in the class. Mr. Kane's just letting me take a makeup test here. So he doesn't have to hang around afterward."

I wished they'd leave it at that, but a guy in a turtleneck said, "You're the one who drove on the football field, right?"

Everyone was looking now. "I guess," I said.

"So what's the exam?" he asked. "You have to take the permit test again?"

I wanted to strangle him with his own turtleneck, but Mr. Kane came in with a stack of exams and everyone froze. Under his breath, he whistled a cheerful version of a funeral dirge. The class tittered with laughter. I felt my stomach drop into my small intestine as I tried to remember everything I'd ever learned about driving.

Mr. Kane handed out the music exam to everyone else. "You've got three hours, although I don't expect it'll take you that long if you've *studied*. Turn it over when I say—*now*." The room filled with sounds of papers shuffling and pens scratching.

"Alex," Mr. Kane whispered, crouching beside my desk. He had one more exam in his hand. I stared at it. "Are you ready?"

Even though I was afraid all the facts about speed limits had flown out of my head, he sounded so enthusiastic that I nodded.

"Great. Take as long as you need."

For a second, all I could do was blink at the exam. It was only a few pages long, mostly multiple-choice and a few short-answers, but the letters blurred into meaningless squiggles. I took one breath, then another, and told myself not to freak out, especially with Mr. Kane sitting at the front of the classroom. If I had another panic attack, he'd probably be really nice about it but secretly think I was just like my mother. Plus, staying up at night was starting to wear on me. My eyes always felt red and raw.

One question at a time, I told myself.

I imagined being in the backseat with Jim, reciting parking laws and identifying road signs. There, it was our own world and there was nothing to worry about. Soon I was circling answers I was sure were correct. Even though my test was shorter than the music exam, I went over it several times, checking my responses until I was the last person in the room.

When I walked up to Mr. Kane, he smiled. "All done?"

"I guess." I almost didn't want to hand the test over, just in case I'd misremembered everything, but made myself place it on his desk. "No use going over it anymore, at least."

"Right. You'll just outthink yourself," he said. As I turned to the door, he continued, "I can grade this now if you want."

I grimaced. "Do I really want you to?"

He laughed, a deep tenor. "I don't have to. I can call you over break to let you know how you did."

I imagined Mom answering the phone. "Now's fine. Pull off the Band-Aid, right?"

"Right. Otherwise you'll be thinking about it the whole time." He uncapped a red pen. I practically collapsed into a seat in the front row, studying the graffiti on the desk so I wouldn't have to look at Mr. Kane making either check marks or Xs. LAURA + ROBBIE, it read, with a bunch of little hearts. THIS SUCKS. '99 LADY MOUNTAINEERS ROCK! A few misshapen stars. I pulled a pen out of my bag and began to sketch a few of my own.

"Alex?" I looked up, thinking Mr. Kane was going to yell at me for messing with school property. Instead he held out my test. "See you next semester."

I grinned. "I passed?"

"Ninety-three percent. Give or take a percent. That's why I don't teach math." He handed me the test, full of delightful little red checks. I'd missed one multiple-choice question about right-of-way and a couple of points from a short-answer.

"Just make sure to practice with your parents in the meantime," he said. "Say hi to them for me."

Say hi, as if they were all friends. As if he knew what was going on at home. He probably thought we'd all be together, stringing lights around the tree. I smiled with my lips pressed together. "Sure thing," I said. "Have a nice break."

At home, Mom was writing addresses on multiple envelopes. She had a whole stack in front of her at the table. Her handwriting was neat and crisp, not her more casual scrawl. She'd been taking time with these.

"What are those?" I asked, getting myself a soda. "Christmas cards?"

"Letters," she said. "Nothing business-related. Mostly to family."

I frowned. "Right. Family. Say hi to them for me."

My tone was cutting, and she noticed. I hadn't expected her to. She lifted her head, pen still midword. "Well, you don't have to say it like *that*. What in the world's the matter?" The way her eyes rested on my face, I knew she didn't recognize me.

"What's the matter?" I said. My face was getting hot, and it was hard to speak. I snatched my driving exam out of my bag, holding it up for her. "I passed my test."

She blinked at me. "That's good—"

"I know," I said. "It's really good. I get to take driver's ed again next semester, and Mr. Kane doesn't think I'm a total idiot now, and I can't even tell you because you'll pretend like it's some stupid flying thing and not what it really is, which is this kind of great thing for me."

"I'm—"

"No," I said, my voice catching. I felt a little cloud of tears form behind my nose and eyes and mouth, and I threw my test onto the floor. "Just shut up, all right? I don't even want to hear whatever you'll come up with. I want you to be happy about this stupid, small thing—actually happy about it. Because it's not that small or stupid to me. But you're writing to family that doesn't exist. We're here, Mom, and we exist and you don't care." Suddenly my face felt wet. I tried to dry it with my hand.

I thought she would start crying, too, and yelling at me. At least I thought she'd run upstairs to her Amelia books. But she regarded me thoughtfully, and a little afraid. Her hands were shaking.

"I don't . . . I know . . ." she started to say, but the door opened and Katy came in, gymnastics bag slung over her shoulder. She looked from me to Mom and back to me.

"What happened?" Katy set her bag gently on the floor as if she thought the room might explode.

"Nothing," I said, grabbing a napkin to wipe my face with.

Katy picked up my test. "You passed?" She tried to smile. "That's really great, Alex. Now you don't have to worry about it anymore."

I shrugged. "Just until I have to pass the actual driving course."

Katy turned the test over in her hands. "Well, now maybe Jim can teach you how to drive through the house."

Suddenly that seemed hilarious. I laughed, and the sound seemed to surprise Katy. Then she started giggling, too, and soon we were both doubled over, more tears trickling down my face. My stomach ached and I could barely breathe, but at least it was a good ache. Mom looked between us, not confused anymore, but smiling, somehow relieved. She looked like she wanted to laugh with us, too, but wasn't in on the joke.

When Katy and I tried to catch our breath, Mom stood and put her hand on my shoulder. She gave it a squeeze. "Congratulations," she said. "Well done."

"Thanks," I said.

She nodded. Then her eyes clouded and her lip quivered, so that for a second I thought she might cry. But she gathered her letters. "There's just so much to do," she said, voice shaky, and went upstairs.

I knew she didn't really understand what was going on with me. But maybe she was trying to. It was all I could ask for at the moment.

Katy took a sip of the soda I'd left on the table. "It could be worse," she said.

"Yeah," I said. "Maybe."

I called Jim that night. He asked me to hold on for a second, since his cell barely got reception in the basement. I imagined him working on something—more paintings of birds, maybe.

When I told him about the test, he said, "That's awesome. And now you'll be ahead of everybody next semester."

"On the first day, I'm going to run somebody over so they'll know who's in charge. Although I think Mr. Kane might be kind of mad at me."

"Depends on who you run over."

"I mean, he did tell me I was supposed to keep practicing."

Jim laughed. "He didn't say what kind of practicing. Seriously, next semester'll be so easy. And after you pass, we can—I don't know—go on a road trip or something."

After I passed—Jim was talking about us being together over the summer. I smiled wider. "Yeah," I said, trying to sound casual, "that sounds great."

Even though the thought of the highway made me dizzy, I liked the idea of a road trip. By then, it would be warm and we could drive off with the windows down and mixes blaring. We could take pictures in front of cheap tourist traps and write real postcards to friends, signing off, *Wish you were here!* We could steal kisses in front of famous monuments and highway pull-offs. It wouldn't even matter where we'd be going, just as long as we were going somewhere and going together.

On the other end of the phone, I could hear some muffled whispers. Then Jim said, "So my parents are having this holiday party thing."

He was quiet for a second, so I said, "That sounds nice."

"It's just some family and my parents' friends, and it's a couple days before Christmas, and you totally don't have to come if you don't want to."

"Hold on," I said. "Are you asking me to come?"

He paused again. "Yeah, but you don't have to. I know it's kind of lame. And somebody'll probably wear a Christmas sweater."

"I hope so. That's all I wear during winter break."

In the background, I could hear Jim tell his mom I was coming and her response, "Good!" I wasn't sure if it was genuine enthusiasm, or if she was just interested in making sure I wasn't a crazy girl who liked making out with her son in their basement. (Although maybe I was.) Either way, I thought it might be nice to be around someone else's family, even if relatives fought and people asked if I was Jim's girlfriend. It would be better than a Christmas with Amelia Earhart. I could pretend it was the Winchester Christmas party instead.

"So when you said, 'Somebody'll probably wear a Christmas sweater,' you meant yourself, right?" I asked.

"Oh, yeah," Jim said. "I've got a collection."

As long as it wasn't a linen scarf or aviator jacket, it sounded all right to me.

"What are you getting me for Christmas?" Teddy leaned against the kitchen table, watching me as I scanned the cabinets for dinner possibilities.

"Bunny slippers," I said.

He collapsed against a chair. "No, *really*."

"No, really. They're the cutest, pinkest bunny slippers I could find, and I'm gonna tell all your friends about them."

He made a gagging noise and I laughed. "I can't tell you what I'm getting you, because then it wouldn't be a surprise."

"What if you gave me a hint? Three hints."

I took a jar of marinara sauce out of the cabinet, wrinkled my nose at it, and replaced it before turning to Teddy. "One," I said, and held up a finger. "It's smaller than you are. Two"—another finger—"it's colorful. Three"—one more finger—"it requires sharing."

Teddy scrunched his mouth and stared at me for a moment. "Okay, three more hints."

"Nope, that's all you get until Christmas." Katy and I had gone in on a Nerf gun set for him, which we were sure would make him the envy of his second-grade class. We figured it was the least we could do, since the rest of the Christmas season had been so nonexistent. Dad was working as much overtime as he could get during the busy season, and neither Katy nor I could muster up much holiday enthusiasm. Usually, the minute Thanksgiving was over we'd drag the box of Christmas decorations out of the basement and fill every corner with snowmen and Santas. One year, Mom showed us how to cut snowflakes from folded paper and we taped them to every window in the house. They stayed up until after Valentine's Day.

Christmas must not have been that important to Amelia Earhart, because Mom hadn't mentioned it at all.

I was resigning us to pasta again when the front door opened and Dad entered, whistling. "Hello, hello!" he called.

Teddy rushed to hug him, jabbering about the bunny slippers I'd teased him about. "But I don't think that's what she's really getting me."

"Oh, I think your sister has something else already worked out." He winked at me. "Have you started dinner?" When I told him not yet, he nodded. "Good. How about we go for a drive instead? Maybe to Greene Valley Farm?"

Teddy shrieked and started jumping as if a tiny explosion had gone off in his sneakers. "We're getting a tree! We're getting a tree! We're getting a tree! Katy!" He bounded up the stairs to collect our sister.

Dad told me to get my coat, but I lingered in the kitchen. "It's okay—you guys go," I said. "Somebody should stay with Mom, and I've already picked a tree a ton of times before. I don't care." I scanned through the cabinets again, as if expecting to find different contents, and tried to wipe memories of cold walks through the Christmas tree fields and the sharp scent of evergreen from my mind.

"Of course you're coming," Dad said. "Barbara Ellis is coming over. I already talked to her and—"

"May I come?"

A few feet away, Mom stood in the kitchen doorway with her hands folded calmly in front of her. She looked from Dad to me and back again. "It's a lovely time of year. My family always had a Christmas tree."

Upstairs, footsteps pounded against the floor. Dad shifted from one foot to the other. "I don't know if that's the best idea," he said.

Mom's face fell a little, but she nodded. "It's all right. There's so much to do anyway—"

"You should come," I said.

They both blinked at me for a moment. "Are you sure?" Dad said, voice low. "Barbara said it was okay—"

"No, she should come." I didn't let myself think about how Mom might act with the Christmas tree farm employees or what might happen if we saw another family we knew there. She never asked to join family activities—maybe she was trying. Even if she couldn't be Mom, she could be with the rest of us.

Katy and Teddy appeared in the kitchen, shoes on and coats in hand. "All right," Dad said. "Everybody into the car." He called Mrs. Ellis on his cell, letting her know that Mom was joining us.

Greene Valley Farm was beyond where Jim and I would practice driving, farther toward the mountains. Katy, Teddy, and I huddled together in the backseat. Dad turned on one of those awful radio stations that played nothing but Christmas music from mid-November through New Year's, but we sang along anyway. In the front passenger seat, Mom mouthed the lyrics as if afraid to hear her own voice.

The parking lot was already filled with cars when we

arrived. "I hope we find a good one," Teddy said, pressing his hand against the car window.

"Oh, I think there are plenty of good ones left," Dad said as he parked. Before getting out of the car, he leaned closer to Mom. "You can stay in the car if you want. There'll be a line—"

"Honestly, Gip," Mom said. "Wait in the car? I'm sure people will be too distracted by their trees to notice me."

Beside me, Katy stiffened and I was afraid she'd end up hiding in the car instead. I squeezed her hand. "Come on, you always find the good ones."

Dad stayed close to Mom, and Katy and I rushed after Teddy, who was intent on running up and down every row of trees before we could examine any of them. Speakers set up throughout the fields pumped in old-fashioned carols. I could hear Mom talk about Christmases with Pidge in Kansas. "We were living with my grandparents at the time," she said. "Grandmother didn't feel the need to raise us like 'good little girls,' thank goodness. It was a happy time."

After scanning a few rows, Katy stopped in front of one tree. "I like this one."

Teddy frowned. "That's not tall enough! We need one that's *at least* three more feet tall."

"I think any taller and it won't get through the door," Dad said. He took a step back and admired the tree. "Looks like a good one to me."

"You have to shake it," Mom said. I waited for her to follow up with some bit of historical trivia about how Amelia Earhart always chose her Christmas trees, but it didn't come. "And run your hands over it. You don't want too many needles to fall off."

Dad followed Mom's instructions and only a few needles scattered on the ground. "Looks like Katy's got a winner. All in favor?"

"Aye!" Teddy cheered. Dad and Katy hoisted the tree off the ground and headed toward the farm stand. Teddy ran ahead of them, dancing along to his own rendition of "Jingle Bells."

Mom and I walked a few feet behind them. Down other aisles, I could see other families inspecting trees and laughing together. I wanted to believe that they were hiding something, too.

"Excuse me." Mom and I turned to see a young couple standing a few feet away, three children under the age of eight bouncing around beside them. Strapped to the woman was an infant, tiny red-and-green-striped legs kicking out of the carrier. "Would you mind taking our picture?" the woman asked.

"I'll do it," I said before Mom could reply.

The man handed me his camera. "It's the big silver button at the top." He looked to his kids. "Okay everyone, smile."

I clicked, hoping to get a picture of everyone open-eyed and smiling so they wouldn't ask me to try again. "Great. Here you go," I said.

The man took the camera back and scanned the picture before nodding. "Thanks. Merry Christmas. Everyone, say 'Merry Christmas.'"

Three little voices trilled "Merry Christmas" at us, and they hurried off to the farm stand. I breathed a sigh of relief that Mom hadn't tried to give them her autograph or tell them about flights over the Pacific.

"Well, that was nice," Mom said to me, voice tight. "People have so much fun this time of year. I love that scent of pine, don't you?"

I was about to agree, but I saw her start to shake, and she tried to cover it with a cough but the tears came anyway. She ducked into an empty row, gasping as she wiped away tears. "I'm fine," she choked out. "I'm fine."

Dad was already out of sight, so I stayed a few steps away from Mom. For a moment, I considered reaching out to her, but she kept her back turned to me and I was afraid I'd startle her if I touched her. I remembered how upset she was with me when I discovered her Amelia Earhart collection, and how she told me she didn't want me around. So I stayed as still and quiet as I could until she was finished.

On the speakers, Judy Garland sang "Have Yourself a Merry Little Christmas."

Mom turned to me again. "I'm fine, really," she said. Her eyes were red, but she forced a smile as she wiped away the last of her tears. "I need to get home. There's so much work to do, and I shouldn't have taken the time off."

"Maybe," I said.

"Come on, let's meet G.P. at the car." She strode quickly through the fields, and I stayed close behind her, not stopping when we passed the farm stand and Katy called to us to wait up.

At the car, she grappled with the door handle, but it was locked. "Oh, for heaven's sake," she muttered. "He has to be in charge of everything. I always tell G.P. —"

"What's the matter?" I hissed. "You were fine and then all of a sudden — it's like you don't want to be with us. Why did you even want to come?"

She crossed her arms and turned away from me. "I don't know what you're talking about," she sniffed. "I'm a busy person; I can't be expected to do everything, you know."

Nearby, footsteps crunched on gravel. "Everything all right?" Dad asked. He and Katy were holding the tree, and Teddy stopped short behind Katy, so he plowed into her, but she didn't yell at him.

Mom and I glanced at each other. "Perfectly fine," she said, smile straining her face. "But I should be getting home. So much to do."

Dad looked to me for confirmation, and I shrugged. "Let's just go."

We strapped the tree to the top of the car and drove home. Mom tried to talk to Dad about flight plans and tour schedules, but he gave her one-word responses. Beside me, Katy murmured, "I think it's a good tree."

"It's really good," I told her. She half smiled and leaned her head against my shoulder. "I think you can still smell it." We inhaled deeply and imagined the scent of pine on our hands and in our hair.

CHAPTER SIXTEEN

*Dawn is a fearful thing to see from the air. Only by wearing
dark glasses can a pilot face the rising sun for any length of
time because of the brilliance of the light.*

—Amelia Earhart

"Alex," Dad said. It was Thursday, two days before Christmas,
and Dad didn't have work. I was watching *Rudolph the Red-
Nosed Reindeer* with Teddy when Dad came in the living room
holding Jackson's leash. "Come walk Jackson with me." He
already had my coat with him.

I turned back to the TV. "It's not my turn."

"I know," he said, "but come with me anyway."

Outside, it was warmer than it had been for weeks. Even
though it wasn't raining, the ground was slick and muddy.
Jackson trotted ahead, sniffing at every tree.

I thought Dad was going to have a talk with me about
something—yelling at Mom, not paying close enough attention
to her, something—but instead he said, "Katy mentioned you

passed your driver's ed test." He glanced at me from the corner of his eye. He didn't look upset, just curious.

"Oh, right," I said, kicking a stone into the gutter. "I did."

"That's great." Jackson started barking at another dog in a yard across the street, impeded by an invisible fence. Dad tugged him along. "Why didn't you tell me?"

For a second, I didn't answer. I didn't even want to glance over at him in case he had that disappointed look again. "I guess I forgot."

"That's a pretty big thing to forget."

I wrapped my arms around myself even though it wasn't that cold. "Not really. I still have to take the class next semester. This just means that I didn't totally fail."

"I think it's a big thing."

One of our neighbors, Mr. Daniels, was hauling bags of groceries into his house. Dad waved at him and I tried to smile but it looked more like a smirk. Jackson stopped to pee under a stop sign. We stood nearby, waiting for Jackson, and I thought Dad was going to let the driving test thing drop. But then he said, "Even though things are really busy with Mom right now, you can still tell me about this stuff."

It didn't feel like it. He was tired and frustrated all the time. Whenever he and Mom came home from Dr. McGlynn's, he'd try to share a piece of good news—Mom was being put on a new medication, or she talked about her feelings without mentioning Amelia—but more often he sounded drained. Dad and I had always had a good relationship; he cheered at my soccer games and taught me how to swim and didn't make me feel stupid about failing driver's ed. But it was like he was a different person now, too. We were all flying through a storm with the clouds pressing against the windows so we couldn't tell which way was up. How could I tell him about normal things like a driver's ed test when we were trying to figure out how to get back on the ground?

"I know," I said. "I just forgot."

Jackson tugged at the leash, in the direction of home. "Let's go," Dad said, and I wasn't sure if it was to Jackson or to me. He put his arm around my shoulders as we walked. "I know it's tough."

It was tough. And it wasn't going to get better. "I know," I said.

"We just have to work through it a little longer," he said, voice cracking. "I'm really trying, Alex. I wish I could make her better." I turned to him, wondering if Dr. McGlynn had given him some good news or a medication was working. Something to make him hopeful, to give him a timeline of his own. But his eyes were on the house, and they were clouded, like he was looking into the storm.

White Christmas lights wrapped around the Wileys' house. Cars filled the driveway and lined both sides of the street. From the front lawn, I could hear glasses clinking and someone's loud, howling laugh. It was a clear night, and I stood outside for a minute, identifying Orion.

"Hello?" A silhouette appeared at the front door. Mrs. Wiley.

"Hi, sorry," I said, approaching the door. "I got distracted for a second. First clear sky we've had in weeks."

She smiled and held the storm door open for me. "It's nice, isn't it? We're so glad you could come, Alex. Can I take your coat?" She was wearing a boxy dress with beads sewn into the collar. For a second, I felt a little stupid in my plaid skirt and black turtleneck, which Katy had called appropriate—"So you don't look slutty in front of his parents"—but now seemed boarding-school bland.

When Jim appeared in the front hall a second later, he was in a button-down shirt and tie. "Hey, Alex." He gave his mom a meaningful look, and she told us to enjoy the party, then disappeared into the kitchen.

"Thanks for coming," he said. "My parents have this thing every year. Sometime tonight my uncle Allen will dress up like Santa for all the kids. When I was seven, I saw him getting ready and freaked out."

"Bet that killed Santa for you."

He shrugged. "My parents said Uncle Allen was just helping Santa out, but I didn't exactly believe them."

In the living room, the Wileys had set up a couple of card tables—one with platters of food, another as a makeshift bar. People balanced small plates and plastic cups as they talked. On one side of the room, the top of a Christmas tree brushed the ceiling. A stereo played pop versions of Christmas songs.

Jim's dad was behind the bar. I hadn't seen him since that day in his front yard, with a chunk of their house missing. Now he was in a bright-red sweater. I wasn't sure if it was the sweater or a few drinks that made his cheeks look flushed. He beckoned us over. "You must be Alex. What can I get for you?"

"Coke?" I said, glancing between Jim and his dad, like I might have gotten it wrong. Jim asked for the same.

Mr. Wiley scooped ice into plastic cups and poured, then waited for the fizz to subside. He extended his hand and the soda. I wasn't sure which to take first. "Glad you could make it."

"Thanks for having me."

Mr. Wiley took a sip of his own drink, something on the rocks. He nodded at us. "I hear Jim's been giving you driving lessons."

Beside me, I could feel Jim tense a little. "He's been a huge help," I said. "The driving teacher at school kind of hated me, so Jim stepped in and it's been a lot better."

"I'm sure." Mr. Wiley kept nodding, as if his head wasn't secured to his neck. "A little tutoring goes a long way. Jim's getting Bs in chemistry now—all it took was a little time after school. Of course, getting tutored by your boyfriend's probably better than getting tutored by Mrs. Frasier."

I blinked at Mr. Wiley. Boyfriend? I made sure to keep my head straight in case Jim's face was suddenly pale and terrified. "I actually just passed the written test."

"Good for you! As long as you know all the rules of the road, you'll be set. Easiest thing in the world, driving." He glimpsed at Jim. "Just make sure he doesn't skip the lesson about stopping. Sometimes he forgets that part." Mr. Wiley laughed so good-naturedly that I wasn't sure if the Wileys had taken to joking about the whole car-slamming-into-a-house thing. Beside me, Jim's laugh sounded more like a cough.

"Well, we're going to say hi to people," Jim said, voice clipped. "Thanks for the drinks." He took my hand and led me through the crowded room, into the kitchen.

I didn't know what to say. Mostly I was still wondering about the whole boyfriend thing, but it didn't seem like an appropriate time to ask. Jim glanced around the room, as if he was looking for a distraction.

"So that's my dad," he finally said.

I tried to smile carelessly. "Parents are fun, huh?" I wanted to tell him that it was a comment my mom probably would have made back before her nervous breakdown, thinking she was being funny or even helpful—a nice reminder to not screw up—and maybe she wouldn't have even realized that it was obnoxious. But now she was Amelia Earhart and thought I was an amazing female pilot, so I couldn't exactly tell him it got better. Besides, no matter what people said to make you feel better about your parents, it didn't work. You still had to come home to them.

Jim grabbed an open party-size bag of chips. "Hungry?"

We leaned against the counter and munched on chips until Jim's mom shooed us away, saying there were plenty of chips in a bowl in the living room, along with lots of other great snacks, so we could go binge on them if we wanted. In the hall, we ran into Will McNamee.

"Hey, dude, I was wondering where you were," he said to Jim.

"Just avoiding people," Jim said, and nodded at me. "You know Alex, right?"

I'd seen Will in school before, but I'd never talked to him. Jim's friends seemed nice enough, but I liked having Jim all to myself and didn't want to share him yet with people who might know him better.

Like Jim, Will was tall and had the build of a swimmer. His hair was dark and slicked with too much product. He wore a button-down shirt, untucked, and no tie.

Will studied me for a second. I wondered if Jim had told Will I was his girlfriend. "You used to be on the girls' soccer team," Will said.

"Yeah," I said. "Freshman and sophomore year."

"My girlfriend, Jess, was on the team with you." He turned to Jim. "She's coming tonight."

They listed a few other people who were supposed to show up—a handful of seniors Jim sometimes sat with at lunch. My stomach churned. I'd thought it would just be relatives and neighbors, not a bunch of people from school. Did they think I was Jim's girlfriend? Or some idiot who couldn't drive? Had they seen my mom at school that day?

The rest of Jim's friends showed up not long after Will. By the time everyone was there, Jim's dad had drifted away from the card-table bar, giving Everett Brown the opportunity to swipe a bottle of vodka. Jim took a two-liter bottle of Diet Coke and a handful of cups, and we escaped into the basement.

We were an even number of guys and girls. Thankfully, Everett and Cameron Colby weren't together; it was weird being around his friends in a dating capacity. I wondered if any of his friends knew about the room off the basement, where Jim had his artwork.

Jess sat next to me on one of the old couches. She was small and used to have long hair, but had recently cropped it. When we were on the soccer team together, she had been pretty cool—really focused on the field, and sometimes made playlists to pump us up before games.

"You were so right to not try out this season," she told me. "The new coach, Ms. Bryan, knows *nothing* about soccer. Plus, a bunch of girls got hurt, so we lost basically every game. Suckiest season ever."

I'd heard about that. But I also remembered running down the field on a clear, crisp day, being part of a group united in this single, simple purpose, and I missed it.

"And it was so annoying that it was our last year. Great way to go out, right?" She cocked her head. "But you're a junior, right? You should try next year."

Will passed Jess a cup. She took a sip and wrinkled her nose. "This much vodka is seriously going to soak into me. You are going to be able to light my hair on fire."

Jim held the bottle of vodka and looked up at me.

"A little," I said. "Not hair-fire amounts."

He handed me a cup, and he started to fill his with Diet Coke and vodka as well. Remembering his epilepsy medication, my stomach dropped a little. "Is that okay?" I asked.

He stopped midpour. "Yeah, I'm fine."

"But what about—?"

"Seriously, it's cool."

Will slid onto the couch beside Jess. "Of course it's cool, dude. You don't even have to drive home this time." He laughed, and Jim avoided making eye contact with me.

After setting up speakers on Jim's iPod, Everett suggested Never Have I Ever. I was kind of relieved—it meant I wouldn't have to make small talk with Jim's friends. Jim and Will pulled over a couple more chairs to form a kind of circle.

Cameron started. She was really skinny; I wondered how long she'd last in the game before getting absolutely wasted. "Never have I ever . . . smoked up in the guys' locker room." Her eyes rested on Will.

He took a sip. "Oh, fine, that's how you want to play? Never have—"

Jess whacked him. "Not your turn. Never have I ever . . . hooked up on school property."

Jim and I glanced at each other and sipped. At first I wasn't sure if anyone had noticed, but Everett laughed. "What'd you do, sneak out during gym class?"

"Behind the library," Jim said.

"Classy."

Giggling, Jess nudged me, like I was part of their group. Now it was my turn. I didn't know anybody well enough to call them out on anything, so I kept things general. "Never have I ever . . . stolen anything."

Everyone except Cameron drank, including me. Everett rolled his eyes at Cameron. "Oh, come on, you're such a liar."

She shook her head. "Unless I stole a pack of gum when I was like three, no. I'm paranoid about being caught."

Jim looked at me. "What about you?"

"Oh," I said. "In middle school, Maddie Richards and I would go to the pharmacy and sometimes we'd dare each other to take lip glosses or nail polish or whatever. Maddie was always really good at it. I got caught once and they threatened to call my mom, but I cried, so they didn't. We kind of stopped after that."

"Maddie Richards?" Will said. "Is she the one who always draws on her hands?"

He made it sound like Maddie was kind of stupid. Even though I wasn't really talking to Maddie these days, I bristled. "Yeah. I've known her forever."

"My turn," Everett said. "Never have I ever . . . started a fight. An actual brawl, not just people being bitchy to each other."

The game went on for a while. *Never have I ever been on a plane; never have I ever cheated on a test; never have I ever been cheated on; never have I ever been arrested; never have I ever . . .* on and on and on. Even though I was sipping my drink, I started to feel loose and heavy, like a wilting flower. Beside me, Jess kept giggling. At one point, she turned to me and said, almost shouting, "Now you're going to know all our secrets!"

"Hey, keep it down," Jim said. "My parents are right upstairs."

"And I'm not exactly on their good list," Will said.

Jess leaned against me. "What about you? You've met Jim's parents, right? Are you on their good list?"

"More than Will," Jim said. "And they still let him come over."

"What about her parents?" Jess wanted to know. "Do they like you? Do they know you almost destroyed your house? I bet they loved that."

Jim rubbed the back of his head. "The first time we were going driving, Alex's dad asked me about it and gave me the whole intense-dad look." He paused. "I only met Alex's mom once, really quick." For a second, I thought he was going to tell everyone about Halloween and I held my breath. Then he continued, "So maybe Alex's dad came back with bad news and now they're getting the shotguns ready."

I laughed a little too loud. "Yeah, that's it. My mom's got all these maps and she's planning an attack. Watch out." Before I could say anything else, I took another sip. That was one secret

I didn't feel like expounding on. At least until someone said, *Never have I ever had a parent go crazy.* My cheeks were red.

"Uh-oh," Will said. "Looks like you're going to have to do a parent intro soon, Wiley."

"I don't know about that," I said.

Just for a second, Jim blinked at me. His face didn't really change, but I suddenly felt like all my organs were rotting. Mr. Wiley had called Jim my boyfriend. Boyfriends were supposed to come over and put on a movie as a pretense for making out and deal with meeting the parents. So far I'd met Jim's parents and friends, seen his secret art room, gone through his old photo albums, and learned about his epilepsy medication. He'd only seen my kitchen.

But I didn't know what I could talk about: How my mom was crazy? How it was hard talking to my dad nowadays? How my friends weren't really talking to me anymore? That'd be super attractive.

"Kids?" Mrs. Wiley was at the top of the stairs. Everett shoved the bottle of vodka under an armchair. "We're all taking a picture in front of the tree."

Cameron handed out mints, each of us taking four. The chalky tablets burned my mouth as they melted. We trotted up the stairs, where the chatter had grown noisier. Empty cups and plates were strewn around the kitchen. In the other room, Jim's uncle Allen was dressed up as Santa and laughing heartily. I felt a little dizzy and disoriented by the commotion as people gathered in front of the tree. I wanted to make things up to Jim but didn't know how. When I tried to reach for his hand, Mrs. Wiley told me to stand by Cameron and Jess instead. Jim didn't object.

The camera was set up on a tripod. Mr. Wiley squinted through the lens. "All right, everybody, squeeze together. Got to get the ends in."

On either side, Jess and Cameron pressed against me. We all smiled, trying not to breathe.

"Looks good." Mr. Wiley pressed the timer and dashed to a spot by his wife. We held our smiles as the camera's red light blinked at us — once, twice, three times, then five quick pulses and a bright flash.

In the back row, someone said, "I think I blinked!"

Mr. Wiley jogged back to the camera. "All right, one more time, just to be sure. Eyes open this time, Bill!" We huddled together tighter and kept smiling, eyes getting blurry. As the red light blinked, I wondered if I would be in next year's Christmas party picture or if I would be another face in a photo album, shoved away in a basement. I couldn't turn to Jim to see if he was thinking the same thing. The red light pulsed and then the camera flashed and we were all captured forever.

Chapter Seventeen

In my life I had come to realize that when things were going very well indeed it was just the time to anticipate trouble. And, conversely, I learned from pleasant experience that at the most despairing crisis, when all looked sour beyond words, some delightful "break" was apt to lurk just around the corner.

—Amelia Earhart

I started watching Mom more closely, trying to follow her personal timeline. If I could figure out exactly when Amelia Earhart's final flight would be, maybe I could stop anything bad from happening to Mom.

One afternoon in January, I was helping Teddy make a poster board about Saturn when I heard the faint, crinkling sound of static. For a second, I thought it might be Katy watching television, but then I remembered that she was at Amy White's that afternoon. I tried to ignore it, but it got progressively louder. I wondered where Mom was.

"What's the buzzing?" Teddy asked. He stopped cutting construction-paper stars and looked around.

"I probably left something on in my room," I said. "Keep cutting, okay?"

"Hurry up," he said. "We need a *ton* of stars."

I followed the static upstairs and into Mom and Dad's room, expecting to find Mom in there, but the room was empty. The door to their bathroom was closed. For a second, I remembered when Mom went into labor and there was all that blood on the bathroom floor. My knees felt weak. Pressing my ear against the door, I could barely hear her voice above the static. "Twelve thousand feet and climbing. Weather fair."

I knocked on the door. "Are you okay?"

The static got louder.

"Can you hear me?" I tried the knob but the door was locked. "What are you doing in there?"

More static.

I banged against the door and twisted the knob. "Open the door! I'm going to break it down and call Dad if you don't open it right now."

There was a pause, then the static almost disappeared. Footsteps padded to the door and I heard the lock click, then the footsteps retreated again. When I opened the door, I half expected to find Mom sitting in a pool of blood. Instead, she was sitting fully dressed—scarf, goggles, a tattered leather jacket, all the Amelia gear—in the empty bathtub. On her lap was a metal serving platter, probably something she got as a wedding present years ago. Taped or glued to it were bits of wire, pieces of broken stereo equipment, digital-watch faces, tiny mirrors from compacts, batteries, Dad's old cell phone, a compass, a thermometer, and one of the controls from Teddy's video game system. On the floor beside her was a cup of hot cocoa. The curtains were drawn, but the windows were open. I shivered in a gust of cold wind. On the edge of the tub was an old clock-radio barely emitting a tinny static.

"What are you doing?" I asked.

She didn't look at me. The goggles were pulled down on her face. "One forty-five a.m.," she said. "Radio frequency failing. Weather continues fair."

"What is that?" I reached for the platter on her lap, but she jerked away from me. "Did you make that?"

She still didn't look over. "So many stars."

I leaned against the sink. A cockpit, I realized. She'd made herself a cockpit out of old electronics and whatever she could find around the house. It looked so pathetic, those bits of nothing pieced together. How could she think it was real? How could a few cogs and wires be more real than me? I wanted to snatch it from her and smash it on the bathroom floor, but I was afraid of what her response would be.

Instead, I asked, "Where are you going?"

She inhaled and exhaled loudly. Then she picked up the cell phone and spoke into it as if it were a two-way radio. "Oakland, do you copy? Oakland?"

"The Pacific?" I said. In Mom's mind, I was interrupting Amelia Earhart's solo flight from Honolulu to California, the first time anyone had ever flown that distance alone. Mom would be so happy afterward. But it was just another big step to the final flight, and I wasn't sure how Mom would manage that and if she'd come back at all. I didn't care what Dad or Mrs. Ellis said. Mom was getting worse, not better, and we could lose her if we weren't careful.

"Fog rolling in," she said into the dead cell phone.

I took my own cell phone out of my pocket and, without dialing anyone, pressed it to my ear. "You need to be careful," I said.

"Everything fine. Four hundred gallons of fuel left."

"No," I said. "Listen to me. Don't try any more long flights. Just land and make this the last one."

She leaned over and turned up the volume on the radio.

"Please," I said. "We need you."

In the tub, she was motionless, staring straight ahead as if into a perfect sky of stars. I waited for a minute to see if she'd react to me at all, but she didn't. Instead, I heard Teddy calling for me from downstairs. I didn't want him to see Mom like this. Putting my phone back in my pocket, I yelled to Teddy that I'd be down in a second.

As I was leaving the bathroom, I heard Mom say, "I am getting tired of this fog." And she was off again, trying to make contact with flying experts who died decades ago. I could hear her going on about how the stars were so bright, how it felt to be all alone, so high above the ocean, and how everyone else in the world was just voices in the distance. I wondered if we were that to her now—a bunch of voices trying to bring her back to earth.

Now at lunch, Jim and I sat with his friends. It felt different from the night of the Christmas party, when all I had to know were answers to Never Have I Ever. They were nice enough and every so often asked me a question, but I didn't feel like a real part of their group yet. I was usually quiet as they talked about people I didn't really know and classes I wasn't taking. Most of them had applied to college and were waiting to hear back. In six months, all of Jim's friends would probably be gone, or at least not at school anymore, and he'd still be here.

My friends, on the other hand, would still be around. One day in late January, I ran into Theresa in the tray return line.

"Hey," she said, eyes focused on the conveyer belt.

At first I wasn't sure if she was talking to me—we hadn't spoken at all during winter break—so it took me a moment to respond. "Hey."

"So I hear you're in driver's ed again. I guess you passed that test."

"I did." I didn't know what she wanted. And after she'd been so bitchy to me in the girls' room, I wasn't sure I wanted to pretend that everything was normal again.

"That's good; at least you don't have an F on your transcript now." I slid my tray on the belt and she did the same; the trays rode into the kitchen together. When I started to walk away, she followed, saying, "Did Jim help you study?"

I didn't look at her. "Yeah, he's been awesome about that. Otherwise I probably still wouldn't be able to go forward or backward." I headed through the exit, into the hall. Theresa was still walking with me.

"You sit with them every day now," she said. Her voice was quieter than usual; I could barely hear what she was saying over the din of the hallways. "His friends. The seniors." When I didn't reply, she rolled her eyes. "Apparently Jim's too cool to sit with the loser juniors and you got cool enough to sit with his friends."

"It's not even like that." I stopped at my locker even though I didn't need to get anything before class. "I met them at a Christmas party, so now I know them."

"We invited Jim to meet us, too. Way back around Halloween." On Theresa's other side, Edward Baker and his freshman girlfriend started to make out against the lockers. "Take it somewhere else, will you?" Theresa snapped at them, and turned back to me. "You know, Jim didn't even know who you were until last semester. And I bet for a while most of his friends thought you were that girl who fucked up the football field."

I was just getting over that. "Stop being such a bitch," I said.

Her laugh was almost a snort. "I'm a bitch? I was the one who stood up for you when you were, like, the worst driver ever.

You're the one who ditched your friends for some guy. And I'm supposed to be your best friend, and you don't even talk to me about it."

When I glanced over at Theresa, her chin was crinkling and her eyes were tinged with red. I'd never seen her cry before, and for a second, I thought she would start right there in the hallway. But then the first bell rang and she rushed away, dodging into a classroom before I could think of what to say.

For a moment, I rested my head against my locker door, wishing I could cram myself inside and hide there forever. I stayed there until the second bell rang and I had to run to my next class.

Everyone else had passed driver's ed. My new classmates knew that. They were mostly sophomores who had just turned sixteen and gotten their learner's permit, and they looked at me like I was the biggest loser ever to enter the driver's ed car. But Mr. Kane smiled at me placidly and asked me to go first.

"We're starting over," he told me when I slid into the driver's seat. "No pressure at all. Just take it slow."

Even though he sounded encouraging, I knew he was worried I'd mess up again, which got me worried, too. I took deep breaths and tried to hear Jim's voice in my head.

Mr. Kane asked me to drive across the parking lot, where he'd set up a series of cones. Whenever I did something small—like turn the key or check the mirror—he pointed it out to the other students in the backseat. "See how Alex adjusted the seat? You need to be at the right distance from the pedals and the wheel." It felt a little patronizing. I pressed the gas gently so the car rolled forward. After a second, I realized I wasn't breathing and had to practically gasp for air.

"It's all right," Mr. Kane said. "You're doing fine."

I kept my eye on a patch of ice in the corner of the parking lot, almost hitting a cone when I made a wide turn to avoid it. Aside from that, I managed the course without destroying anything. Mr. Kane was ecstatic.

"Wonderful!" He turned to everyone in the backseat. "Who else wants to try?"

Mindy Johansson volunteered, and we switched places. I squeezed in the back between a JV football player and a blond sophomore girl whose named I'd already forgotten. Neither of them glanced at me. I tried to concentrate on Mr. Kane's voice as he guided Mindy through the course. I pretended it was last semester, and he was talking to Caroline Lavale. Instead of the blond sophomore girl, I imagined I was sitting next to Theresa, who would whisper sarcastic comments to me all class.

In early February, Mom was planning her flight from L.A. to Mexico City. Whenever I sat with her late at night, she'd be pouring over dozens of maps—really high-quality ones, too, with aeronautical symbols and notations I couldn't recognize. Dad had caught her ordering them online. He saw it as a good sign that she was using the computer—something Amelia Earhart couldn't have done—but I thought she was taking bolder strides away from us. The maps covered the table, the counters, half the floor space, and most of the walls. She'd get so close to them that she practically brushed her nose against the paper and would write notes to herself. But she didn't seem as happy with it anymore. I remembered a few months ago, when she wanted to show off her maps. Now she would mutter to herself, "Doesn't look right," and "Not that path." Sometimes she didn't even notice when I sat at the table with her.

One night I didn't hear anything from the kitchen, so I crept downstairs to check on Mom, hoping she was engrossed in her work. But even though her notes and maps were on the table, she wasn't standing over them. I padded softly into the living room, whispering, "Mom?" and hoping she'd suddenly appear. Nothing.

It was suddenly hard to stand and breathe all at once. How could I have lost her? She wasn't planning her final flight yet. I thought we still had time.

I was about to run upstairs and wake Dad when I heard the distant sound of metal against metal. I rushed outside to find Mom standing in the driveway, regarding the car engine thoughtfully, a mismatch of tools on the pavement beside her. It was freezing out, but she wasn't wearing a coat.

No one else was on the street. Windows of neighboring houses were dark. Maybe I could get her inside before anything happened.

"It's three in the morning," I hissed. "What are you doing?"

She reached down for a wrench. "I need to make some adjustments. I'll never make the record without my plane in top shape. Need to make sure it's ready for Mexico and New Jersey."

"Don't," I said, rushing over and grabbing the wrench. "Do not touch the car."

"I'm doing just fine on my own, thank you." She tugged back, pulling the wrench out of my hands and going back to whatever kind of work she thought she was doing. Before I could stop her, she pulled at one of the tubes and it came off, spilling greenish liquid.

We both screamed and jumped back from the car.

A light came on in Mom and Dad's room. Another window illuminated across the street. I wondered if I could drag Mom back inside before anyone noticed.

Mom was too busy frowning at the car to notice that we'd probably woken up half the neighborhood. "It wasn't supposed to do that."

"You think?" I said.

Dad appeared in the driveway, dressed in pajama bottoms and a backward T-shirt. Suddenly I felt guilty, as if he caught us trying to set the car on fire. "I found her like this," I said.

"I'm doing the best I can," Mom told Dad. The lines of her face hardened and her hands were shaking. "You know how these models are."

I thought Dad might put his arm around Mom and appease her, but he sighed and shook his head at his bare feet. "It's three in the morning. I don't care who you are; it's not the right time to be messing with machinery."

"Gip, I—"

"I don't want to hear it. You shouldn't be out here on your own in the middle of the night anyway. And then to start playing around with the car—what were you thinking? Do you want to get hurt?"

Mom's hands clenched. "I know what I'm doing."

"You don't." Dad was almost shouting now. "You really don't. You want to make notes on maps, write letters to no one, that's fine, go ahead. But this could get you killed, do you realize that?"

"I'm trying very hard." Mom's voice cracked. "We need to get ready for this flight. I want everything perfect and so do you."

"You're not listening to me. Listen to me!" he said. For a second, I thought he might grab her and shake her.

Then I saw something else: across the street, a man stood in his doorway. It was our neighbor, Mr. Daniels. He was wrapped in a plaid bathrobe and staring at us. I nudged Dad and motioned to Mr. Daniels. Dad waved, trying to smile.

"Everything all right over there?" Mr. Daniels shouted.

"Yep," Dad said. "Just a little car trouble. Have a good night!"

Mr. Daniels hesitated, then waved and went back inside. We waited for a minute, staring at his front door to see if it would open again but it didn't.

Dad stooped to pick up the tools. He held them close to his chest the way he would hold a small child. "Come on. We can talk more about this tomorrow." He started for the house, not turning to see if we would follow. For a moment, Mom stared at his back, looking like she might either scream or cry.

"I told him I would leave if I had to," she whispered.

I wasn't sure if she meant for me to hear that. "He's tired," I said. "You don't have to leave anyone. I'll work on repairs tomorrow. Everything will be fine for Mexico."

She smiled at me wearily and started toward the house without responding. At the door, Dad called for me to come inside. I slammed the hood of the car down and rushed after them. Even if Mom went to sleep now, I was sure I'd be listening for her footsteps for the rest of the night.

After that, Dad was adamant about making sure she didn't leave the house alone. He told her that he didn't want her going outside because of reporters. I thought she'd argue, but she nodded conspiratorially. "Can't take any chances," she said, "not with a flight like this."

"What do you mean?" I asked. "What kind of flight?"

But she shook her head, lips pressed together. "Nope. Can't breathe a word. Not even to you."

I kept trying, though. I'd join her in the middle of the night as she spread charts out across the kitchen floor and tried dismantling various appliances. In the morning I'd be exhausted, but it was better than lying in bed, imagining the ways she could leave us. But mostly she worked without talking. She used to tell me everything about being Amelia—the flights, the tours, the people she met. Now she was more serious.

Once I came downstairs and found her sitting very still at the kitchen table. At first I thought she might just be pausing before scribbling notes on one of her maps, but then she took a deep, choked breath and I realized she was crying.

When she saw me, she wiped her face with the back of her hand. "Hello," she said. "Didn't know anyone else was up."

"Are you okay?" I asked. What did Amelia Earhart have to cry about? Maybe she was back to being Mom again and we didn't have to worry anymore.

"Of course. Just working on these plans." She picked up a pencil and pressed the tip against paper but didn't write anything. "It's a long one. We have so much to work out before it happens. It's more—" Her voice cracked, but she pretended it was a cough. "It's more than I would have thought. . . ."

I sat at the table beside her. "You don't have to," I said. "Just don't go."

"Everyone is expecting—"

"Screw everyone," I said. "Stay here."

She shook her head. "That's not how it works."

"It works any way you want it to."

Mom finally looked up at me, her eyes red and shining with tears. But instead of crying, she took a deep breath and smiled at me. "It's fine. It's going to be fine. It's the last flight, I promise, and then I can rest. Now, are you here to help?" She handed me a chart, which I couldn't read, and busied herself with planning her final flight.

"You kids all right?"

Mrs. Wiley peered into the living room, half her body hidden by the door. Jim and I were curled up on the couch in front of a really bad sci-fi movie. We'd missed most of the plot since we started making out during the opening credits, snapping apart when we heard footsteps approaching.

"We're fine, Mom," Jim said.

She stepped into the room. "Hungry? Alex, have you had dinner yet?"

"I'm good," I said. "We had pizza at home." It was frozen pizza, of course, that I popped in while making sure Mom didn't try to get outside and work on the car again. I wondered what the Wileys had for dinner. Mrs. Wiley seemed like the kind of person who roasted chicken and made sure meals included vegetables.

"Thirsty?" she asked. "We've got water, juice—"

"Mom," Jim said. "We know where the kitchen is. I'm not letting Alex starve."

"All right, I can take a hint. Alex, make sure to help yourself if you need anything." She glanced at the TV, where a giant crocodile-shark hybrid was eating a team of scuba divers. "Do you really enjoy this?"

"Yeah, it's my favorite movie ever," Jim said. "We really don't want to miss this, so . . ."

Mrs. Wiley rolled her eyes and disappeared back into the hallway, leaving the door open behind her.

Jim peeked over the edge of the couch to make sure his Mom was walking down the hall. When he was sure she was gone, he settled back down. "Sorry about that. She likes hovering."

"I mean, you are alone on a couch with me, watching a really bad movie." On-screen, the crocodile-shark was now walking around a beach. "I think she can put two and two together."

"What do you mean?" Jim laughed. "I'm totally into *Croc-Shark*. I had no other motive when I asked you over to watch a movie."

"I bet." I leaned my head against Jim's shoulder, and he put his arm around mine. Hanging out with a cute guy and not really watching a lame movie—it felt so normal. It was like slipping on a costume of a totally regular girl who didn't have any secrets at home.

A helicopter was trying to take down croc-shark. "This has got to be the worst movie ever," I said over a yawn.

Jim nudged me. "You can't be bored during the helicopter fight scene. Look at the computer animation on that croc-shark."

"Masterful," I said, and yawned again. "Sorry, I got the worst sleep last night. It just hit me all of a sudden." It wasn't just last night, of course. Waking up to sit with Mom was starting to wear on me. I'd started using my free periods to nap in a corner of the library. A few times I nodded off during class and was jerked awake by the sound of a teacher snapping at me.

Jim pulled me in a little closer. "It's okay. We can just hang out."

"Make sure to tell me about croc-shark if I miss anything."

"You got it." He kissed the top of my head, and I could have melted right into his lap. I wanted to ask him how he knew what to do to make me feel better, even when things were so messed up, but my breathing was heavy and my eyes couldn't stay open. I fell asleep on Jim's shoulder, and when I woke up, he drove me home.

CHAPTER EIGHTEEN

In the air, as with automobiles, many accidents are due to
the human equation.

—Amelia Earhart

For Valentine's Day, the student council sold carnations to raise money. You could buy a carnation—pink, white, or red—for a dollar, and the student council kids would deliver it to whomever you wanted, which meant that a lot of the girls with perfect hair and polo sweaters walked around with armfuls of flowers all day. I always hoped that one of them would be stricken with a terrible carnation allergy and swell to three times her original size. Usually my friends and I didn't waste money on school stuff, so I was surprised when one of the student council reps handed me a pink carnation.

"You sure you have the right person?" I said.

"You're Alex Winchester, right? Check the tag."

Sure enough, it was my name. I made my way through the crowds to Jim's locker and held up the flower for him.

"Happy Valentine's Day," he said, as if he'd been caught without a hall pass.

"Thanks," I said. "It was really sweet. I've never gotten one of these before. Which, saying it out loud, makes me sound like an enormous loser, so maybe we can just forget that part."

He shoved his hands in his pockets and looked at his sneakers. "The carnation table was right there and I had exact change with me and everything. And since I guess we're kind of together and all—"

"Are we?" I said. "Together? Officially?"

"You're the only person I'm helping to drive, so I think so." He glanced up at me.

"Good," I said. "I was kind of thinking that, too. I mean, as long as you're not giving anybody else driving lessons."

"Well, nobody does a three-point turn like you." He laughed. "And that sounds like some really weird innuendo."

"So . . . I guess we're together." Since Mr. Wiley had dropped the boyfriend bomb and since I'd been sitting at Jim's lunch table, this conversation wasn't exactly out of the blue. And I really liked being with Jim. Not just because he was an amazing kisser, either. He made me laugh and didn't get frustrated with me when I avoided parallel parking. So far, he was the one thing about my junior year that didn't suck. I'd just have to make sure that he never came over. Most boyfriends didn't want to meet their girlfriend's parents anyway—I thought Jim should consider this a blessing. As long as he stayed out of my house, why couldn't we date?

"I didn't get you anything," I admitted. "For Valentine's Day. I didn't know—"

He shook his head. "No, it's fine. The carnation was everything I had planned. Unless you want to have pizza and watch a movie or something later."

"At your house?"

"Sure," he said. "My parents are probably going out to dinner, so they won't be around for a couple hours."

"Subtle hint," I said, tapping his arm with the carnation. Jim and I hadn't had actual sex yet, but were getting close. Being around Jim made me feel comfortable and excited all at once. But it was my first real relationship, and I was worried about getting so serious. If anything went wrong, I wasn't sure I could handle losing Jim in addition to all the other crap I'd been dealing with this year.

The bell shrilled. "That's Spanish for me. Can I give you a call after school? I've got to babysit my brother until my dad gets home from work."

He agreed. I wasn't sure how to leave now that we were actually dating, but Jim leaned over and kissed me. One of the teachers walking by told us to break it up, so it was a quick kiss, but I felt my cheeks get pink and my head get light. Trying not to giggle like an idiot, I wondered what the Spanish word for carnation was.

Mom and Dad didn't really do anything for Valentine's Day. Dad had left a card for Mom on the table in the morning, which Katy thought was a good sign, but Mom didn't seem to acknowledge the day at all. Teddy brought home a paper bag filled with store-bought valentines and candy, but Mom didn't say anything except that the other kids in his class must have thought very well of him.

Katy teased me about the carnation but seemed fascinated by the idea of a real boyfriend. "He's cute," she said. "Are you going to bring him over?"

"Yeah, right," I said. I was in the midst of trying on and rejecting different sweaters for going over to Jim's. "We'd have to hide Mom in the attic like Mr. Rochester's wife."

By the time I had a new outfit selected, Dad was already home and making dinner, more than the usual frozen pizza or waffles. It was some kind of pasta dish from an actual cookbook and required actual cutting and measuring of ingredients. He was even going to make brownies with Teddy; the carton of eggs and box of brownie mix were already on the counter.

"Not too shabby," I told Dad, surveying the kitchen, which was a mess of chopped vegetables and empty plastic bags. "It actually smells like food."

"Exactly what I was going for," he said.

I snagged a stray mushroom. "I'm going over to Jim's for a little while."

Dad wiped his hands on a dish towel. "Are his parents going to be around?"

"Yeah, I think so," I said.

Mom strode into the kitchen with an armload of papers and sniffed the air. "That smells delightful."

Dad grabbed a ladle and stuck it in the pot. "Try it for me, will you?"

"I'm not sure I have time—"

"One bite?" he said, pouring sauce into a mug. "I think I should add some more oregano—give it a try for me, please?"

She breathed in and out, then nodded. "All right." She sat stiffly at the table as Dad set the mug and a spoon in front of her. Smiling without showing her teeth, she dipped the spoon into the mug and lifted a tiny amount of sauce to her lips. Another deep breath. After a second, she swallowed.

"It's my mom's recipe," Dad said. His voice was a little softer. "Remember? I used to make it all the time, the first year we were married."

I thought of Mom and Dad, not a lot older than I was, setting up their first apartment and not even knowing that any of this would happen. I thought of them in their wedding picture, which was still missing.

"One time you added a tablespoon of hot pepper instead of a teaspoon," Dad was saying, crouching beside her. "We could barely eat it. Remember?"

Mom wouldn't look at him. She took another bite.

"And you always made that chicken dish, with the cream of mushroom soup, and you could always get the butcher to give you a deal. So we ate that a lot because it ended up being so cheap." He sounded so hopeful.

Mom set the spoon down. "It's a lovely sauce," she said, her voice a little shaky.

"You think?"

"Yes." She folded her hands over her lap. "Where did you pick it up, George?"

At the sound of that name, he stood and marched to the counter, leaning against it like a boxer leaning against the ropes. For a second, everything was quiet. Then he grabbed an egg from the carton and hurled it against the wall.

"Goddammit!" he said. "Goddammit!"

The eggshell lay, split and oozing, on the tiles. The wall was splattered with yellow from where the yolk had exploded. At the kitchen table, Mom had started to cry, very quietly and almost imperceptibly. It wasn't like the other times she'd gotten upset, the frantic cries and frustrated shouts. Her fingers uncurled themselves from around one another, and she grasped her papers but didn't move from the table. Dad took a few deep breaths, then tore a few paper towels off the roll and began to clean up his mess.

I stepped noiselessly to the door and left before either of them noticed I was gone.

By the time I got to Jim's, his parents were already gone. "I was just going to text you," he said, letting me in. "I thought you weren't coming or something."

I took off my coat and hugged it against my chest. "Sorry, my parents were having a thing. And I walked."

"I could have driven you." He pulled the coat out of my arms. "Cold?"

I was shaking but hadn't realized until Jim mentioned it. "Oh, yeah. You know, winter." A lump was forming in my throat. I was desperate to not cry in front of Jim. Not after he bought me a carnation and invited me over when his parents were out of the house.

Jim rubbed his hands quickly over my arms and back. "Let's get you warmed up."

I followed him into the basement. We started kissing before we were even halfway down the stairs, then fell onto the couch together. Every part of me he kissed felt warmer—the tops of my ears, nook of my collarbone, my bottom lip—like they were slowly starting to glow. All I wanted was to forget everything except Jim and this feeling. Nothing else existed but us and how perfect we felt together. Zippers were unzipped, clothing disappeared, and I was on top of him.

"Are we?" I managed to ask.

He stopped kissing me. "Are we?"

"Maybe?" I pulled away a little. "I mean, I haven't. Do you have, you know, something?"

"In my room. One second." He kissed me hard and then bolted up the stairs. I could hear his footsteps above, moving into his room.

Suddenly it was cold again. I grabbed a fleece blanket and

wrapped it around my shoulders. The door to Jim's art room was open, so I peeked in. He was working on a new series of what looked like portraits of people, but everyone looked almost like they were underwater—hair bled into the background; eyes were glossy; colors ran together. It was ethereal. I didn't recognize any of the faces until I saw one in the corner that could have been me. Her eyes were almost closed, and her hair was dark purple and floated around her. She was separate, peaceful.

I heard Jim hurry down the stairs, and a second later, he appeared in the doorway. "Sorry about that."

"Don't be sorry," I said. I wanted to ask him how he made me feel calm and excited all at once. How he got me so well. How he made me forget about everything else. Instead, I said, "Your new paintings are so good. How are you so good?"

He smiled. "I'm good at other things."

"I bet." I laughed. He moved closer, and I wrapped the blanket around both of us. Maybe it was fast, maybe not. But for a little while, I was warm and happy. I wasn't shaking anymore.

At home that night, I lay in bed with my cell phone clutched to my chest. A couple of times I pulled up Theresa's number from my contacts list and held my thumb above the call button and rehearsed what I wanted to say in my head. *I just had sex with Jim Wiley—yes, the Jim Wiley. It was nice and kind of what you think it's going to be and not at all what you think it's going to be. He was nice during and afterward and I don't think anything's going to change except that everything's changed, right? I'm different now except I don't feel all that different, but I am, and I'm holding it all inside and I want to tell you.*

Except Theresa and I weren't exactly talking, so I couldn't tell her.

"Hey." On the other side of the room, Katy was huddled under her comforter. I had thought she was asleep, but I turned to see her staring at me. "What's the matter?"

"Nothing. I'm fine. Go back to sleep."

She sat up. "You keep typing and looking at your phone and not doing anything, and you look like something's up."

In her pajamas and her hair half a mess, she looked younger than thirteen. But I felt like it would burst out of me if I didn't tell anyone. "Can you keep a secret?" I asked, and we both laughed a little. "Seriously, you can't tell anyone."

She nodded solemnly.

"I had sex tonight." It felt strange to say the words, and for a moment, they hung between us.

"With Jim?" she asked.

"No, with Brad Pitt. Of course with Jim."

Katy shifted under her comforter. "Was he nice?" I assured her that he was nice. "Were you safe?" Yes, we were very safe. My sister stared at me for a moment as if she were working out a math problem in her head. "What's it like?"

"It's nice," I said. "It's like running and laughing, and like when you look at someone and you know you're both thinking the same thing. I don't know. It's hard to explain." I frowned. "Maybe I shouldn't have told you."

"No, I'm glad you did," Katy said, but suddenly she seemed smaller and farther away. "Just be careful, okay?"

I promised I'd be careful. "Sorry, you can go to sleep now." Katy nodded and rolled over. For a moment, I watched her body rise and fall with each breath, but she was clutching the comforter so tightly that I was sure she wasn't asleep yet. On my phone, I tapped out a text to Theresa—*hey can we talk?*— but immediately deleted it. I set my phone aside and joined my sister in mock sleep.

"If you could be anyone else, who would it be?"

Even though Dad assured me Mom wasn't leaving the house anymore, I still woke up most nights and spent a few hours with her at the kitchen table. They hadn't spoken a lot since Valentine's Day. Dad was unusually stoic and Mom was on edge, saying she just needed to complete this last flight and everything would be fine. So I figured it couldn't hurt to look after her in case she decided that George Putnam didn't know what he was talking about. A few times, I almost told her about having sex with Jim; since she wasn't acting like Mom, she wouldn't have been upset with me. Maybe she would have asked how I felt about it and him.

Mom was sifting through papers on the kitchen table. She claimed to be filling out new forms for landing visas. "With the new route, we need to completely reapply for all clearance. Such a waste of time when there are so many other things to be doing." When I repeated my question, she scribbled something on a piece of paper and said, "I'm happy with who I am."

Yeah, right, I thought. "It's a game. Just pick someone. Anyone. Real, imaginary, I don't care."

"Wilbur Wright," she said, not looking up from her notes.

I frowned. "Wilbur Wright? Why not Orville?"

"Orville, Wilbur, it doesn't matter."

"Just because they could fly?" I stood up from the table and got myself a glass of water. "You have such a one-track mind."

"They didn't just *fly*," she said. "They were the first people to fly. They went up in the air before anyone else. For a little while, they were the only ones who knew what that felt like. Nowadays all it takes to go up in a plane is a trip to the county fair. But back then they had something special, didn't they? They'd accomplished something great, and it was something no one else had ever even felt before."

Her face was so blissful, it was hard to get mad at her. She set down her pencil. "What about you?"

I sighed. "Me? Oh, I'd be you." I gulped water before I could say anything else, and she returned her attention to her so-called visas.

When I put my glass in the sink, I saw something outside — snow. It was drifting through the air and settling on the lawn. There was already enough for white clumps to have gathered among the grass. Even though it was a cold winter, we hadn't gotten snow all year. For a second, everything was soft and quiet. I remembered when we were little and there was a snowstorm one year, a shocking three feet of snow. School was canceled, but Mom woke us early anyway and told us to get our coats on so we could build a snowman. Having grown up in Florida, Mom loved the first snow. We spent the morning putting together a pathetic snowman—Teddy, at two, kept trying to knock him over—and then had a snowball fight, shrieking whenever any of us were hit. Afterward, when we were sufficiently rosy and exhausted, Mom made us hot chocolate and put on Disney movies. This was before she tried getting pregnant again, before she stayed in bed for a month, before the idea that she was Amelia Earhart had even occurred to her.

Mom had noticed, too. She walked away from the table and stood at the window, arms crossed in front of her like she was cold. Her face was illuminated by the snow. "It's beautiful," she said, then looked at me and smiled. "Isn't it?"

I smiled back. "Want to go for a ride?"

I knew it was stupid while I was doing it, but everything was so lovely outside that I didn't care much. With the snow floating silently to the ground and the rest of the neighborhood dark, it didn't feel real at all. It was more like a dream, and in a dream, why couldn't Mom and I go for a drive through the snow?

The keys were kept in a cupboard, behind the cereal bowls, in case Mom ever tried to drive on her own. Upstairs, Dad would be fast asleep. He'd never have to know.

Mom and I put our coats on over our pajamas. When the first gush of cold air hit us, we shivered. She looked up at the sky, thick with gray clouds. "Are you sure this is good flying weather?"

"Sure it is," I said. "High air pressure."

Satisfied, she nodded and climbed into the passenger seat. It was the first time I'd been in a car without Jim or Mr. Kane or even Dad. Mom hadn't taken me out for driving lessons before she went crazy because she claimed we'd end up fighting, which was probably true. There was a light dusting of snow on the windshield, so for a second, it was like being in a cave. I flipped the wipers to brush it away. Unlike getting caught in the rain with Jim, I wasn't afraid. I knew where all the buttons and knobs were and how everything worked. And everything felt so dreamlike, it would have been stupid to be afraid. Of course I could drive. Of course my mother was Amelia Earhart. Of course we were going for a drive in the snow.

"Where are we headed?" she asked, clicking her seat belt in place.

We rolled down the driveway, and I took a left for no reason at all. "Newfoundland," I said.

Her face brightened. "Oh! That was our starting point for the Friendship flight. Have I told you about that one?"

"Once or twice," I said. "But why don't you tell it anyway?"

She did, from the beginning, about how Captain Hilton Railey called her, asking, *Would you like to fly the Atlantic?* How excited she'd been but how she calmly asked for details about the flight. How the project coordinators—George Putnam included—thought she had the right look for it. How Railey was the first person to call her Lady Lindy. How she hadn't really piloted anything aboard the Friendship—she might as well have been a sack of potatoes—but it was about the opportunity. She'd become the first woman to cross the Atlantic, and look at all that happened as a consequence.

I only heard about every other word. I knew the story already, and I had to focus on the road, which was slowly being obscured by a layer of snow. But more than that, I didn't want to be distracted from the moment. We were the only ones awake, it seemed. Ours was the first car to drive through the snow. The snow falling looked like tiny, frozen stars. Maybe this was what flying looked like, I thought. All those stars, all that solitude.

"It's a lovely night," Mom said suddenly.

"Yeah," I said, not turning my head to catch her expression. "We haven't gotten much snow this year."

She pressed her palm to the window. "I never mind the cold. Usually on flights, I drink hot chocolate to keep warm and awake." For a minute, she was quiet, and then she gave my shoulder a squeeze, saying, "You're a solid pilot. You know that? Even in foul weather."

At first I thought it was a part of her delusion. I was just some other Ninety-Nine, the daring girl pilot of her mind who would win races and fly impossible distances. But then I glimpsed her out of the corner of my eye—she was looking at me so solidly, so tenderly, I wondered if she was thinking of me as something more. Maybe somewhere in her brain, she recognized me. Me, Alex Winchester, her daughter, who fought with her constantly and barely passed driver's ed and was a general disappointment. Maybe she was actually talking to me, and this was the only way she knew how to say it.

"Thanks," I said, blinking at the windshield. "I've been practicing."

A gust of cold air filled the car. Mom was rolling down her window. I opened my mouth to ask what she was doing, but then I saw her stick her hand out the window, feeling the air rush against it. Instead of asking her what she was doing or complaining about the cold, I rolled down my window and stuck my hand out, too. It was the first time I'd allowed myself to take a hand off the wheel. For some reason, Mom and I both started giggling. Our laughter and the wind were the only sounds we heard. I reached out as far as I could, trying to catch snowflakes in my palm. It seemed like a better idea to go faster—more snow, more wind. My foot pressed against the gas pedal and soon we were soaring down the street. People in their houses were fast asleep while we were zipping through the snow, laughing all the way. It was our own secret.

Until the car hit a patch of black ice.

The world spun around us. I wanted to scream, but the sound died in my throat. I didn't know what to do; I'd never learned how to handle ice; I wasn't even supposed to be driving, really. So I did the only thing my body could do at the moment—slam my foot against the brake. It didn't matter much. There was a sudden hit and pop, and the car stopped.

For a minute, I didn't move, in case I'd died and didn't know it yet. Then I felt my entire body start to shake, and I knew I couldn't be dead.

"What . . . what happen—?" I tried to say, but once I could form syllables, my throat swelled and I started to cry.

Mom unbuckled herself and slid her arm around my shoulders. "It's all right," she said calmly. "Deep breaths. No one was injured, and that's the most important thing, right?"

I choked back a sob and nodded. Mom's voice was so steady that for a moment, I believed she was going to handle this for me. She'd pull it together and help me deal with whoever owned the mailbox I'd just smashed. She'd act like my mom instead of a famous historical figure.

"And it doesn't seem like the vehicle took much damage, either. With a little maintenance, it'll be up and flying again soon."

"Driving!" I looked at her like she'd betrayed me, so she backed off a little. "It's a car, not a fucking plane."

"I was just trying—"

"Well, don't." It didn't feel dreamlike anymore. It was cold, and hot tears were blurring my vision, and the car was half on someone's lawn. I didn't recognize the house—a blue split-level. Wiping my face with the back of my hand, I stumbled out of the car to assess the damage. One tire completely blown out, a dented bumper, and someone's totally demolished mailbox. (A mailbox in the shape of a cow. Perfect.)

I kicked the deflated tire. Of course I didn't remember how to change it. "Dammit."

Mom had gotten out of the car as well. "It's not so bad," she insisted.

I didn't answer her, just shook my head and sniffled. A few yards away, lights flicked on in the blue house.

"I guess I'll have to call Dad," I said, even though I didn't want to think about what would happen when I did. I'd have to explain why I was out with Mom in the middle of the night. Why I was driving without actually having a license. Why I was driving in the snow. Why I'd crashed. Why it had all seemed so nice until I lost control of the car. Hugging myself on some stranger's front lawn, I wished I could be anywhere but there. I would rather have been miles under the Pacific Ocean, in the cockpit of a plane, never to be seen again.

Chapter Nineteen

Not much more than a month ago I was on the other shore
of the Pacific, looking westward. This evening, I looked
eastward over the Pacific. In those fast-moving days which
have intervened, the whole width of the world has passed
behind us — except this broad ocean. I shall be glad when we
have the hazards of its navigation behind us.

—Amelia Earhart, several days before
she left for Howland Island and disappeared

I'd never seen Dad so upset. He couldn't even talk—just kept shaking his head like he had to jostle the information around for a little while. He apologized to the owners of the mailbox, but with me, it was like he had to struggle to get any sound out. And it wasn't only outside, with the smashed mailbox and banged-up car, either. For a few days after, it was like he tried not to look at me, his eyes glazing over whenever I was in the room. At first I would try to make insignificant conversation—"Weather's better today"; "We need more cereal"—but his responses were so brief that after a while I stopped.

He did speak enough to mention that I was grounded for a couple of weeks, and, when I wasn't at school, I had to call him every hour to let him know I wasn't destroying the neighborhood. I also wasn't allowed to see Jim outside of school, not even for driving lessons. Whenever I said I needed to practice, Dad said he'd take me out instead. But we never got near the car.

Things were tense between Mom and Dad, too. They were arguing a lot more: Mom would blame Dad for not paying enough attention to her flight plans. "I can't do it all myself," she'd say, and shove charts at him. Usually Dad was calm as he explained that he wasn't George Putnam and they weren't planning anything, but now he'd snap a response, and soon they'd be yelling at each other behind their bedroom door.

A little part of me thought that maybe it was a good thing—that Mom was working out whatever issues she had—but I didn't get my hopes up. Once I warned her that if she tried to fly around the world, she wouldn't make it home, but she waved me away, claiming I was unnecessarily nervous and that she was taking the proper precautions. I argued that it wasn't about proper precautions, that it was going to happen, that it had already happened. She started muttering to herself about heading west instead of east, wondering if the weather patterns would be more favorable that way.

No one else seemed worried about her disappearing. Dad looked distracted all the time, and not only because he was upset with me. I would have asked him, but no one was talking about anything. We were all standing still, waiting for things to get worse.

In bed, I would listen for Mom downstairs. More specifically, for the sound of the door opening. For Mom trying to make her exit and vanish forever. Eventually I would fall asleep listening to the sound of maps crinkling and her footsteps on the kitchen floor.

About a week after the accident, Theresa came up to me before homeroom. Since she'd accused me of ditching my friends for Jim, we hadn't really spoken. Instead of switching off between lunch with them and lunch with Jim's friends, now I sat with the seniors. So I was surprised when I heard her say, "I was at the dentist yesterday."

I took a random book from my locker. "Okay?"

"Your mom works for Dr. Forrester, right?

"Um, right." I paged through the book, like I was trying to find something specific. "Not every day, though."

She leaned against someone's locker. "Well, I asked if your mom was there, because I was your friend from school, and they said she'd taken some time off because she wasn't feeling well."

I tried to focus on page 320 of my calc book. Even though I didn't look up, I knew Theresa's eyes were on me.

"Alex," she said, "what's going on?"

"Nothing," I said. "Did you get this equation at all?"

She took the book from me. "Alex, you've been acting

really weird all semester, and if it's because of something with your mom, you can tell me. I mean, if she's really sick, that's serious and you should talk about it."

It was the perfect intro. She sounded genuine, and maybe it would make her understand why I'd avoided her and everyone else for the last few months. I could have told her about how I wanted everyone—my friends, my family, Jim, his friends—in their own little bubbles, far apart so no one else could get hurt. We could have skipped homeroom and our first classes—English lit for her, calc for me—and gone to the bagel shop on Archer to talk about how messed up this year had been. She could have told me how much it sucked and how she knew somebody else whose mom was depressed or whose Dad had shot himself or whose sister had schizophrenia. I could have told her about the It Could Be Worse game. We could have laughed about something.

But I couldn't make the words form in my mouth. If I said it, it would be real. It would be out there, and maybe Theresa would ask questions about it that I didn't want to answer. Maybe she'd bring it up at lunch with Josh and Maddie, and then they'd know. And maybe everyone would find out. And even if they kept it a secret, maybe Theresa, Josh, and Maddie would want to come over, saying it wasn't such a big deal, and what if they did something to upset Mom? What if it sped up her final flight plans?

"My mom, um, just gets these migraines," I said. "Like,

she stays in the dark and can't have any noise. She's trying different medications for it."

When I looked up, Theresa was staring at me. "Really?"

I pulled my book out of her hands. "Really. I've had to take over some stuff at home. It's not a huge thing."

The bell rang before she could reply, and we filed into homeroom. Behind us was Nick Gillan. "Hey, Winchester," he said, snickering, "I heard you demolished a mailbox. You must be the dumbest fucking driver ever."

I cringed. We didn't exactly live in a bustling metropolis, so if someone's mailbox got plowed over in the middle of the night by a teenage girl and her mom, people knew about it.

"Hey, Gillan," Theresa said, not even turning around. "I hear you're the dumbest fucking person in our school."

Our homeroom teacher, Mr. Pianci, looked up from his desk. "Language, people."

"At least I can drive," Nick muttered as we took our seats.

"Yeah," Theresa said, "drunk."

"Whatever. I'm a better drunk driver than she is sober."

I kept my eyes on the blackboard, where Mr. Pianci had already written the date, with huge slashes in between the numbers.

"And look," Nick said. "She knows it. She's got to let *you* fight back."

"Oh, it's not that," Theresa said. "I just love seeing your face scrunch up when I use words with more than two syllables."

"Settle down, people," Mr. Pianci said, and started to read the announcements for the day—there was a girls' basketball game that afternoon, students were reminded not to park in the faculty parking lot, the drama club's performance of *Oliver!* still needed people to help build sets, and so on. I wanted to thank Theresa for sticking up for me, but when the bell rang, she popped up from her seat and left before I had the chance.

That afternoon, Katy and I taught Teddy how to play BS (we refused to play any more Go Fish). He liked it once we convinced him that saying "BS" wasn't swearing. Katy was thrashing both of us.

"Can you, like, see my cards?" I asked, picking up the pile and adding it to my hand. "Because that's cheating."

Katy smirked. "I know what you look like when you lie. Maybe you shouldn't do it so often."

I grabbed a pillow from the couch and whacked her with it. Teddy tried to do the same, but Katy was too fast for him and snatched it away. They were struggling with the pillow when I heard Mom in the kitchen: "Hello? Is Fred there?"

At first I thought Mom was off in her delusions, but after a short pause she said, "No, I need to talk to Fred. Noonan. It's important."

I told Katy and Teddy to play the next hand without me and went to find Mom. Standing over the kitchen table with maps spread out in front of her, she was punching digits into the phone. Then she pressed it to her ear and said, "Fred? Fred, I have to talk to you. . . . You know what it's about."

Fred Noonan was Amelia Earhart's navigator for her final flight and disappeared with her. I grabbed the phone away from Mom.

"Hello? Who is this?" a man was saying into the phone. I didn't know who it was. "There's no Fred here." Instead of replying, I clicked off the phone. I hoped whoever that was didn't call back.

Mom was beside me, hands on her hips and eyes narrowed. "What in the world did you do that for? I need to talk to Fred Noonan about our flight. It's absolutely essential."

"That wasn't Fred," I told her. "That wasn't anyone. You can't call strangers and pretend they're whoever you want them to be."

She grabbed a handful of papers and held them up for me. "How else is this going to get done? Look at how much work we have left!"

"There's no rush—"

"Yes, there is!" she insisted, then slumped into one of the kitchen chairs, touching her fingertips to her forehead. "I can't manage it alone. I need Fred on board for this one. We've already had a false start, and I can't risk that again."

I sat down beside her. "When is it going to happen? When are you leaving?"

She pawed through maps. "We have to finalize the route

and supply lists, make sure the Electra is in shape, get the finances —"

I took her hand in both of mine and stared into her eyes, hoping that a little part of Mom was listening. "Whenever it happens, you have to let me know. Before you leave. I don't care if it's in the middle of the night, but I need to know. I get that you want to keep it all secret, and I promise I won't tell the reporters or whoever. I just want to make sure things are okay. You trust me, right?"

For a moment, she didn't react at all. Then, slowly, she nodded. "You're an excellent pilot."

"And you'll tell me before you go?"

She paused again. "I'll tell you."

"Good." I stood. "Just try to handle things without Fred for now, all right?" I took the phone with me. Maybe if Fred Noonan wasn't available, she'd stay with us a little longer.

I was sitting down with Katy and Teddy again when the doorbell rang. "Got it!" I shouted, in case Mom thought it was Fred coming over to work on the Electra. Assuming it would be Mrs. Ellis, I swung open the door. It wasn't.

It was Jim.

"Hey," he said, smiling.

I stepped onto the front steps and shut the door behind me. "What are you doing here?"

He took a small step back. "Thought I'd stop by and see you."

"I'm grounded," I said. "You know that."

"Yeah, that's why I came over here instead of asking you to go somewhere." He craned his neck to look behind me. "Is your Dad at home or something?"

At the window, Katy and Teddy were spying from behind a curtain. I didn't see Mom anywhere. Why wasn't one of them watching her so she wouldn't open the front door? "Yeah," I said, "that's it. Dad's gonna be really pissed if he catches you here, so you should probably go."

Another backward step. "Okay, I'll go. See you at school, I guess."

"See you." Immediately I was mad at myself for being so short with him, but I also didn't want to say anything else that might make him stick around. I turned to let myself back in the house, but the door was locked. "Dammit. Katy, open up!"

I heard footsteps approach, then a voice: "Is Fred here?"

"Katy!" I banged on the door. My sister opened it a second later, with Mom close behind.

"Take forever, why don't you?" I pushed past her.

"Don't you want to talk to him? I thought Jim was your boy-friend?" Katy asked, peering outside. Jim was standing at the end of the driveway, watching us. I tried to smile at him and waved, and he waved back without smiling.

"Kind of," I said, and shut the door.

I texted Jim later to say I was sorry for brushing him off like that, but he didn't respond. I started typing out a lie about my mom and I having been in a fight and that it was bad timing, but I erased it. It would be too complicated to start making stuff up about what was going on at home. Instead, I decided to just pretend like nothing happened. Jim hadn't asked a lot of questions about my family before, so I didn't think he would now.

The next morning, I found him in one of the stairwells, sitting with a few of the seniors. They were all crowded around Will's cell, watching a video. I walked up to them as they started laughing.

"Oh, my God, his face." Cameron giggled.

"I've watched it like nine times this morning," Will said. "I lose it every time."

Jim had been laughing, but when he looked up at me, his smile faded. "Hey," he said.

"Alex, you need to see this," Jess said, and nudged Will. "Hit play again."

Even though the video was only about a minute long, I didn't really pay attention and only laughed when everyone else did. I noticed that Jim didn't laugh this time, either. We weren't the kind of couple that clung to each other like barnacles, but when I moved next to him, he didn't kiss me or try to hold my hand.

Mr. Hunter entered the stairwell and frowned at us. "Fire hazard, people," he said. "Move along. First bell is—" As if on cue, the bell rang, and Mr. Hunter smirked as he continued up the stairs.

"Mr. Hunter has evil powers," Cameron said as we all grabbed our bags. I followed Jim even though we didn't have homeroom together.

"Hey," I said, "did you get my text?"

He nodded. "Yeah, last night."

I dodged a group of freshmen trying to share homework. "Well, I'm really sorry about being so weird. My parents are just so mad at me right now."

Jim stopped at his locker and turned the knob back and forth. "Sure. Fine."

"So we're okay?"

He shifted through books but didn't take anything. After a second, he turned to me; the lines in his face seemed sharper. "Actually, we're not. At least you don't seem to be that okay with me."

A couple of junior girls slowed as they walked by, so I kept my voice low. "What are you talking about?"

"You've been to my house tons of times," Jim said. "You've seen my art; you came to my family's Christmas party; we always end up there. And for some reason, I haven't been inside your house since that first time we went driving. So if you're, like, embarrassed to bring me over, just say it. Is it that I'm repeating my junior year? Or the crashing-into-my-house thing?"

I was so stunned, I could barely get my mouth to work. "That's not it at all."

"Then what is it?" When I couldn't answer, Jim slammed his locker shut and darted into homeroom.

The hall was almost empty now. For a second, I couldn't do anything but stare at the space Jim had just occupied, hating myself for not telling him what was going on and potentially ruining the one good thing I had going. But I still didn't know how to explain everything.

The second bell rang. I ran to homeroom, where Mr. Pianci snapped at me for being late and I had to take deep breaths so I wouldn't cry in front of everyone.

Even though I hadn't sat up with Mom since the car accident, I wanted to tell her about Jim. She wouldn't understand what had happened and would probably try to relate it to flying, but I had to talk to someone. With my friends mad at me and my still not being close to any of Jim's friends, I went almost the entire school day without saying a word to anyone. All day I felt like I was underwater. I could practically feel the weight on my lungs.

Things still felt off when I went downstairs that night to see Mom. I heard papers shuffling and her talking low. She was telling herself to be calm, that it would all be fine.

"Hey," I said, and she jumped a little.

"I didn't think anyone was up." Behind her, the kitchen table was bare and there were no maps taped to the wall. She was wearing her battered leather jacket and best linen scarf. Goggles hung around her neck. A small canvas bag stuffed with papers sat on a nearby chair.

I took a step toward her. "What are you doing?"

She sighed. "We were trying to keep it secret."

My heart started beating faster. It was the same feeling I'd had all day, but worse—like the room was filling with water and I couldn't breathe. "What secret?"

"A flight around the world," she said. When she tried to smile at me, her lips looked strained, as if they might crack. "It's going to be most important thing I'll ever do."

CHAPTER TWENTY

The most difficult thing is the decision to act, the rest is
merely tenacity. The fears are paper tigers. You can do
anything you decide to do. You can act to change and
control your life; and the procedure, the process is its own
reward.

—Amelia Earhart

I barely heard Mom as she spoke. She and Fred were ready
this time, she insisted, not like that first try in Hawaii. It was
an entirely different route. They were going to see so much—
Brazil, Ethiopia, India. This was going to take flying one step
further for everyone. This was going to mean something.

"You were just going to leave?" I managed to ask. "Like
none of us mattered to you?"

She stopped flipping through one of her notebooks. "I
never said that."

"You promised you'd tell me before you left."

"I know." She reached into her bag. "I wrote you a letter—"

"That's not the same thing," I said. Now I was shaking. If I hadn't come down to talk about Jim, I would have gotten up the next morning to find her gone. To maybe never see her again. I hated her and loved her so much in that moment; it felt like falling.

The floor swayed underneath me. "I have to get Dad."

I was two steps out of the kitchen when Mom grabbed my arm. "No, you can't. I'm leaving now."

I stopped. It was a bad idea. But if I turned away now, maybe we would lose her forever. "Let me go with you. Either I go with you or I tell Dad."

"No." Her voice shook. "We can't take passengers."

We, I thought. "Fred. I know where Fred is."

For a second, neither of us breathed. Then Mom let me go, snatched her bag from the table, and headed toward the door. When I followed her, she didn't object.

Before we left, I snagged my coat from the closet. In the pocket was my cell phone, where I'd left it since I didn't expect to hear from Jim that night. I tapped out a quick text to him: *need help now please.* I hoped he would get it, and I hoped when he did I would know how to explain everything.

The car was already full of Mom's things—the cobbled-together cockpit, cardboard boxes filled with maps, compasses and canteens, some extra clothes. She wasn't planning on coming back.

I automatically slid into the driver's seat. Mom didn't protest.

She didn't even look at me as we rolled quietly out of the drive-way and down the street. I'd thought that whenever she'd try to leave us for Amelia's final flight, she'd be calm and happy as she moved determinedly toward nothing. But whenever I snuck glances at her, her face looked strained and stretched, as if it hurt just to sit there.

Amelia Earhart was tired, I thought. She wanted to be done after this big flight.

When we pulled up to Jim's house, I saw a light on in his room, but it quickly switched off. I tried to pretend that didn't hurt. I was about to shift the car into drive when the Wileys' front door opened and Jim stepped outside, peering at our car.

I told Mom to wait a second and met Jim halfway up the front walk. I wished he'd hug me, but his hands were stuffed in the pockets of his hoodie. At least he didn't look mad at me. "I need your help," I said.

"Yeah," he said, voice a little scratchy. "I got your text. What is it?"

I took a couple of breaths. Outside of home, I hadn't said the actual words before. And they seemed so ridiculous in my head that I didn't know how they would even make sense when I actually said them. "My mom thinks she's Amelia Earhart."

Jim blinked. "She what?"

If I didn't say it now, I never would, so I kept going. "She had, like, a nervous breakdown and thinks she's Amelia Earhart—you know, the woman pilot who went missing in the 1930s?" Before Jim could even ask any questions, I started telling him everything quickly and all out of order—how I had to find her on Halloween because she wasn't supposed to go off alone; how she freaked when Mr. Kane called her by her real name; how I had a little sister that was born too early and died; how Mom and I went driving on that snowy night and broke a mailbox; how now she wanted to go on Amelia Earhart's last flight and I didn't know what that meant, but I knew I had to stay with her and I needed Jim to be our navigator.

"I'm sorry I didn't tell you before," I said. "I just didn't know what to do."

Jim didn't say anything for a second, glancing between my mom waiting in the car and me. Then he nodded. "Let's go."

We held hands as we rushed to the car. I got behind the wheel, and Jim took a spot in the backseat. Mom didn't turn around to see Jim. "Do you have everything we need?" she asked coolly.

"Um, yeah," Jim said. "Right here."

"I hope you haven't been drinking."

He glanced between Mom and me. I shrugged. "Not recently."

"Good. I expect you to control yourself during this trip. The world will be watching us."

I didn't know where I was going when I started the car again, so I followed familiar paths from when Jim and I practiced driving, only now everything was dark and there was no one else on the street. Mom started pawing through her papers again. Every few minutes, she would pass one back to Jim to get his opinion on distances they'd have to travel and how much fuel they'd need. For the most part, Jim tried to agree with her, but nothing he said seemed to calm her. My hands stayed firm on the wheel without my even having to worry about it.

"Are you sure it's enough fuel?" she asked. "I don't know if we'll make it. But we can't take on the extra weight for fuel. It's a long trip. It's such a long trip. I don't know."

"Maybe you should wait," I said. "You don't have to leave now."

Mom extracted a notebook from her bag.

"We can go back—"

"No." Mom's voice was so sharp, I nearly hit the brakes in surprise. Amelia Earhart was never this upset. "No, we need to go. Now. I can't—" She took a deep breath and didn't exhale for a while.

From the backseat, Jim reached out and rubbed my shoulder with his hand.

We were outside of town now, winding our way through the countryside. Barely any streetlights lined the road. The dark and quiet pressed against the glass and metal of the car.

"We'll send the parachutes home once we get to New Guinea," Mom said. "No use for them over the Pacific."

Jim and I glimpsed each other in the rearview mirror. "Why not?" I asked.

"Even if you survive the crash, you've almost no hope for rescue," she said. "No one would ever find you."

"They won't ever find you," I said without meaning to. I

knew arguing would upset her even more, but the words pushed themselves out. "Don't you get that? Amelia Earhart never finishes her big trip. She dies somewhere out in the ocean."

Mom tried to laugh, but it came out as a gasp. "What? I don't—"

"Amelia never came back." I hit the brake. We stopped in the middle of the road, vast fields on either side. "That's the great finish to the story. You have to know that. Why are you doing this?"

For a second, she didn't move. Every breath came faster until I thought she'd cry or scream. But then she threw the car door open and rushed into someone's fields.

Jim and I ran silently after her. She was faster than I'd thought she'd be. We were halfway into the field when she slowed to a walk and wrapped her arms around herself. Jim circled around to her right, in case she turned toward the road. I stayed a few steps behind her, ready to run after her again. It was dark enough that I could have lost her if she got too far ahead of me.

Mom tilted her head toward the sky. "Clear tonight," she said, sniffling. "It'll be a good start. It will."

"Mom, please." I couldn't remember the last time I'd called her that. Usually I avoided saying her name, or went with Amelia if I had to. I'd missed the sound of it and wanted to say it again. "Mom. Mom. Please."

She stopped suddenly, shaking her head and trying to

shield her body from me. "I need to go," she whispered. "There are so many plans."

"It's not real," I insisted, expecting her to run away again, but she stayed. "Amelia died. Years ago."

Mom turned to me, her eyes red but unblinking. "No one dies. No one."

There was a heartbeat, and then I saw everything before me, like clouds parting to reveal the earth below. "Amelia Earhart never dies," I murmured. "She disappears. They never find her, so she never dies." I thought of Mom curled up in bed after losing the baby; Mom in a hospital waiting room, waiting to see if she would die of cancer like her mother, always steeped in death. She must have wished she could float above it all, never letting death touch her again.

"Mom," I said, "we're still here. Don't disappear, please."

She inhaled, waited a second, then exhaled. Her face softened a little and she tilted her head to the sky. "Look at all those stars."

I took a step toward her, and she didn't back away. When I reached for her hand, she curled her fingers around mine. We stood there for a moment, leaning against each other and looking at the stars, Jim watching from a few feet away.

"That's Vela," Mom said, pointing to one part of the sky. "It means 'sails,' like on a ship."

I tried to find the constellation she meant, but they all looked the same to me. I was about to ask her where it was exactly, but I saw someone walking toward us from the far end of the field. I turned to Jim, who had seen him as well. "We should go," he said. Then we heard the wail of approaching sirens. Red and blue lights streaked across the fields. I gripped Mom's hand in case she tried to run away.

"It's okay," I said to Mom and Jim and myself, but I didn't think it would be.

We were caught trespassing. I tried to explain that we weren't just kids messing around, but the man who owned the strawberry fields didn't seem to buy it.

"This is my livelihood," he said. "I can't have a bunch of people tramping through my strawberry fields at any time of the night."

"We weren't tramping," I said. "My mom just needed to get some air. She wasn't feeling well."

Mom didn't say anything to back me up, but at least she wasn't introducing herself as Amelia Earhart. And the police officer wasn't taking my word or Jim's, especially after he found out that Jim also crashed into his home last year.

"You're all going to have to come with me," the officer said tiredly.

We trudged through the fields and climbed into the backseat of the police car. He didn't use the sirens as we sped back into town, leaving Mom's car behind us at the side of the road.

I'd never been inside the police station before, but it was smaller than I'd expected and not very active at three in the morning. Instead of being shoved into a cell, we were directed to a wooden bench by the wall. Mom and Jim sat, but the police officer pulled me aside.

"Is your mom all right?" he asked me.

I stared at him for a second. He hadn't been a jerk to us so far, and his eyes seemed genuine. "She's been depressed," I said. "She was feeling really bad tonight. Can I call my dad?"

When Dad answered the phone, he was still half asleep and didn't quite understand what had happened until he heard the words "police station." He rushed through the station doors, what seemed like seconds later, in rumpled clothing, his hair a mess. He took a step toward me, but the police officer waved him over. For a moment, Dad stood apart with the officer, talking in low voices. Then the officer strolled over to us and nodded to the door.

"Sounds like this was just a case of wrong place, wrong time," he said. "You weren't causing any real mischief, so we're gonna let you go with a warning. Just make sure it doesn't happen again." He looked at me. "Take care, now."

Dad guided us out to the parking lot. I didn't even know how to begin to explain what happened, so I stayed quiet. Dad didn't ask questions, either.

When we dropped Jim off, the windows in his house were still dark. "See you later," he said to me, and I nodded. I watched him run up the front walk and disappear inside the house.

In the backseat, Mom stared at the houses flashing by, all

dark. She hadn't said anything since we were alone in the field. I wanted to tell her that I was glad she hadn't disappeared, that things might still suck but they would be okay eventually, that we weren't going to leave her, either. But instead I just said, "Mom," and it came out as a sob.

She turned. Her eyes were still red, but she looked at me, waiting for me to speak.

"That was Jim," I said, wiping away tears with the cuff of my shirt. "He's my boyfriend."

The edges of Mom's lips curved up. "He seems like a nice young man."

Dad glanced between us as he eased the car back into our driveway. But after he turned off the engine, he didn't move. I braced myself for a lecture about how dangerous it was to drive into the middle of nowhere with Mom, or how lucky we were that the police officer was so understanding, but it didn't come. His face was wilted, not angry. At first I thought he might be tired or disappointed, but there was something softer behind his eyes. He brushed his face with the palm of his hand.

"I'm really sorry," I said. "I—"

"Alex, you can't keep doing stuff like this," he said. "First it's the mailbox, and then you're nearly arrested. You could get everyone seriously hurt."

"She was leaving." My voice was small and calm. "I couldn't let her go alone."

He caught Mom's eye in the rearview mirror. After a

moment, he sighed. "It's okay. I'm just glad you're safe. Come on, let's get a few hours' sleep."

Outside the car, Dad took a step toward the house and stopped. Suddenly he turned back on his heel and pulled me into a fierce hug. "I'm sorry," he said, and pressed a kiss on the top of my head. "I'm so sorry." I held tight back, as if we'd both fly apart otherwise. When I pulled away, I saw I'd left tearstains on his shirt, but Dad didn't seem to notice or care.

We trudged back into the house, walking so close together that our shoulders touched.

Chapter Twenty-One

The soul's dominion? Each time we make a choice, we pay
with courage to behold restless day and count it fair.

—Amelia Earhart

I wanted to wake up and find everything better. Mom would be down the hall, shouting to us that the bus would be here any minute so we needed to get ourselves out of bed right now. Instead, when our alarm went off, my head ached, and Katy, who'd slept soundly, sprang out of bed. I made sure everyone had breakfast and got out the door in time for the bus. Mom was still asleep when we left. Mrs. Ellis was coming over as usual. I kept wondering if last night had happened at all.

At school, Jim was leaning against my locker, so I knew it hadn't been a dream. But I didn't rush over to him. Maybe texting him for help in the middle of the night was fine, but the next morning it would be too much. I wished I could erase it all from his memory and briefly considered running into a random classroom to avoid him altogether. But he'd also been my navigator last night. That had to count for something.

"Hey," I said, leaning against the locker beside mine. "Did you make it back in okay?"

"Oh, yeah. My parents asked me how I slept." He grinned. "I should sneak out more often."

"Less trespassing next time."

"Depends on what we want to do." He lowered his voice. "I'm glad you told me, though. That was a lot to deal with."

I thought he meant that it was a lot for him to deal with and he was glad because now he knew that he should book it, because I had too much baggage. Girlfriends were fun girls who weren't surprised about getting carnations. They invited their boyfriends over and weren't afraid of ending up like their moms. I turned my head farther away from Jim because I thought I might start crying, and I was sick of crying. But then I felt one arm reach around my shoulders and another cross my collarbone, so I was half pulled into his sweatery arms.

I probably should have cried, just let myself have this huge release. But instead I took deep breaths and felt Jim's warmth.

"Thanks" seemed like such a small word. Instead, I said, "Sorry I got you almost arrested."

He laughed. "That's okay. Next time I can get us arrested."

Next time, I thought. Even with all the craziness going on at home and how I'd hidden it, he was still thinking of a next time. I kissed him until the bell rang and Mr. Hunter yelled at us to break it up.

That afternoon, Mom and Dad went to see Dr. McGlynn. It wasn't their usual appointment. I knew it was because of Mom trying to leave the night before, but part of me had hoped that Mom didn't need to see doctors anymore. That wasn't the case.

Dr. McGlynn seemed to think that Mom had a good break last night. Mom was relying less on the Amelia persona, she explained, which meant she was getting ready to work through her issues. But it wasn't like an on/off switch, and Dr. McGlynn was worried that Mom would be overwhelmed by the emotions she'd been hiding and try to hurt herself. So Dr. McGlynn suggested that Mom spend some time at the Saint Giles Behavioral Health Center. "Somewhere she can get the help she needs in a safe environment" was how Dad explained it.

Dad signed papers and made phone calls. Mom would get group therapy, individual therapy, grief counseling, and more, in a series of squat brick buildings all clustered together. Mom was quieter than usual and told Dad that it all sounded fine.

While I packed for Mom, I thought about what it would be like: not to hear her in the middle of the night; not to have her around to talk to about Theresa or Jim or driver's ed; not to see the maps and the scarf; not to hope that one day I'd wake up and things wouldn't be like they were before—they would be better, because Mom would be Mom again but we wouldn't fight as much.

It was a long drive to Saint Giles, so Mom and Dad were going to leave early the next morning, before any of us were awake. I didn't know how to say good-bye, so instead I wrote a note and tucked it inside my mother's suitcase.

You have to come back, I wrote. *I don't care what really happened. Screw history. You have to come back.*

I didn't know if she would read it, but that night I slept without dreaming and didn't wake until morning.

It was still my job to get everybody ready for school, but now we left an empty house. Even though I slept through the night, I felt like kind of a wreck. Katy and Teddy were both sluggish, too. Since it took Teddy forever to get out of bed, I didn't have time to shower. I felt like everybody could see the grime all around me and know the reason. I hid in a baggy sweatshirt and a pair of jeans with the hem all frayed in the back because they were too long.

In Spanish, Señor Oria asked me to translate a sentence on the board, and I stood with a piece of chalk in my hand for about five minutes without managing a single word.

"*Abejorro*, is that . . . is that 'butterfly'?"

Señor Oria crossed his arms over his chest. "*En español, Alejandra!*"

"*Es ese* . . . something. I don't know the word for butterfly, so I can't ask about it."

"*No es una mariposa.*"

I looked at the class to see if I was the only one who wasn't getting it. The other ones who didn't understand weren't paying attention, and the kids who did understand stared at me like I must have had help dressing myself that morning.

Finally Señor Oria let me sit down and basically ignored me for the rest of class. After the bell rang, I seriously considered skipping the rest of the day and was halfway to the door when Jim saw me.

"Hey," he said. "I missed you before homeroom. You coming to lunch?"

I didn't want to sit with Jim's friends, who had no idea what was going on with my mom and would think I was just an unshowered mess. I was about to make up some excuse when Jim asked if I was okay.

"Yeah. I look okay, right?" I'd told Jim that my mom was going to a treatment center, but I hadn't mentioned when and I didn't want to rehash yesterday in the middle of the hall. Instead, I took a breath. "Sorry, it's just not a great day. Let's go."

I followed Jim into the cafeteria, which was thick with loud voices and the smell of grease. At one end of the room, Jim's friends had already claimed a table. Theresa, Maddie, and Josh were at the other. It looked like Maddie was cramming for a U.S. history test, while Theresa and Josh were hunched over

Josh's phone. Then Josh said something and they all laughed. I used to be a part of that.

Even as Amelia Earhart, Mom had Mrs. Ellis to sit with her. Who would stay with me if I couldn't be myself anymore?

"I'll be right back," I told Jim. I took a step forward, then another and another until I was at my friends' table.

They all looked over at me like I was Caroline Lavale asking them to go to the football game. It was hard to remember that a few months ago, I was right there with them.

"Hey," I said.

Maddie and Josh mumbled hello. Theresa spun a fork between her fingers. "Hey."

I eyed an empty seat. "Can I sit for a second?"

"You can sit anywhere you want."

I perched on the edge of the chair, back straight. Everything I'd planned on saying evaporated in my head. "I was . . ." I said. "It's . . ." It must have been like this for Mom — the longer you go without talking about something, the harder it is to start, until eventually you don't know how to.

Theresa munched on a French fry. "Thanks for stopping by."

"Will you stop being a bitch?" I snapped. "I'm trying to apologize."

I expected Theresa to tell me *I* had been the bitch, but she didn't. She stared, face stolid.

"I'm sorry I disappeared," I said. "It sucks when your friends go off and forget you." I didn't say anything about Mom, even though Theresa had asked about her. It wasn't something

I was ready to talk about with everybody yet, especially when I didn't know what was going on or what was going to happen. For now I looked each of them in the eye, trying to appear as genuine as possible.

Theresa scowled. "What did you do, break up with Jim or something?"

"No, we're still together. I just wanted to say that." I pushed the seat back. "So I guess—"

"Oh, sit down," Theresa said. She tried to hide a smile. "There are like ten people in this school who don't suck, so we might as well keep you around."

I smirked. "Thanks for the vote of confidence."

"Yeah, well, it was either you or Caroline Lavale, and she tried to get us to join the color guard. Josh was really into the color guard thing, but fortunately we got to him before he performed in public."

Josh rolled his eyes. "That's friendship for you."

Maddie and Josh looked over my shoulder. Theresa and I turned to find Jim standing there. "Hey," he said, "can I sit here?"

My stomach gripped. What if Jim brought up my mom, assuming I'd told my friends about her? What if they were still upset with him because I'd been ditching them for the last few months? But I nodded for Jim to take a seat beside me. Maddie and Theresa raised their eyebrows at each other.

"Jim, right?" Theresa said, like she didn't know. "We're Alex's friends. She likes to save us for a special occasion."

"And what's more special than shepherd's pie day in the cafeteria?" Josh said, frowning at his plate.

"Man," Jim said. "If I'd known that, I would've put on my tux. The lunch ladies expect that level of class from me."

The tux got Maddie talking about prom, and how she thought it wouldn't suck too much to go. Theresa couldn't believe it, and they argued about that while Jim and I grabbed food. At the table, Jim didn't say a whole lot, but every so often he would cast me a half smile.

After lunch Jim left to find Will, and Theresa linked arms with me, as though she thought I'd run off, too.

"So what do you think?" I said.

"About Jim?" she said, and paused for a second. "Not bad, Winchester. He can keep up, which is good. Just don't go MIA on us again."

I meant to smile. "I'll try."

Even after a couple of weeks, everything was too quiet at home. I kept expecting to find Mom at the table, maps scattered all over the kitchen table, but every time I unlocked the front door, the house was quiet. If Dad wasn't at work, he went to visit Mom, so even he wasn't home a lot. I felt like I should have been doing stupid things just because I wouldn't get caught. Of course, if I did try anything—hooking up with Jim, breaking into the liquor cabinet, starting an illegal gambling ring—Teddy would be only too thrilled to tell Dad about it.

So instead I tried to make as much noise as possible, to fill up the space and the silence. With music blasting, maybe Mom really was in the next room and I just couldn't hear her.

Teddy didn't mind the noise because I let him pick out songs every so often. "Nothing Disney-ish," I told him. "This is, like, your musical education."

Teddy and I bounced around to the Fratellis in the living room. When Katy came home from gymnastics one afternoon, her eyes were wide. "Oh, my God," Katy shouted. "I could hear you all the way down the street."

"What?" I said. "Sorry, can't hear you."

"People are going to call the cops," Katy said.

I rolled my eyes. "If they do, we'll turn it down."

She pulled a pack of vocab cards out of her backpack. "I've got homework!"

"Oh, right, because you're not already weeks ahead in everything." One song faded away and another started. I snatched the cards away from her and tossed them into the air so they rained over us. For a second, she stood very still and then started to smile. I grabbed Katy's hand, pulling her farther into the living room. Teddy leaped off the couch and started to dance around her.

Soon Katy was bopping along with us. We went through the whole album, and then Vampire Weekend, until we were all sweating and starving and exhausted, prostrate on the living-room floor. Teddy and Katy were still singing the refrain of the last song, both off-key. Their cheeks were red, and they laughed when Katy jumped up again to mimic Teddy's dance moves.

It could have been any day. We could have been waiting for Mom and Dad to get home from work. I hadn't thought about Mom the whole time, and I hoped they hadn't, either.

My road test was scheduled for the day after our junior year ended, so Jim and I decided we needed to practice a lot before then. In exchange for babysitting Teddy most days, Dad let me drive with Jim every night. We did spend time going over three-point turns and reversing next to a curb, but we also drove out in the country, with the windows down to catch the new spring air, and parked beside the reservoir. I didn't freak out anymore; instead, I was amazed to find that driving could be fun.

One night it was so warm and clear that we lay on top of the hood of the car and invented new constellations.

"That's the circus elephant," I said, pointing. "See, there's the trunk."

"Pretty small trunk."

"You're looking at it backward. Maybe after we finish with driving lessons I can give you astronomy lessons."

"You're a way better tutor than Mrs. Frasier." We turned sideways to kiss. "We're gonna have to think of a new excuse to get away from our houses after you pass the road test."

"*If* I pass."

"*When* you pass."

I smiled. "We're going to have to schedule some extra driving lessons, since Mr. Kane's going to be out for the next week or something." That afternoon in driver's ed, Señor Oria appeared instead of Mr. Kane and made us watch a video about train safety that I'd seen the previous semester. The rumor was that after years of barely hanging on, Mr. Kane's mom had died. I wondered how it had happened — if Mr. Kane was home at the time; if he woke up in the morning and realized that she wasn't brushing her teeth or making coffee; if he got a chance to say something nice to her before she died. I wondered if he had anyone helping him plan the funeral.

"I really want to pass," I told Jim. "Mr. Kane is going to come back and find me a parallel-parking master."

Jim sat up a little. "Whenever I bring up parallel parking, you always look like I'm talking about shooting puppies."

"I've got to do it sometime, right?" I pulled him back down with me. "And when I pass, we should go somewhere. To celebrate. Like a road trip." Aside from a couple of soccer tournaments and family vacations, I hadn't really been outside of Virginia. I wanted to go places with Jim — drive along the coastline and run through the surf, talking to everyone we met along the way. Maybe we could pass it off as a college tour. Possibility flickered around us like fireflies.

We talked about all the places we wanted to go, until the stars shifted position and we had to climb back into the car. I drove, but along the familiar country roads, it didn't feel like I was behind the wheel. It felt like I was running and I could run forever.

Mom had been at Saint Giles for a month when Dad brought home the first letter. I was sitting on the couch with Jackson curled in the crook of my legs, spacing out in front of some reality show. I barely noticed Dad was around until he dropped the letter on the coffee table.

"Special delivery," he said.

Jackson leaped up and followed Dad into the kitchen. I picked up the envelope, plain and white, with no address or stamp on the front. I ripped it open and pulled out the pages inside. They were lined and torn at one edge—from a notebook. Immediately I recognized Mom's handwriting and all the ventricles in my heart froze. I hadn't seen her or talked to her in so long that holding her letter was kind of a shock. After a few weeks of her not being around, it was like she had gone forever. Now here she was again, in my hands.

I told myself not to get my hopes up.

There was no greeting. It might have been a journal entry, except she kept saying "you," which I assumed was me, or otherwise Dad wouldn't have given me the letter. She talked about the weather—how it was going to be spring soon, with the daffodils flowering in the front yard—and how she was getting some rest. Mostly, she was vague on details or mentioned names without explaining them. Was Deborah her roommate or someone in her therapy group? Or was it a name she remembered from one of her Amelia Earhart books?

Then I noticed. She didn't really refer to Amelia Earhart at all. I flipped the pages over again to make sure—no G.P., no Fred Noonan, no Lockheeds, nothing. Nothing about us, either, but maybe it was something.

In the last paragraph, she wrote:

> I'll be glad when it's all over. I'm learning a great deal, of course, and I don't think this will be for nothing. But I'll be glad when I can recognize everything out the window again. A few times I've dreamed that I was back, and you were at the table, having hot chocolate and waiting for me. I didn't drive or fly home—I was soaring, like you can in dreams. Even though the window wasn't open, I could feel the air around me. Flying aside, it all felt real. Then I woke up and it was another day. I'm pushing forward and I hope to see you soon.

There wasn't a signature, either. But it was like she remembered me. The real me, not some imagined girl pilot. We would keep searching for her, and she would keep searching for us. Even though Amelia Earhart's plane was probably at the bottom of the Pacific Ocean, people kept looking for her. No one knows when or how rescue could come. Mom was out there, somewhere, too. We were trying to find each other again.

ACKNOWLEDGMENTS

Thank you to my family for all their love and support, especially my parents, who encouraged my love of words in every form. Thank you for reading to me, for punning with me, for driving me to and from writing camp, and for believing this was a possibility.

To Taylor Martindale, whose encouragement and hard work are invaluable. Your e-mails always leave me with a smile, even when we talk business. I'm so glad to have you in my corner.

To Hilary Van Dusen, the best editor anyone could ask for. Your editorial judgment is flawless, and your comments always left me enthusiastic about the next draft. Thank you also to the entire Candlewick team. Your talent and dedication to children's literature are unparalleled.

To the PEN New England Children's Book Committee, especially Susan Goodman, for changing my life.

To my critique partners—Akshay Ahuja, Andrew Ladd, Heinz Healey, Michelle Fernandes, Kim Liao, Kirstin Chen, Bridget Pelkie, Tara Sullivan, Lauren Barrett, Lisa Palin, Julia Maranan, and Katie Slivensky. Thank you for your thoughtful feedback, your writerly gossip, and for making conferences way more fun.

To Ben Brooks and Pam Painter, who first helped bring this novel to life. Thank you for taking a chance on YA.

To the 2014 debut community, especially the Fourteenery. You make this debut ride a little less scary and a lot more awesome.

To writers, researchers, and publishers of works about and by Amelia Earhart, including the George Palmer Putnam Collection at Purdue University, the official website of Amelia Earhart, and books such as *The Fun of It, Last Flight,* and *20 Hrs., 40 Min.* Your resources were so helpful in the creation of this novel. Special thanks to Candace Fleming for her wonderful *Amelia Lost: The Life and Disappearance of Amelia Earhart.*

Saving the best for last—thank you to my husband, Walt McGough, a brilliant playwright and my favorite person in the world. Thank you for your endless encouragement, for the quiet nights writing in separate rooms, for making every day better than I could have imagined. We have fun!